OVERS

VOLUME I OF THE F

OVERSTRIKE

VOLUME I OF THE FIXPOINT TRILOGY

CM ANGUS

Elsewhen Press

Overstrike
First published in Great Britain by Elsewhen Press, 2020
An imprint of Alnpete Limited

Elsewhen Press, PO Box 757, Dartford, Kent DA2 7TQ
www.elsewhen.press
British Library Cataloguing in Publication Data.
A catalogue record for this book is available from the British Library.
ISBN 978-1-911409-60-1 Print edition
ISBN 978-1-911409-70-0 eBook edition

Printed and bound by CPI Group (UK) Ltd, Croydon, CR0 4YY

To my wife
You are my rock.
You are my foil.
A widow to my endeavours;
Belief when I dare not dare to dream.
You are my heart,
and forever will be.

FACT

Operation Unthinkable was the name for plans drawn up by the British Armed Forces' Joint Planning Staff at the end of WWII. Requested by Winston Churchill, these plans proposed a pre-emptive Anglo-German attack on the Soviet Union.

In most realities, these plans were never put in place...

PROLOGUE

LONDON 1948

"Captain Howard. They're waiting for you."

The military escort opened the door to show Joseph Howard into the Westminster cabinet bunker's crowded meeting room.

All but one seat was already filled, and at the head of the centre table sat the Prime Minister, her face stern.

"Howard," she said, her relief apparent. "Thank God. Sit, and we'll begin."

"Yes Mother."

Staff withdrew, doors were closed and fifteen pairs of eyes focussed intently, as they waited for her to speak.

"Gentlemen. We stand on the brink of defeat; however, I must insist that no words spoken today leave this room."

What sounded like distant thunder could be felt through the floor. Trails of dust fell, and glowing filaments briefly flickered in electric lights. Seemingly unperturbed, the thin woman pressed on.

"Stalin may be upon us. However, Churchill's move was not the overzealous act it seemed. Nor was it the rash decision widely reported. It was taken with the knowledge that, come the day, come the worst, come the situation we find ourselves in now, we, at least, would have options."

The Prime Minister paused and surveyed confusion in the room.

"In the dossier in front of you is such an option. *Operation Overstrike*."

Overstrike was the name that The Commission had given to applying a reality-graft far beyond what had ever been back-propagated and fixed before. The safety net that they'd discussed prior to mounting *Operation Unthinkable*, the pre-emptive Anglo-German attack in '45; the abortive attack that had led them to Total War.

Since then, Joseph had watched through the RIFT, tracking a number of outcomes. But he now struggled to hold *Overstrike*, their single-last chance to graft themselves out of trouble.

Hope... Fading...

If only it were as vibrant as the pre-war branch that Joseph still held for his wife, a potential reality where he'd never signed up and where Ruth had survived.

Of course Joseph had petitioned for that alternative; to graft to Ruth's branch. However, concerned that their work in avoiding Nazi atrocities would be undone – that the war with Germany would be extended, or even lost – The Commission had flatly refused him and even warned that any unilateral action would suffer the direst of consequences.

The Commission had called it regrettable.

Regrettable!

The word still stuck in his throat.

Back in the room, the PM – or *Mother*, as she had affectionately become known – rose from her seat to stand, arms locked with her weight resting on the clenched knuckles of each hand.

"So – Gentlemen," she said, "If we are agreed, only a select few of us will even remember this conversation. We will, however, with God's grace, be spared what is inevitably to come. Now is the time for unity. Therefore I must ask that if any one of you has an objection, for it to be raised now..."

Round the chamber, the silence was deafening. Joseph looked from face to face, the tension palpable. Seconds dragged by and Joseph Howard swore to always recall this moment.

"Thank you, gentlemen. That concludes this, and likely all, sessions; may God have mercy on our souls.

"Captain Howard, if you'd be so kind?"

Joseph nodded and again focussed through the RIFT. He knew what he needed to do, but it was still not going to be easy – not with the branch so distant and so withered. With his mind's eye he searched and attempted to bring it into focus.

To his surprise, he felt resistance – something was pushing back against him – trying to stop him.

How? – Stalin didn't know about The Commission – did he? Unless he had his own...

Slowly the branch began to sharpen, but this was hard, too hard. He'd expected that he'd be able to yank it toward him, to graft it to their timeline, but – no; beads of sweat formed on his brow.

Through the haze, the sound of gunfire and voices was heard outside. The doors opened.

"You will stop this immediately!"

He looked over at the Russian officer, who now stood in the doorway, gun in hand.

"Captain Howard. As you no-doubt have discovered, we have men opposing you. You will not succeed. It is over."

He raised the narrow-barrelled pistol at Joseph and began squeezing the trigger.

"With a gift such as yours, this is a shame, but I have no choice. I'm sorry."

Gasping, Joseph felt the searing heat of the rounds hit his chest.

The room spun as he fell, his head smacking into the floor. In seemingly slow motion, all grip of the branch tumbled out of his mind and disappeared back across the RIFT; out of his reach – lost forever.

His head began to swim.

Gone!

It was over.

Unless...

Losing consciousness, he grabbed desperately at Ruth's pre-war branch, the forbidden fruit that still shone like a star, and with all his might, he pulled...

CHAPTER 1

"Matt – it's coming!"

Matthew Howard was aware of someone next to him, shaking his arm.

What's happening – where am I?

"Matt, don't do this, not today. I swear, if you don't wake up – the baby's coming for God's-sake."

Slowly, the fog started to clear from Matt's mind, and he began to rejoin the world around him.

"Matt – wake up."

Blinking he focussed on the face of his wife, Jane. He was always like this when woken, unable to separate the multiple tendrils of dream-state from reality. He would always come-to in the end, but it was rarely quick and today was no exception.

Since he was a child it had ever been the same; he would dream of events yet to come, or witness variants of past events that had typically happened the day before. These were never the same, but then again, they were *always* the same. His dreams were never what he thought dreams should be; of flying, of fighting dragons or some romantic tryst. If Matthew Howard dreamt of these things at all, it was rare. He was instead *continually* short-changed and treated to a theatre of the unremarkable, a prosaic daily helping of mundane slices of life – each one as vivid as the next.

"What's going on?" he mumbled groggily, attempting to determine whether he was yet awake.

"Matt, I think the baby's coming."

He shifted his weight, still confused, struggling, trying to force himself to focus.

"Are you sure? How far apart are you?"

"About twenty minutes."

Managing some clarity, he looked at his wife's enormously distended abdomen and smiled.

They had been trying for a baby for the best part of three years and for a while they'd wondered whether Jane was ever going to catch-on – wondered if it was ever going to happen.

When it finally did, they'd intentionally avoided being told what it was, *boy or girl*, but Barbara, Matt's mother, had been in little doubt.

"*It'll be a boy*," she had insisted. "*It's your father's side. Howards are always boys, for as long as records go back. Always a boy and always only the one. I think they put something in the water.*"

I'll be happy either way thought Matt, and it was true.

"This could be it then," he said, gently stroking her bump. "Are you sure it's real – I mean could it be Braxton Hicks?"

Jane threw a pillow in his direction, her brown doe-eyes glaring. She was in no mood for debate. "Look, just get woken up, get my bag, and get me to the hospital; and don't zone out. OK?"

Matt had a tendency to slip into distraction, to daydream or to *zone out* as Jane called it. He'd done that ever since they'd met, but that was just Matty.

I may as well try to catch the wind as change him, thought Jane, *like father, like son.* However, for all her understanding, today was different. Today she needed Matt to be her rock, to be 'with-it' a little more than normal, to be a grown-up.

Still dozy, Matt swung his feet out of bed onto the floor; the thick rug that covered most of the room felt warm under his toes. He paused, remembering buying it with Jane only yesterday, bringing it home, how she almost convinced him not to bother.

"For God's sake Matt!"

"Uh?"

"Get a move on – and by the way, you have dog-breath."

Matt rubbed his eyes and mashed the palm of his hand into his stubbled cheek to wake up, before padding across the bare boards that made up the bedroom floor.

We definitely should have bought that rug.

Jane Howard lay on the bed like a beached whale, her recent contraction now abated. She looked around the room at the browning, hand-me-down pine bedroom-set. She and Matt were not wealthy, they did not have the latest things, but she was happy – she knew that much.

Simple pleasures, she thought, *all this will change soon, lazy mornings would be a thing of the past*; if her mum-friends were anything to go by, she was in for a rough ride.

...But it would be worth it.

In the bathroom, Matt caught sight of his reflection.

Matthew Howard was twenty-eight, but since dropping out of college, his work as a plumber had put five years on him. It was as unglamorous as it came, but he was always in demand. It was like he was born to it. He could tell what joints would last and which would fail just by looking at them.

It was like he had a sixth sense; like he had intuition. In one sense it was ideal; regardless of what technological advances would be discovered in the future, people would always need plumbing and would always have things go wrong. But in a much more real sense, it was far from ideal; crawling under other people's sinks and through their sludge was not something he could do forever.

In the mirror, picturebook memories of his grandfather's face stared back at him. Maybe it was his father's lack of hair, but Matt had always resembled his grandfather, more than his father ever had.

Good grief – I look old... and tired.

He grabbed his crusty electric toothbrush and began to work it around his mouth.

"When you've done that, get my bag," shouted Jane from the bedroom. "I'm nearly ready."

"OK," he attempted to say, before spitting the foam into the sink.

C'mon fella, keep it together, he thought. *Wake up.* He was *always* like this when woken. A bomb could be going off, and it wouldn't get a reaction.

Dog-breath sorted, he threw the cheap plastic toothbrush back into its glass and splashed water on his face.

Should have bought an electric toothbrush. He was starting to come around. Finally, he felt the first hint of adrenaline kicking in.

Jesus, Jane was having a baby, and he was on another planet. Well, at least she couldn't say he wasn't consistent.

Jane lurched around the house checking she had everything she needed. She knew she should ask for help, but she also knew that there was little point – she loved Matty more than life itself, but he really was a disaster waiting to happen. In the kitchen she attempted to calm herself with a fruit tea – strawberry and camomile; what Matt would have called *Fancy-Nancy* – well his opinion could wait, she was determined to enjoy it. Jane tied back her light hair in a high ponytail; an Apache preparing for battle. Invigorated, she was as ready as she would ever be for what was to come.

OK… let's get this show on the road…

In the bedroom, Matt pulled on his jeans and looked over at Jane's identical bags.

Two bags…

Why two bags?

"You ready?" Jane waddled back into the room; slowly rocking side to side to transport the weight – legs bowed like a gunslinger from the old west.

"This baby's not going to wait for you…"

"Pretty much," came Matt's muffled reply as he struggled to pull on a polo neck. Through the rough-knit weave, he could vaguely make out that Jane was moving, possibly muttering at his inept attempts to get ready.

"OK – when you *eventually* do escape from that, I'll see you in the car. Don't be long – OK?"

Dressed at last, he cast his eyes around the room for what he needed to bring.

One bag…

He grabbed Jane's remaining bag and joined his wife.

Parenthood, he mused, *bring it on.*

****

Joseph Howard lay on his back, exhausted, unable to sleep. This was nothing new: he'd been living like this for the best part of a year. He looked at the ageing polystyrene tiles and tried in vain to focus. It was no use, he continued to see double.

He felt claustrophobic as he looked into the approaching graft. It reminded him of the woodblock print he'd once seen, years before, in the British Museum: *The Great Wave off Kanazawa* – by the Japanese artist Hokusai.

The picture depicted three boats being tossed around by a tsunami-like wave which, due to a trick of perspective, appeared to dwarf Mount Fuji and be on the verge of crashing down on the mountain itself.

This feeling of impending peril resonated strongly and provided him with a visual metaphor for the reality-graft that he'd become aware of for the last year.

Like the wave in the Hokusai print, the graft hung in the foreground of the RIFT. Unlike the wave, however, it was not a snapshot in time – progress might be glacial, but it was progressing. It was growing.

Should he try to oppose it? How could he know? It'd been so long… Would he even know what to do?

As far as he could tell, nothing in the graft looked different. But, all the same, it ominously pressed on the fabric of his mind and fractured his vision. It haunted his dreams and waking hours in equal, dreary, measure.

The events in the war-rooms had been over fifty years ago; more than half-a-century since he'd last seriously looked into the RIFT – since he'd changed history. What he hadn't foreseen was that this world's Joseph Howard had challenges beyond anything he'd experienced before. This world's Joseph Howard would probably have been categorised certifiable, had he ever sought a diagnosis. He always wondered whether that had been what had made the difference; whether that had been why Ruth had lived here, in this world, when Ruth had died there. It was like one of those movie-house retellings of *Faust*. It was like he'd done a deal with the devil where nothing ever turned out the way that he'd imagined. *There was always a sting in the tail.*

For more than fifty years he'd been a composite, two personalities in a single head, neither one thing nor another. He'd been the stabilising influence on this world's otherwise-stricken Joe. And this *alter-Joe* had kept him from returning to the RIFT – there would be no way that *that-Joe* would cope with that, and therefore there would be little chance that *he* would cope with that either.

But after so long, did it even make sense to separate the two sides anymore? There were no longer two Joe's, there was just Joe. He was what he was.

In '48 he'd turned his back on all of that and tried to put it behind him. Until last year, he'd thought he'd succeeded. But now, here he was – *and there it hung.*

If he had to, could he even be that person again? He didn't

know. Would it be the final straw; would it send him over the edge?

Sleep denied, he opened the notebook that he always kept with him, and wrote.

Who is doing this?
Why, after so long?
Is this retribution?
Consequences?

****

"Come on Jane, push, just a little more…"

Matthew Howard clutched his wife's hand and felt helpless; the NHS labour room bustled with attending staff.

Jane was exhausted, he could tell that, but somehow she kept going.

He wiped her sodden hair out of her eyes and mopped her fevered brow with a cold compress that the nurse had just handed him.

"Come on Jane, you can do it; breathe…"

Getting this far hadn't been easy; they'd arrived at the hospital nearly twenty-four hours earlier, thinking they knew what lay ahead.

It had been a slow, drawn-out process, but Jane's contractions were now coming thick and fast.

"I can't do it," she sobbed grabbing the rails on the institution bed's functional metal frame.

"Yes you can, Jane," Matt told her, "I'm here, we all believe in you."

"I can't. I can't do it."

Across from Matt, the midwife, who had just changed shift, rubbed Jane's arm in encouragement. "We'll have none of that," she said, admonishingly, "Baby's being born, and that's the end of it."

To Matt's surprise, this scolding appeared to actually invigorate his wife. With steely determination, she once again began to push.

C'mon Jane he thought against her rhythmic panting.

Jane grimaced and kept pushing; her back arched with pain.
C'mon Jane…

Through gritted teeth, she voiced her agony with a drawn-out guttural cry.

C'mon Jane...

With her whole being, Jane began a scream that seemingly had no end.

It's commmiiinnnggg...

Throwing in everything she had, Jane Howard continued to push a brand-new life out of herself, into the world and into the midwife's waiting hands.

The infant wriggled in the nurse's arms, ruddy and squirming.

It was over.

"Well done *Mum* you can relax. You've done it."

Exhausted but frantic, Jane peered down.

"Is it OK?"

Jane had dreaded *that question*, dreaded all the possible outcomes that it could bring. She had told herself that it would not make a difference. But could she be sure? Did she know herself that well?

The midwife swept the baby up, coddling it in a blanket.

"He's a boy, all the right number of fingers and toes, and he's beautiful. *Aren't you pet?*" Lifting him up she handed the baby to Jane to ensure the all-important skin-on-skin bonding happened as soon as possible. "There you go."

Even though he was still spattered with blood, he was indeed beautiful. Jane, now calmer, gently stroked his head.

My son, thought Matt.

My family.

With the baby's arrival, the previously clinical surroundings seemed to take on a far more organic feel, the machines and medical equipment faded into the background, and all that was left was the wonder of a new life.

"Do you have a name picked out?" asked the midwife.

"Ethan," Jane and Matt said in unison, their eyes never leaving the newborn.

Ethan Joseph Howard.

The midwife continued to speak, but neither Jane nor Matt heard a word she said. Their attention was, utterly and completely, focussed on the newest addition to their family.

Matthew Howard looked from Jane to Ethan, welling with pride and knew at that minute that he'd do anything for them.

Absolutely anything...

Anything at all.

CHAPTER 2

Thomas Howard straightened the potting tray in front of him and tipped out the packet onto a small saucer. One by one he took a pinch of tomato seeds and pushed each into the array of compost plugs that he'd arranged in a regular grid.

He sat, perched on the edge of a battered stool, within the greenhouse that lay at the far end of his garden. The greenhouse had seen better days and been patched-up any number of ways, but that only increased Tom's affection for it. He had no time for *brand new*, not when it came to this. Growing was about playing the long game; that was part of its attraction for him. None of it was about appearance; it was about understanding nature; it was about gentle encouragement; it was about finding peace.

Why did such a simple thing relax him so?

It was like knocking his brain into neutral. Thirty-six years as a civil engineer had taken its toll and left him balding, hypertensive and overweight. Recently he'd increasingly felt uneasy, but the time he spent tending his plants removed all that, made him forget that he bore little resemblance to his former self. It took Tom elsewhere.

The sound of the phone interrupted the silence of the Sunday morning.

Barbara would get that.

"Tom!" Barbara's voice, calling from the house, caused him to look up.

"Tom! Matthew's a dad! We're grandparents!"

Tomato seeds forgotten, Tom hurried into the house to where his wife stood. Barbara was next to their ageing telephone-table, speaking into the receiver, her fingers wrapping themselves around the worn spiral cord.

"That's wonderful, I'm so glad for the two of you. Your dad's here now – I'll put him on."

He knew she wanted to talk for longer, but Barbara was always like that, looking after the pennies.

Tom took the phone from Barbara as she excitedly did a little dance, mouthing *A boy! Told you*!

"Matthew?"

"Hi Dad, or *Grand-dad* I should say" came his son's crackling voice. "It's a boy – Ethan. I'm a dad! *How mad's that?* I'm on a payphone in the hospital, so I'll have to be quick, but I wanted to let you know."

Tom inwardly felt his feathers plump with pride. *A grandfather – how about that?* It had not seemed five-minutes since Matty had been born and he'd become a father himself.

Time...

"That's fantastic Matt. How's Jane?"

"She's fine, great even, but knackered – all good – she's even asking for chocolate. Dad, I haven't got much change, have you got the number for Grandpa's place?"

Tom's heart sank.

Why couldn't Matt let it go? Why couldn't he just leave it?

"Matt, you know I do, but are you sure that that's a good idea? You know what he's been like recently. He's *always* been a crazy old man but now... I don't know."

It was true, Tom's relations with Joe had always been strained but, over the last year, the old man had started making less and less sense. It was like Tom's childhood, the *bad old days*, all over again, but this time Tom had fallen out with him completely.

"Dad, I know you think he's lost it, but I need to let him know..."

****

Joseph Howard looked out of the window into the street, so sleep-deprived he barely registered the events around him.

Like a museum case of Victorian dolls, the residents sat motionless behind the veranda's glazed panels. Each with uncomprehending eyes, they watched the ever-advancing world as it passed them by.

The curator of this particular display weaved her way between them before stopping and lightly touching an arm.

"Joe. You've got a phone call."

Joe, roused from his daze, looked up from the worn-out

high-backed Chesterfield to where a member of the nursing staff held a chunky cordless phone, its antenna extended.

"It's your grandson, I think he's got some exciting news."

Joe put down his notebook and reached for the receiver.

"Hello?" he croaked.

"Grandpa-Joe, it's me, Matt. Jane's had the baby; it's a boy: Ethan Joseph Howard."

The words stunned Joseph into silence.

"Grandpa?"

Joseph said nothing. What could he say? At the mention of Ethan's name the graft had jumped, ever so slightly, but more than that, *worse than that*, he could now see what the variance was within it.

Within the graft. This conversation did not happen. And now he saw it; within the graft – Matt did not have a son; Ethan had no existence.

He drew in his breath and steeled himself for what he was about to say.

"Matty. Listen carefully, don't rush here, but it's crucial that you come see me as soon as you can – it's time."

The graft hung there, suspended, but thankfully, it hadn't moved further.

Good.

It was static for now and sufficiently distant.

It just needed to stay that way.

Joseph continued, "Don't speak to anybody – especially your father. Especially Tom."

"Grandpa, is everything alright?" asked his grandson, the concern evident in his voice.

"No Matty, the very opposite, I think Ethan's in serious danger, grave danger. I need to talk to you about your son and some other things I should have told you a long time ago, but not over the phone. Come and see me, Matty. *It's time*, just make sure it looks natural. They could, already, be watching."

Without speaking further, Joseph Howard thumbed the phone's power switch and pushed its antenna back into its body before placing the handset on the table beside him. He once again picked up his notebook and continued to stare blankly out of the window.

Joe sighed heavily.

Why Ethan?

Other than him, what connection could there be?

"There will be dire consequences..."

If old debts were to be called in why wait a lifetime to do it?

Unless...

Unless there was a new ACL.

Unless they needed to make an example of him, an object-lesson, to keep other fixers in line. It was perfect, brilliant in its monstrosity – get with the program or after you're gone we'll erase your family. Like we did with poor Joseph Howard.

That delicate balance...

Joe's mouth dried, as a horrific realisation washed over him.

They were likely waiting for him to die or become too old and decrepit to oppose them – a soft target. Even though his family had the gift, it was latent; undeveloped. With no perception, or interaction with the RIFT, they would never even see this coming.

But the ACL, or whatever they called themselves now, didn't know that he was on to them. Until his family was in a position to defend themselves, he needed to keep it that way.

The veins on the back of his hands rose, and his knuckles whitened as his grip on the notebook tightened.

If they thought Joseph Howard's family were going down without a fight, they were sadly mistaken.

CHAPTER 3

Matthew Howard was speechless – stunned, his grandfather's words still ringing in his ears.

Ethan's in danger? Who would want to hurt Ethan?

No, he'd said he thought that Ethan was in serious danger, grave danger – even. What did that mean? Who even knew about Ethan? Who could be watching?

As he tried to comprehend what he had heard, he felt the panic rise within him. His heart hammering so hard in his chest that he fought for breath.

It made no sense. No sense at all.

Absent-mindedly, Matt replaced the pay-phone receiver back on its hook to stop its drone, and slumped heavily against the hospital corridor wall. A sigh escaped him as though he were punctured.

Maybe his father was right. Maybe the Grandpa-Joe he'd known, or Joe as he preferred to be called, was gone. He'd said not to speak to Tom, his own Dad. Did Joe think his dad would hurt Ethan? Surely not!

What else had he said?

It's time. Something about that phrase and the way that he'd used it was strangely familiar.

He searched his memory and recalled the time he had spent with his grandparents during a school holiday, before Grandma-Ruth had passed away. They'd gone to a once-popular seaside town in the south of England that had held memories for the two of them.

"Matty, not everything in this world makes sense," his grandfather had said, looking out to sea, "The world is not as you think – especially for people like you and me.

People like you and me...

"In your lifetime, God-willing, you'll see many things, some of them dreadful, some of them wonderful, some of them mundane. But Matty, if you think you're going mad, if you think the very world is splitting apart, come see me, talk to me. Will you promise me that?"

Joe had unsettled him, yet he'd promised all the same. Then had come the wave of unease, "What do you mean, people like us? I don't understand."

"One day you may, Matty. Or maybe you won't; hopefully you'll be spared that guilt. There's a quote, I don't know who said it, but it goes something like *All that is needed for the triumph of evil is that good men do nothing.* I tried to be that good man Matty, but I loved your grandmother too much. I did try though Matty, believe me, I tried..."

Wistfully, Joe had broken off; his mind had seemed to have travelled elsewhere, his eyes looking out over the slate-grey waters.

"One day we'll talk further, and you may come to understand, but I think that I've burdened you enough with the tiresome ravings of an old man for one day. Come on, let me buy you an ice cream."

Joe had tousled Matt's hair and had even managed to force a smile.

"Someday, when it's time, promise you'll hear me out. *When it's time*, promise you'll trust me, Matty?"

Through the false smile, his grandfather's beseeching manner had shocked him.

So unlike the man he knew.

He remembered how Joe had looked like he had the weight of the world on his shoulders. None of it had made any sense. Later he'd looked up the aphorism his grandfather had quoted, but that had thrown little light on the subject. All that mattered was the response he'd given.

"I'll always trust you Grandpa" he had said, the memory so strong that he could still taste the cold of the ice cream on his tongue.

But now he was an adult, things were no longer so clear-cut.

I'll always love you, Joe, he thought. *But I've no idea whether I can trust you anymore.*

It's time...

Almost by surprise, he found himself considering the now fading phone-conversation with his grandfather as marginal, categorising it as '*Yet more of the old man's craziness*,' as his father would have put it.

But Joe had warned him not to tell his father...
Why?
He did love the old fool, but could he afford to humour him when the immediate here-and-now had to take precedence?
I'm a dad myself now. I've responsibilities. I need to grow up. I need to be the grown-up. Not only that, I'm exhausted, and Jane needs chocolate.
The ebullience he felt earlier at the birth of his son had faded, and tiredness now deflated him once again. Dazed, he headed off to the hospital kiosk.
Coffee...
As was often the case when he was as tired as he was now, he struggled to focus on details, like the text of the newspapers racked on the shelves. Ignoring them, he instead headed for the display of soft toys, where he selected a powder-blue rabbit which he took to the cashier.
"That's nice. For a boy?" asked the young girl behind the counter as she took the toy from him.
"Yes – my first" he replied.
"Could I also get a bar of chocolate and a coffee – white no sugar?" Jane had been desperate – *buy me chocolate* she'd mouthed threateningly while feeding Ethan. More than that, though, Matt needed something to wake him up. He needed to get back to Jane, get organised – it wouldn't be long before they would be heading home.
As the girl retired to make his coffee, he looked again at the rack of soft toys with the powder-blue rabbits.
Ethan's going to love that. Looking round, he struggled to find where he'd put the rabbit he'd picked up earlier.
C'mon Matt where have you put it now? Maybe the girl still has it?
He was about to ask but found that an older grey-haired woman had returned with his coffee.
"One coffee, white no sugar."
Mentally-shrugging, he picked up another rabbit, the midwife had switched shifts, mid-labour, too.
That was unions for you.
"This as well, please."
"That's nice. For a boy is it?" asked the woman at the counter.
"Yes – my first" he replied. "What happened to the girl

who served me earlier?" he asked as he picked up the coffee.

The woman looked up. "Julie? Yes, she was meant to be working tonight, but she asked me to swap with her. Why, do you know her?"

Matt blinked and shook his head, "No – I must have been mistaken."

Bearing gifts and coffee in hand, he navigated the hospital's magnolia corridors and made his way back to the ward, his mind returning to the conversation with Joe.

No matter how he was to resolve his twin dilemmas: whether to tell his father and whether to believe Joe. It was not something with which he was about to burden his wife.

CHAPTER 4

Barbara and Jane peered into the Moses-basket as Ethan gurgled merrily back at them.

Ethan Joseph Howard was now a week old, and Matt's parents had come to stay.

He was beautiful – perfect even.

Leaving the girls to their cooing, Matt returned to where his father sat at the kitchen table, sipping tea.

"So how's fatherhood?" asked Tom.

The question caught Matt off-guard, so obvious yet so strange. It was as if Tom had asked 'so how's breathing working out for you?' It was what it was, and to Matt, it felt that it had ever been this way, almost as if there had never been a time before Ethan.

"Fine," he answered.

Ethan was yet to develop his voice and, for the most part, quietly ate and slept.

"How was... *he*?"

For a second Matt considered being cute and replying 'Who?' – however as it was obvious his father meant Joe, there seemed little to gain from playing dumb.

"He was, you know, Joe. You know how he gets. You know how he is."

Matt was already finding this conversation difficult.

Could Ethan really be in danger? If so, he could really do with confiding in his father, but Joe had explicitly told him not to.

After a lengthy pause, he opted for the middle ground.

"Dad, he said some stuff, *bizarre* stuff, none of which made sense. I think you might be right. I'm worried about him. Maybe I should go and see him."

His father offered up a sigh. "Matt, at his age, there's little you can do for him. I'm no psychologist, but in my opinion, there's always been something going on, whether that be undiagnosed schizophrenia or something else – all is I know

31

is when I was a kid he was a real git! You know I've told him countless times to seek help, but he never listens; he never will. If his ravings are getting worse then, to me, it's those birds that are coming home to roost. But at his age, what's going to be gained by going down that route now? I've told you before Matt; *let it go.*"

Unperturbed, Matt pressed on. "He thinks something is going to happen, something bad, something really bad." He was fishing now, "What do you think he could have meant?"

Tom paused, thinking carefully about how to frame his response, "I think that when you become a father, you see and imagine all sorts of dangers, some real, some imaginary. But with the help of friends and family, you get through anything that life throws at you. Is Joe saying he can tell the future now?"

Matt shook his head, saying. "Stranger things have happened; what about you and the bridge?"

'The bridge' had been a project that Tom had worked on years earlier, back when Matt was young. He had finished his part in minor works to the Clayfeth river-bridge and was due to go home. Packing his case to leave, he had flicked on the hotel's TV to a news report.

Witnesses say the bridge gave way during the morning rush hour leading to three deaths and multiple injuries... The camera had panned past the reporter to the bridge.

On the TV, Tom had seen an image of where the bridge had collapsed near its largest extent; the weak point where they'd had to join girders years before.

The pin and hanger assembly Tom had thought, watching the TV in mounting horror. *I'd better get down there.*

Tom had hailed a taxi and had arrived at the scene where, rather than a news crew, work had been completing just as he'd left it yesterday. The bridge was intact, it was fine.

Just how I left it...

I've just seen this collapsed on the news – the pin and hanger assembly. What's going on?

It was bizarre, he'd watched the bridge in ruins on the TV, was he going mad?

After much pleading he'd managed to, finally, convince the crew to shut the bridge to investigate.

"Tom, that area's not even what we're working on. If

you're wrong about this, they're going to have my hide," his boss, Charlie, had warned.

But just as he'd said, they'd found the assembly on the verge of collapse due to corrosion.

"I think someone up there likes you..." Charlie had joked nervously afterwards.

How could it have been?

How could he have known?

Was Joe right? Surely not.

Tom brushed away his dark thoughts, submerging his doubt, and shook his head.

"It's simple enough," he told Matt. "All of that was likely a dream that pieced together information that my subconscious had picked up on throughout the day. It was a lucky break. I must have still been dozing and imagined the TV news."

Matt wasn't convinced; he was sure Tom wasn't convinced either.

"If you say so, Dad. All I'm saying is stranger things have happened. Why can't you give Joe a break?"

"Matt, you don't know what he was like, if you'd been through what I had, and had a childhood like mine, you'd understand. You only know him as a grandfather; he'd mellowed by then. As a dad, he was never in the here and now; but look... can we drop this? I thought you and Jane were going out – after all, isn't that why your mother and I came here?"

Tom was suddenly cross and looked more and more uncomfortable; Matt was certain his father was hiding something.

Nothing sinister – he would be safe leaving Ethan with them tonight, he was sure of that – but enough to convince him he should pay Joe a visit.

CHAPTER 5

Jane Howard busied herself in front of the mirror.

Earrings...

She could not remember the last time she and Matt had gone out, so Matt's parents' offer was a real boon.

Foundation, last touches to her lipstick...

There – done!

Happy with the result she bounced out of the room and made her way downstairs.

"Right then," she said, "if you're sure you'll be OK then we'll get going."

It had been Barbara's suggestion to babysit, so she and Matt were going out for a meal. She couldn't wait.

"We'll be fine," Barbara answered. "Stay-out as long as you like. We've got everything organised."

Needing no more prompting, Jane grabbed Matt's arm and ushered him to go, gently pushing him outside.

With the closing of the door, silence descended on the room; Ethan continued to sleep quietly in his basket in the corner.

Peace at last, thought Tom. *If only I could still my mind.*

But rather than the silence he craved, he felt his thoughts returning to the conversation earlier and Matt's assertions about Joe.

If he could bring himself to be honest, there was an element of truth in what his son had said.

Matt was right – stranger things do happen...

Like now – looking around him, Tom soaked up the room. It was familiar but somehow wrong, he couldn't explain what he was feeling. *Everything was real but not quite real*, almost as if existence itself was a bubble that could be burst at the slightest touch.

Why couldn't he stop himself feeling this way?

For the last year, there had been a weight that had pressed on the fabric of his mind, ever so slightly, making the world around him take on an almost-translucent quality.

Sometimes things would be in the wrong places, or would disappear, and then turn up where he'd least expected, only to later be back where they started – with alien memories of never being anywhere else.

Sometimes things were how they should be but changed; either the wrong colour or the wrong shape.

Some days he even doubted what was real and what was not.

It was like the bridge. When you can't tell the difference between dream and reality, thought Tom. *When you can't trust your memory, who are you?*

Today had been like that. The conversation with Matt had been hard. He knew none of what he was feeling could be real, but that didn't help.

Not when I can't tell the difference. But if Joe's feeling this too, could there be something more to it?

"Barbara, I need to talk to you," Tom said, "It's happening again. It feels like a storm building in my mind. Matt says Joe feels it too."

Barbara's face was filled with love but was cold and stern; they'd had this same conversation what seemed like a hundred times before. Raising her palms to the side of her head she suddenly looked ten-years-older – and desperate.

Oh God Tom, Not this again!

"Tom – don't do this to me. Not here; you promised. We agreed; these feelings you have aren't real, and I'm not going to sit by and watch you torture yourself with them."

I've got to be strong, Barbara thought; *I can't give him an inch. For his own sake; don't entertain this.*

"Your dad has always had issues which he refuses to acknowledge, I'm not going to see you go the same way."

Softening, she sat by Tom and rubbed his arm, attempting to comfort him.

"You have to stop with this *there's a problem with the universe* stuff, and the first step is acknowledging that the issue is with you. We need to get you some help, Tom. Like we've said about your dad. There's a problem there which he refuses to confront. The difference is that you're not him, and he's a long way down the road – you're not. Joe needed help a long time ago and should have got it. I'm not going to let you make the same mistake."

Tom knew Barbara was right; she always was, with stuff like this.

"I know. I know, and that's what I said to Matt, but I don't know Babs – if you could see what I could see, feel what I could feel, would you still be saying that? You don't know what it's like. Some days, *none of this* feels real."

"So now I'm not real? Is that what you're saying?" said Barbara, her voice wavering. "Listen to yourself. Ask yourself, what's more likely, that the world around us is broken, and only you and your dad can see it… Or, that your dad has some congenital form of schizophrenia and you're your father's son?"

Sensing the indecision in him, Barbara became stern and reached out, taking hold of both his wrists.

"Tom," she said, "look at me… I'm here, and I promise you, *this is real.*"

Barbara was right.

Barbara was always right.

"Tom, you need to see someone; someone professional. I can come with you if you like, but we need to do this before you get worse. You'll likely need a referral – I'll make an appointment with Doctor Dickinson."

Tom felt a thousand thoughts clamouring to be heard. *Was he mad? If he were, how could he tell? He had no choice but to trust Barbara.*

"OK, you're right. Let's do that."

With that decision made, Tom felt an element of calmness flow over him.

His wife was right; he needed help and the sooner, the better.

Barbara stood up, "Good", she said, "now should we have a nice cup of tea?"

Tom nodded, "Please." Standing up himself he wandered over to Ethan's crib.

It's alright for you, he thought. *You've got all this to look forward to. But for now, you haven't a care in the world.*

He watched, as Ethan slept at peace and contented. The gentle, rhythmic sound of his breath calming Tom like a ticking clock.

Looking closer, he took in every detail of his grandson.

Enjoy the moment, Tom, he thought. *He'll be grown up*

before you know it. Remember how he is now, from his nose to his toes. What will the world be like when he's my age?

As if to answer Ethan shifted in his cot and sighed, but as Tom watched he realised that he could see the base of the cot through Ethan, as if he were ever-so-slightly transparent.

No, 'see' wasn't the right word. But, if not 'see' then what? He didn't know.

In front of his eyes Ethan seemed to shimmer, as if becoming more, and then less, real. Tom watched, transfixed, as the colour of his grandson's bedding appeared to change from blue to yellow, and Ethan himself seemed to jitter and flicker in and out of his consciousness, for a split-second disappearing.

What the hell's happening to me? Tom panicked – his heart suddenly racing.

But then as soon as it had begun, it was over. Ethan was asleep in his basket, and his wife was handing him a mug of steaming tea, strong and sweet. Strangest of all was the juxtaposition of two competing memories drilling into his head. One memory where he had panicked at Ethan's disappearance and one where he'd calmly watched Ethan sleeping.

The two sets of alternate events grated against one another, but there was also something else, a voice, disembodied and without ownership, repeatedly conveying one single word.

Hope.

What did it mean?

Hope?

Am I losing my mind? thought Tom, his heart in his mouth.

I can't get this weight out of the front of my head, and now I'm hallucinating too.

None of that could be real... Could it?

Glancing briefly at Barbara, it was evident that she'd witnessed none of it, none of what he had.

If it were not real, why could he remember it so vividly?

But if it were real, how could he remember it not happening?

Was he losing himself?

"Tom!"

The sound of a woman's voice, speaking his name, caused him to turn his head to the right. Tom Howard glanced towards the side of the hospital room where a nurse now busied herself. Looking down, he saw that restraints on his wrists and ankles hampered his movement and held him securely to the metal-framed bed.

"OK then Thomas, shall we get you up?"

The nurse banged on what looked to be a heavy door.

Tom watched in silence as the scene unfolded around him. It was strangely unreal yet also reassuringly familiar.

"Two-Seven-One requesting assistance removing restraints from patient Thomas Howard…"

A name resonated in his head – *Kathy?*

"Tom?"

Another voice called his name, causing him now to turn suddenly to the left.

"Tom – you're spilling your tea."

There stood Barbara, exasperated, and just as before, he was in his front room with his wife and Ethan.

What the hell just happened?

Where the hell had he just been?

The only thing he knew for sure was that he needed help.

CHAPTER 6

Matthew Howard pushed the buzzer of the residential care home where Joe now lived.

For a while after his wife had died, Joe had struggled on alone, but found that he craved company, or, as he'd put it, hated silence.

At the time Matt had been in no position to take him in, and Barbara would have none of it.

"He's not living here," Matt remembered his mother reiterating.

His father had objected at first but had inevitably caved into Barbara's wishes, as he always did.

"As much as I hate the idea, he is my dad," Tom had protested.

"But Tom, he's as mad as a box of frogs," Barbara had said before finally delivering an ultimatum. "If he comes, I go."

The net result was Joe moving to the West Verity residential care home, where Matt now stood, baby-carrier in hand.

From outside it looked a nice-enough place, if a little pedestrian.

Matt shifted his grip on the carrier – Ethan was now six-weeks old and starting to get heavy.

"Yes?" The door was answered by a stern looking woman in a fading pastel-yellow gingham uniform. Her face instantly softened on catching a glimpse of Ethan.

"I've come to see Joseph Howard." Matt explained, "I'm his grandson."

A flash of recognition flickered across the nurse's face. "Ah yes, Joe's grandson, you rang up didn't you, that's right – My word, you certainly look like him in his younger days – come in. My name's Mary, I look after Joe."

Matt followed the nurse into the lobby, where he signed in.

"I must warn you that your grandfather hasn't really been himself lately. He's been increasingly withdrawn and insular.

Maybe seeing you two will cheer him up, though. You never know."

Mary led him through the sitting room to the veranda where, as before, Joe sat alone in the corner, staring out of the window.

"Joe, you've got visitors!" Mary half-shouted.

Joe looked up, "I'm not deaf," he grunted grumpily before turning to Matt. He half-smiled but mostly his face wore a look of relief.

"Thanks for coming Matty – and you must be Ethan."

Unperturbed, Mary patted Joe affectionately on the shoulder.

"Should I bring you boys some tea?" she asked. "I'm not supposed to, but since you've come all this way."

"That would be lovely," Matt replied as she left him and Ethan with his grandfather. "So, what's this about?" he asked.

"All in good time Matty," said Joe, not taking his eyes off his great-grandson. "What's this about? In order to explain that, I need to tell you who I am; and I need to tell you what *you* are… Where do I even begin…"

What I am? wondered Matt, leaning in.

"Years ago, Matty, during the war, I did some work for the government. For an organisation that until recently I thought was long gone, or perhaps never even existed – not in this world anyway. I went against them Matty, and now I believe that they're after Ethan as a punishment; as a lesson to others."

What Joe was saying didn't sound like real-life. *What was he talking about?* But the from the tone of his voice he was obviously concerned about Ethan.

"What do you mean 'after him'?" asked Matt. "Are you telling me someone wants to hurt him?"

"No Matty, they wouldn't hurt him. They would just make it so that he was never born."

CHAPTER 7

Thomas and Barbara Howard sat patiently in their GP's surgery, waiting to be seen. Scribbling notes and leafing through the spiral-bound pad he'd brought with him, Tom struggled to relax. Barbara, in comparison, was a picture of tranquillity, sitting silently, her hands placed on her lap.

"Thomas Howard, Consulting room four," came the receptionist's voice over the tannoy.

Roger Dickinson had been the Howards' GP for as long as they could remember. Back in the day, he'd both treated Joe and seen Matt through his childhood ailments.

Now he was a regular visitor to their home, and they to his, as part of a round-robin bridge school. Part of Barbara's grand plan to go up in the world.

A friendly face, thought Tom, *but it was still not going to be easy.*

"Barbara, Tom; how can I help?"

Tom sat down and, slowly, began to open up.

Not too much detail, Barbara had said. Concentrate on how you're feeling, not on the specifics; we still want to play bridge with him, after all.

He explained, just as Barbara had coached him, that he had been feeling '*not right*' for some time and thought he ought to see someone.

He confided to Roger that he had been having a crisis of confidence at home and at work and how he didn't seem to be able to think as fast or as clearly as he'd done previously, how he'd been in a haze.

He mentioned that things did not always seem *completely* real to him, how he could recall events which happened earlier in the year but not the background to them – and how, just as clearly, he could recall events that could never have happened, and *could* often recall the background events to clarify these *non-events* further.

He recounted finding things very uncomfortable and

painful and, as a result, panicking regularly.

"I need to get my head in a better place; I don't feel like I'm the same person I once was," he said. "Sometimes, *I don't know* – sometimes it's all fine for days, but sometimes I don't know what the hell is going on."

As he continued to speak Tom felt the misery rising as a thousand repressed feelings bubbled to the surface.

"My heart is in my mouth almost all the time. Why can't I get this panicking about the world out of the front of my head?"

He was now becoming progressively more agitated and, as he continued, he began bunching his fists through his hair, almost ripping at it in frustration.

He spoke at length, explaining how Barbara was getting increasingly annoyed with him, as well as his problems day-to-day.

"Small things continue to panic me, and I'm hallucinating – I don't feel like the same person."

How could he explain it when he didn't understand it himself?

Filled with a tumult of emotion, he sat in silence rocking backwards and forwards.

"Sometimes, none of this seems real," he said finally. "Sometimes, it feels like I'm not living this life at all – that all of this is some kind of weird dream that I'm going to wake-up from. What's wrong with me?"

As Tom opened-up further, tears welled and flowed.

"I feel like I am losing my mind and myself. I can't seem to think straight and have these panic attacks. I feel like I can't tell what's real, and I can't focus or concentrate. I feel like I'm living a lie, trying to give the outward impression of being in control, but inwardly... Inwardly, it's another story."

Exhausted, Tom had no more to give – he was done.

Dr Dickinson was silent, thinking before calmly beginning. "OK, Tom: You're right to look for help, I believe that you're right about needing to see someone. The way that this works is that I believe a psychologist may be most appropriate, but to verify that I need to first refer you to a psychiatrist. I believe your medical insurance covers you privately, so if you like, I can make a recommendation, unless this is something that you wanted to look into yourself."

Dr Dickinson flicked through the pages of the directory in front of him before suggesting a name of a specialist that, he said, came highly recommended.

"No – he sounds perfect Roger," said Barbara. "The key thing is that we move at pace. Thank you, Doctor."

CHAPTER 8

"No Matty, they wouldn't hurt him. They'd just make it so he was never born."

Matthew Howard fell silent, not knowing how to respond.

"What do you mean, destroy his records? So, he was a non-person? We have pictures, paper copies of his birth certificate. His name was in the newspaper. What you're talking about, that couldn't happen. Could it?"

What his grandfather seemed to be suggesting just wasn't feasible. *Was it?*

Joe reached out and touched his hand.

"No Matty, that's not what I mean – I wish it were that simple. I don't mean that there would be no official records of him. What I mean is…" he paused thinking how to phrase his words. "What I mean is that, if they succeed, Ethan will have *literally* never have existed. There would be no record of him, not because those records would have been destroyed, but because those records would have never have been created in the first place."

How could he make Matt understand, that not only would Ethan not exist but, for most people, all memory of him would be gone too?

Matt felt the anger welling inside him.

"You keep saying *THEY*," he spat. "*WHO ARE THEY* and what do they want with *MY SON*?"

CHAPTER 9

Thomas Howard sat in the consulting room at the private clinic. Recounting his recent issues and how they had continued, he now felt drained.

It was always different, but always the same. *Scenes of unreality but, to him at least, as lucid and as real as any other.* Either there were marginal inconsistencies, making up the chatter and clamour of everyday life, or there were sharp differences and discontinuities, typically around Ethan. Finally, there were the recurring images and scenes of psychiatric treatment and restraint. These were always the same, with always the same nurse – *Kathy*.

Dr Anish Kumar finished the notes that he had been writing and put his pen gently down on the desk.

"Right, Mr Howard, I'll provide your insurance company referral details in a few days and let them know that my recommendation is that you see a psychologist and that you start a programme of cognitive behavioural therapy. After that, I suggest that you return to me in six months for review. You should be able to choose whom you see. However I would recommend my colleague, John Williamson."

Tom stood up and thanked him before pulling on his coat and rejoining Barbara in the waiting room. He felt tired but invigorated.

He was taking control; things were going to improve, he was sure of it.

Waiting until the door had closed, Dr. Kumar lifted his Dictaphone.

"Case: AK/BA/186427

"To Dr Roger Dickinson, Janet: add address and date.

"Dear Dr Dickinson, with reference to Mr Thomas Howard: date of birth 16/12/1946, Janet: add address,

"Thank you for referring the above-named patient whom I saw today.

"He reports psychotic episodes of sporadic hallucination,

delusion and experiencing imagery and autonomic arousal on a number of occasions.

"His sleep is affected by rumination on this topic but otherwise he is free from biological symptoms of low mood.

"He was born in Hampshire of normal birth and milestones. He is an only child and his father is alive. He left school at 18 and attended Winchester University. He works as a civil engineer. He has been married for thirty-two years, and the couple have one child aged twenty-eight, and recently one grandson. He describes his premorbid personality as enquiring, and his interests are in gardening. There is no history of cigarette, alcohol or illicit drug misuse. The couple live in a three-bedroom house and are financially secure.

"There is no family history of mental disorders, although he believes his father presents similar symptoms and is undiagnosed in this regard.

"He has had no previous psychiatric contact and has been a reasonably healthy man, albeit overweight and suffering from hypertension, for which he takes a diuretic. He has no known allergies.

"On mental state examination, he was casually dressed and well-kempt with good eye contact and appropriate behaviour. His speech was of normal flow and content and his mood eurythmic with no ideas of harm to self or others. He has some evidence of schizophrenic episodes. However there is limited ongoing psychosis, and his cognitive functions are intact with good insight.

"I feel that the intensity of his episodes would benefit from a psychological intervention in the form of a course of cognitive behavioural therapy alone. Should I be mistaken I am in no doubt that he will benefit from a pharmacological approach.

"Yours etc, Anish Kumar, Consultant Psychiatrist."

Dr Kumar stopped the machine and paused, as if in thought. Restarting the recording he continued:

"New message, memo to Director Rountree – Branchford Institute.

"Sir, without violating doctor-patient-confidentiality, the patient I have just seen has made reference to the area you asked be monitored for.

"Yours etc, Anish Kumar,

"Janet, please send each of these straight away."

CHAPTER 10

WHO ARE THEY? Matt had asked.

They were the ACL – The Anti-Catastrophe League, Joe thought. *The Reality Commission for Acceptable Outcomes – how do I explain that? Acceptable to whom, by whose definition?*

"*They* are, or *were*, an organisation that I was involved with a long time ago. An organisation that was created because of me. An organisation set up to find, take advantage of, and control, people like me, people like you. People like Ethan."

Matt, concern rising within him, held back the obvious question and looked at his grandfather. "I'm listening."

"For as long back as I know, Matty, the men in our family have had a kind of gift which we'd always thought of as unique. Depending on the individual or circumstances, it surfaces at different points in their life, or maybe not at all, but it's always there if you know where to look, if you know how to develop it. I have it, your father has it, you have it, and Ethan will have it. This gift gives us a window into different possible worlds where events are played out to different outcomes, where *different causes* trigger *different effects*. This may sound hard to believe Matty, but you can pick these outcomes, like picking apples from a tree."

Matt looked sceptical. Eyes narrowing, he asked, "What's this got to do with Ethan? You said that Ethan was in danger."

"I'm coming to that Matty. During the war, I saw what was happening with Germany, the way that things were going, so I signed up. Your grandmother tried to convince me otherwise, but I didn't listen. I thought I knew it all."

Matt was confused, *Joe had been an electrician, he had never been in the forces, had he?*

Humouring him, he asked, "Signed up, what to?"

"The Army, a foot soldier. I got a reputation for having a sixth-sense, like I could see around corners – like I could see the future. That wasn't it, of course, I could just see other worlds where things happened on a slightly different timeline. Like your father, that time with the bridge he was working on."

Matt was suddenly shocked; he'd mentally begun to pigeon-hole Joe's story into fantasy, but his reference to the incident with Tom rattled him severely.

"So now you're telling me that you were some war hero and Dad can see through time?" Matt asked.

"Not *time* Matty, *other worlds*, but yes, he can, as I'm sure you can too. However, he's in denial deeper than you know. I've tried to have this conversation with him more times than I can remember. He just refuses to listen, thinks I'm crazy."

Are you? thought Matt. He looked his grandfather up and down but remained silent.

"When I was in the army I once got a chance to speak with a top brass – a General Envaneer. He wanted to know my secret, wanted to know what my trick was, what my luck was. So, stupidly, I told him. He just laughed, of course; laughed in my face and looked at me like I was nothing – so I fixed him."

The phrase caused Matt to prick up his ears.

"What do you mean *fixed him*?" said Matt.

"I'll tell you, 'cause I can remember as if it were yesterday. I looked at Envaneer and I felt my anger rising. I thought *how dare you laugh at me like that, in front of everyone?* Who did he think he was? But then I saw something else, through the RIFT, what I saw was a course of events where he did believe, where he truly believed, a world where I must have either looked at him differently or said things in another way, because I saw real comprehension on his face."

As Joe continued, he had become more animated than Matt had seen him in a long time.

"To my shame and in my anger, I selected that world out of arrogance, forced that reality into being. Just to prove a point. Of course, he became like a man possessed, but by then it was too late."

"What do you mean?" asked Matt.

"He was evangelical – 'We need to get you to London. Find others like you; think what you could do.'"

Matt sighed. This was too much to take in. He loved Joe,

but he was quite obviously delusional. Joe was never in the army – as far as Matt knew he'd never even left England. Joe had worked as an electrician during the war, a reserved occupation, and lived in Hampshire with Grandma Ruth, end-of-story.

And this story that Joe was telling him? Well, what could he say?

He looked from Joe to Ethan, who continued to sleep peacefully in his carrier, and felt a tumult of mixed emotions. Sorrow at having Joe rave like this, but relief at what that meant for Joe's warnings about his son. Ethan was not likely to be in danger – Matt was convinced of that now.

But he's still my grandfather, he thought, *even if he has lost it. I still love him, and he's telling a good tale.*

Settling into his chair and sipping the tea Mary had brought them, Matt said "So, what happened, Joe? Tell me it all."

CHAPTER 11

LONDON 1941

Private Joseph Howard sat in the back of the staff-car, an Armstrong Siddeley 25, as it weaved a path through South London. Bomb-damaged wrecks of unnamed, unfamiliar streets flashed in front of him before he could fully take them in. As he passed them, he found his attention drawn to a shawled woman who stood motionless, statue-like, at the corner of two devastated roads; baby on hip, her smudged face a picture of desperation and angst.

Who was she? What stories from the night did her grief-stricken face hide?

But, before he could consider her more, she was gone, and the car sped through the early dawn.

The devastation more than shocked him. *Was this carnage really England?* From the point he had left France, none of this had seemed real. What was he getting himself into?

He had been the solitary passenger of the plane that had flown him overnight into Biggin Hill, and as the sun had begun to rise over the capital, he'd been immediately transferred into the car in which he now found himself.

Whoever this general was, he was clearly connected.

After becoming enthused with Howard, Envaneer had made a number of phone-calls that resulted in him being immediately re-assigned with new orders to report to one Prof. Branchford, who would meet him near King's College Hospital, London.

The car pulled into Denmark Hill and stopped in front of an imposing Edwardian brick building with white porticos on its doors and lower windows.

Just as tight-lipped as he had been en-route, and as his pilot had been from France, his driver wordlessly opened the car and ushered Joe out towards the entrance. The street around him was still and eerily quiet. The driver deftly produced a large key, which he used to unlock the expansive door, before finally breaking his silence.

"Through here Sir; someone will collect you."

Joe stepped through the doorway into the dimness that lay beyond, but to his surprise, once inside, the driver heaved the oak timbers shut without following him through. The sound of the massive door closing and the subsequent clank of the heavy lock resonated, causing echoes along the apparently empty corridor.

Joseph Howard looked around and found himself in a vast but seemingly abandoned building. The hard, polished surface made his footsteps echo as he paced. In the half-light, the checkerboard design of the floor seemed to give it an unreal quality. He walked forwards and backwards deciding what to do next. Trying the door, he found it locked tight, as he knew it would be.

What have you got yourself into this time, Joe? he thought.

Onwards and upwards.

Crossing the threshold of the weighted inner doors, Joe moved along a dim corridor. No lights guided his path, however for all its desolation, the surroundings were spotless; clinical, as if fastidiously cleaned.

He felt like a rat in a maze.

Come on Joe, don't get spooked, keep with it.

He paused, waiting for an alter-world to give him an indication of what could be to come, waiting for any bifurcation in the event-line that could give him some insight into what lay round the corner.

Come on... he thought.

Nothing. All world views remained stubbornly empty.

That in itself was unusual. Normally, when he felt for other worlds there was typically a huge amount of divergence, but here, *in this place*, there was nothing. All worlds were somehow in unison.

Strange.

That almost never happened...

How could that be?

What did that mean?

At the far end of the corridor he had a choice of paths – *right or left*. Joe could now see the glow of an electric light emanating from the far end of the passageway to his left.

Choosing the left path, he carried on towards the light, aware that, in the silence, his footsteps were more than announcing his presence.

Like a moth to the flame?

As he approached the light, he was acutely aware of what looked like hospital wards, one after another – all empty.

Like the Marie Celeste...

He finally reached the room which emitted the light and found himself looking into a small office where a middle-aged man with greying hair and a clipped white beard sat at a battered desk, poring over a set of documents.

"One moment..." came his voice without looking up, continuing to methodically make notes, alternating between writing and refreshing his pen from the old-style inkwell on his desk.

Eventually finishing, the man at the desk slowly blew, right-to-left over the text that he had just completed, to aid its fixing. Satisfied, he calmly placed it down and looked up.

"There," he said. "Joseph Howard, I presume, it's a pleasure to meet you. Professor Arthur Branchford at your service."

The man proffered his hand.

"You must be parched. Can I offer you a cup of tea? It's not very good I'm afraid, and we have no lemons, but we make do."

Branchford slowly worked his way up from his desk and shuffled past Joseph, before, almost as an afterthought, beckoning him to follow, "Come..."

Bemused, Joseph followed him like a lost lamb, through a maze of unlit silent corridors until he eventually reached what looked like a staffroom, where Branchford lit the small gas burner in the corner and placed a battered copper kettle over the heat.

Busying himself with a cracked bone-china teapot, Branchford heaped a generous helping of tealeaves into it before finally adding the now boiling water.

"Milk and sugar?" he asked, picking up a tall milk bottle that stood semi-submerged in water in the sink.

Wondering what this was all about, Joseph simply nodded, "Please."

Preparations complete, Branchford set a silver tray with the teapot, milk jug, two bone-china cups and saucers and a sugar-bowl that held two bright silver spoons.

With that, he shuffled off down the dim corridor back to his office, this time beckoning with his head, again simply saying, "Come..."

When they reached it, Branchford set down the tray.

"I'll be *mother* then, shall I?" he said, pouring the tea into the cups and adding the milk and sugar. He handed a cup and saucer to Joseph before settling back into a chair and taking a long sip from his own.

The tea was strong, sweet and hot, but most of all, after his journey, it was extremely welcome.

"That's better, isn't it?" said Branchford, "Now, where should we begin?"

Joe didn't know whether the question was rhetorical.

Was he supposed to respond? What had Envaneer said to Branchford? He had no idea.

"Where am I? What is this place?"

"This *place* is, or *was*, the Maudsley Hospital for early and acute psychiatric cases. But that was then. Now they let me use it. Before the war, this was set up by Henry Maudsley as a centre to treat early-onset schizophrenia rather than waiting for patients to be so-far-gone as to need institutionalising in an asylum. Maudsley's view was rather than treat chronic cases that there needed to be somewhere that tackled early and acute cases. He wanted this to be inclusive and have an outpatients' clinic, also support teaching and, most importantly for people like me, research. In the beginning this was progressive, but it slowly turned rotten as many took it upon themselves to experiment without much regard for the outcome for the patients."

As Branchford continued Joe wondered who it was the man was really addressing. Was it him, or was Branchford justifying his position, speaking his confession to the wider world?

"Back then, there was no drive to properly understand the condition. It was all random pot shots, either so-called electro-convulsive therapy or pumping patients full of animal hormones. It was a mess. I would have none of it. It was a completely unstructured search for the silver bullet, for a magical cure for what may not even be a disease. Sargant was the worst of them. Chemists and electricians the lot of them – what happened to *First do no harm? The Hippocratic Oath?*

"My view was that we can't effectively treat psychological conditions until we can understand them, not only in their symptoms but also in their mechanisms, their causes – determine what is going on below the surface. So that brings us to you Joseph, and why *you* are here. For a while, I've had a theory that schizophrenics actually see the world in a less-filtered way than so-called normal people. I believe they actually see the world how it really is, rather than being modified by expectation.

"Take this mask Joseph," said Branchford gesturing at a hollow, porcelain-visage mounted via a thin wooden shaft on what appeared to be a gramophone player. It looked like a makeshift comic mask from Greek tragedy. Branchford wound the handle which caused the face to slowly revolve.

"Most people are unable to see this mask for what it is, Joseph. As it rotates, most people look at this and see the inside of the mask as facing outward, even though they know this is not the case. My question to you, is what do *you* see?"

The words hung in the air as Joseph looked at the slowly revolving mask. What *did* he see?

"Joseph, do you see the mask, as it is, *sometimes inward, sometimes outward*, or do you see it looking outward?"

Joseph continued to look at the mask. *How could he explain that what he saw was neither of those things, but it was also both of those things?*

Finally, he submitted, "I see whichever I choose to see, I see both at the same time; what does that mean?"

"Now I was hoping you were going to say something like that," said Branchford. "If I'm right about you, it could mean that you are the missing link I've been waiting for. If I'm right, you could maybe even see the world as it actually is – but you can also see it how the rest of us see it. Have you or your family a history of schizophrenia, Joseph?"

"Stay hidden Joseph," his father had told him. *"There're many that would seek to put us in a freak-show, stay hidden and stay low, and whatever you do, keep your own counsel on what 'normal' means."*

"No, not as far as I know" replied Joseph, pushing away

the memories of the agonising demise of his own grandfather, which the family had kept hidden. *Where was this questioning going?*

"And I don't feel that I have a split personality."

"Not a split personality, that's a common misconception. I'm convinced that schizophrenia is, as far as I can tell, although many would disagree, a disconnection between the multiple possible realities and the intrinsic filter that keeps these at bay. The average person cannot see reality for what it is – *like the mask*. The average person sees what they expect to see and cannot see the truth, even if it's before their eyes. I believe schizophrenics don't have that veil, I believe that they have the scales removed from their eyes but, for the most part, can't cope with this in any way that could be considered normal.

"My theory Joseph is that some of the different worlds that torment them are actually real, different *elsewheres,* but real nonetheless. My theory is that all things that could happen, *do happen,* somewhere; and that for all their psychosis, schizophrenics have a window into these worlds. For a number of years, I've been putting out feelers throughout the community to get notified of anyone treating patients who could be thought of as high-functioning schizophrenics who lucidly describe *other worlds*. And recently with the army generating so many patients I'd gone down that route too. However, after so long I was beginning to think that it would never bear fruit."

"And then you found me," said Joseph.

"And then we found you." echoed Branchford.

"So, now that you've found me, what is it that you want to know?"

CHAPTER 12

OXFORD 2005

Eli Phillip Rountree lifted the ageing handset and dialled. He sat in an opulent office with a collection of leather-bound books behind him. Tomes of wisdom, there predominantly for show. Finally, the phone yielded an answer.

"Kumar?" he asked.

A voice squawked on the other end of the line.

"Good, I got your note. You say you referred him – to one of ours I hope?"

Rountree listened to the reply, taking notes.

"Good. Williamson's a good man. Thank you for your help, Doctor."

Replacing the receiver, Rountree fidgeted nervously with his pen.

They had better break ground soon, or the funding for the programme would dry up.

For the last sixty years, the Branchford Institute had slowly burned through a segment of the funds left by the late Arthur Branchford to 'locate and investigate high-functioning schizophrenics who lucidly described other-worlds'. It offered generous bounties for referrals and had also previously been funded by the army, but that had been years ago. After countless patients over more than half a century, each attempt to find *subject zero* had always come to nothing.

Maybe this one would be different. Williamson would know – if only he were available a little earlier.

Once found, there was more funding available and a programme ready to go, but this was conditional on there being at least one confirmed subject. Maybe this was finally the one. If not, he feared it would be time to wrap it up and go home.

CHAPTER 13

THE MAUDSLEY 1941

"So, I understand that you can see things," said Branchford, "Things that might happen, but not dreams or inventions – you can see things that give you a view of events you could never have known."

Joe thought. Where should he start?

It had always been that way. How much should he share? Or was he well past that stage already?

"You could say that," said Joe. Playing it coy, he continued, "I'd never really thought about it until I signed up. Like I said to the general, and like what you just said, it's not that I can tell the future. It's nothing like that – nothing even close. It's that I can see other possibilities, and *more often than not*, if I wait long enough, one of these plays out in *this* world."

Becoming more relaxed, Joe began opening up…

In his unit, the way it used to work was that they tried to play it cool. Joe would be on point, flushing out Jerries that were typically holed-up after the main hostilities had moved on somewhere else.

At each intersection they went through the same drill. He'd sit them down behind cover and he'd wait, and wait, and wait. They'd wait until he could see the 'alter-them' advance like shadows into the street ahead of him. Like pages of a flick-book, he'd see himself and the others dancing like ghosts along the roads, and then, either nothing would happen or, a hidden shadow would open up on them. When that happened, more often than not, he had them. He knew where they were. It was a waiting game. Once found, he'd call it out to Charlie, his sniper. *"There, in the old church, far left window,"* or *"Behind the tree line, to the right."*

All his unit saw was him sit and quietly think before pulling one rabbit out of the hat after another. They called him 'bidet', an infantile play on the French *BD*, for 'bullet dodger'. They'd joke that he was deep in thought, waiting to squeeze one out – but they always took his advice.

Under his watch, they'd only lost one man, and that had been foreseeable. Jackson had been removed for personal reasons, and he'd been replaced by a young Irish kid, name of Riley. He'd been full of himself, boasting how he'd seen action on numerous fronts and how the unit was full of old men. He'd lasted all of about two hours – stupid kid. At the first choke point Joe had sat down, as ever, and waited. The rest of the lads had broken out their sandwiches, knowing that this could take a while. Riley however, was made of different stuff; he would have none of it. Unwilling to be told, he wandered out on-scout, and that was the end of him. Dead, for the sake of waiting half an hour.

"*What are we going to do without you, Bidet?*" they'd asked. "*Without you, we're all... Well y'know... like Riley.*"

He'd had no words for them; not then, not now. All he could do was make the best of things and try to relate to Branchford as well as he could.

Behind the desk, Branchford was rapidly making notes in what Joe thought was a particularly elegant leather-bound journal. For some reason, Joe felt drawn to it; wanted to touch it.

It was as if the scratch of the Professor's pen in the small book had a hypnotic quality that drew him in, calmed him. He watched the old man write and, for a short time, he was strangely at peace. *Everything else was gone.* There was only the book.

"And did any of these, let's call them *premonitions*, turn out not to be the case?"

"Sorry. What?" said Joe, once again aware of the conversation.

"These things you saw, did any of them turn out to be false; not happen?"

"Certainly," replied Joe, "but that would be maybe one in fifty times, and, like I said, these weren't *premonitions*. The trick would be to either wait things out or wait for multiple confirmations from multiple shadows. The more confirmations, the more confident I'd be. Then of course, if I suspected there was a sniper somewhere, there would be a good probability we'd see him. On some occasions, however, they'd have already left, moved out, and all we found was traces of where they'd been. Those were the better ones. The ones where nobody died, on either side."

"And what about *you* Joe," said Branchford. "Could you see yourself in these other worlds?"

"In a sense, yes, but in a sense no," said Joe. "It's not like I could see another me, it's that *I was* that 'other-me' – see through his eyes, walk in his footsteps, think through his thoughts."

"And how did that feel?" said Branchford. "Were you able to differentiate the two memories?"

"I wouldn't say it's easy, but with practice, it's possible and becomes less of a problem," said Joe.

It was difficult, but his father had shown him how to deal with it, how to feel for the triggers and box-in the errant feelings and memories. How to tell the straight for the variance and how to limit the effects.

"That is unless of course, I pulled in..." he trailed off, realising he'd revealed far more than he'd intended to.

"What do you mean?" asked Branchford.

A sickening feeling rose in Joe's stomach.

He'd said too much.

How could he have been so stupid?

"I think I'd like another cup of tea, and to rest," muttered Joseph, searching...

Branchford would have none of it.

"All in good time Joseph. First, what did you mean by *pulled in*?"

Joe ignored him.

How could he be so careless as to mention that? It was one thing to 'see' different worlds, it would be quite another to admit being able to manipulate them, to change reality itself.

He was sure that he wasn't ready to share that information – not yet.

Joe searched for possibilities within his grasp; no longer hearing Branchford's questions. Finally, he saw it; the graft-point he was looking for where he'd avoided mentioning pulling in different worlds. He reached for it and deftly replaced this reality with that one.

He felt the movement in his memory, but this was only a minor shift; after all, it was just a little nudge. In his mind the events seemed to halt and then repeat, overlaying his previous memory.

"…and what about you Joe," Branchford had said. "Could you see yourself in these other worlds?"

"In a sense, yes, but in a sense no," said Joe. "It's not like I could see another me, it's that *I was* that 'other-me' – see through his eyes, walk in his footsteps, think through his thoughts."

"And how did that feel?" said Branchford "Were you able to differentiate the two memories?"

"With practice, that was no problem," Joe said, this time making sure he stopped without elaborating any further.

Fixed, he thought. *Good, I'd rather that particular box stays shut until another day.*

Filling the gap, Joe smiled and asked, "I don't suppose there's any chance of another cup of tea, is there?"

Branchford blinked repeatedly and held the side of his head. Seemingly confused, he said, "Tea, yes of course." Then looked at Joe and his face blanched.

"What the hell just happened?

"What did you just do?

"…and what did you mean *pulled in?*"

CHAPTER 14

Matthew Howard was startled by a hand lightly touching his arm.

Mary gently smiled, "I'm sorry boys, but it's almost dinner time." She turned to Joe and half-shouting said, "Joe, it's time for your dinner dear – shepherd's pie – *your favourite.*"

Glaring, Joe snapped, "You don't need to shout woman – and how can everything be my favourite?"

Turning to Matt, he waved Mary away.

"Matty, you can't go. I've only just begun – I've so much to tell you, so much to show you... I haven't even got onto Ethan."

Joe was increasingly agitated, Matt had to calm him down. Staying longer would be impossible – he'd happily humour Joe further, but he had to be home. Had to get Ethan home. It had been a long drive to get there and would be a long drive to get home again. Ethan continued to sleep, *bless him*, but now the time was up for today. It was time to go.

"Don't worry Joe, I'll be back, and soon. And next time, I'll make sure we have more time – I promise."

How could he not? He was more than intrigued by Joe's tale. It was clearly fantasy, but where was it all coming from?

"Joe," he said giving the old man a hug, "you take care, and I'll see you soon. Okay?"

As Matt settled into the long drive back to Newcastle, he thought about what the old man had said. Joe was obviously delusional, but, with everything else that had happened, could there also be grains of truth sprinkled through it?

His father...

The bridge...

His own inability to focus that had led to him dropping out of college.

There was definitely something there, something that resonated.
But what?

CHAPTER 15

Thomas Howard sipped his coffee as he waited to be seen. The two weeks since he'd been given the referral had dragged by. His issues had continued, with denial being his primary strategy – a tactic that, given where he was, would be difficult to maintain.

He now sat in a comfortable waiting area of the private clinic. It was luxurious by hospital standards; in his experience anyway. Coffee was on tap – not instant either – and each of the broadsheet weekend editions sat in pristine condition, waiting to be read.

Tom poured himself another coffee from the percolator jug that sat warming and settled in to read *The Telegraph*. If he had known that it would be like this, he'd have arrived earlier.

Although these small things served to mask the nervousness that he felt – they could not remove it altogether, and he found himself paying scant attention to the paper as the gearwheels of panic spun uncontrollably in his mind.

It was one thing to sit at home and ignore his feelings, it was another to force himself to confront them.

What was the institution where he invariably found himself restrained and being treated?

Was any of that real?

Was any of this real?

Where would this end up?

In an attempt to distract himself further, he resolved to read – *in detail* – the business pages in front of him. However, before he could, he was interrupted by the receptionist, who sat behind the rather formal administrative pedestal.

"Thomas Howard. Dr Williamson is ready for you – room number two."

John Williamson was in his early forties, and, in contrast to Dr Kumar, was casually dressed. "Mr Howard?" he said, "Come in, come in – how are you feeling?"

In between episodes, Tom had actually been feeling fragile, but he had also feeling better of late – *good even*. But then, he'd been pretty much living in his greenhouse, letting the rest of the world go to seed.

By avoiding Ethan, he'd limited his episodes as much as possible. His hallucinations had continued to come, but, more often than not, he simply let them wash over him like the fabrication they were. Attempting to push away the panic he'd felt in the waiting room, he tried to concentrate on the positives.

"I'm good," he replied. "How are you?"

"I'm very well thank you, Tom. I'm sorry, may I call you Tom?"

Tom nodded, "Sure."

"Good, please take a seat." Williamson gestured to a comfortable-looking upholstered chair in front, but not directly in front, of him.

"I thought I'd be laid-up on a bench," joked Tom.

"Would that make you more comfortable?" Williamson answered with a degree of levity, "The main thing today, Tom, is that you tell me what's been going on and that I listen to you. From there we can work out what is going to be the best thing to do."

Tom sat down, settled in, and described what he'd been feeling, what he'd been seeing, and all that had been bothering him. Time had passed, and he was now no longer tearful. The wound was no longer open, but there were still grains of sand in it; still areas to be explored.

Williamson listened intently and, when Tom was done, he sat in silence, consulting the set of notes before him.

Finally, he spoke.

"So, you think you can see things," he said. "Things that might happen, but not dreams or inventions – you can see things that give you a view of events you should never have known about."

Tom paused, "In a sense, yes," although he'd not thought about it in those terms. "Sometimes it is vivid. Years ago there was a bridge... but more recently there was my grandson, that was the weirdest thing. That really shook me up. He seemed to shimmer and blink in and out of existence – and then, as I said, there is this psychiatric hospital where I'm a patient, but I'm restrained to the bed. That's like a waking dream, and then I'm back in the room as if none of it happened. You're going to think I'm crazy, right?"

"It's not for me to say, Tom," said Williamson, "I'm just here to listen and to try to give you the tools to help yourself. Tell me, Tom, directly before these episodes, did you feel different?"

Tom thought. How could he explain it; what had he said to Barbara? "Yes," he said, "it was like a storm building in my mind, like electricity – like when you know it's going to rain, but you don't know why. It's always like that."

"Good," nodded Williamson, "The first thing we need to do is identify what your triggers are. Although, as that's still not clear, we can use that feeling in the meantime. What I want you to do is be mindful, and *really* recognise how you feel, well before you begin to panic, and then box this in so that you're in control. What I want you to do, is sit quietly. Just focus on what we've talked about for five minutes, and then, as we've discussed, you need to keep a detailed record over the coming days which we'll go through at the same time next week."

Tom sat quietly. He didn't know what he'd expected, but he also felt more settled than he had in a long time. He was a little bemused.

They had simply talked, apparently done nothing, but strangely, it seemed to have helped. It was bizarre.

Session complete, Tom stood up and thanked Williamson before helping himself to another coffee on his way out. For a second, he considered liberating the copy of *The Telegraph* that he'd begun reading earlier, but then thought better of it.

No Tom, he thought, *that just wouldn't be right.*

Suddenly his mind flickered, and he found himself in a dressing gown, eating bland stew, opposite Simon, the other patient in the hospital dayroom.

Simon...

And then as soon as it had come, the vision was gone, and Tom found himself outside in the car park, unlocking his car. Getting in, he put the newspaper that he'd just taken onto the passenger seat, started the engine and drove off.

Williamson waited for Tom to go before reaching for the phone. Punching the raised square buttons, he dialled the number written across the card that read:

Dr Eli Phillip Rountree

Director of Research

Branchford Institute

It was a Saturday, but he was nevertheless surprised when he reached an answerphone.

"This is John Williamson, leaving a message for Director Rountree. Regarding the subject who was referred to me today. Future visits will be needed to confirm. However I believe there are extremely strong indications that this could be *subject zero* and I think we should assume that this will be subsequently proven. I am sending you details under filename 'Subject Z1'."

CHAPTER 16

Matt stood again in front of the West Verity residential care home. This time he had come alone. It was now four weeks since his previous visit, and he'd had to fight tooth-and-nail with Jane to come this time.

"Why Matt?" she'd pleaded, *"Don't you have enough on? Don't you have enough to worry about?"*

Home life had become increasingly tough over the last weeks, and Jane considered his wanting to go see Joe as a case of him abandoning her – leaving her with *IT*.

Since his last visit, Ethan had transformed in size and temperament, but most importantly, in audible volume. They now lived a shadowy existence where everything revolved round getting him to sleep at night. Matt had become a night owl and frequently slept in their front room, next to Ethan; gently rocking him to try to keep him under. That was plan A. Plan B was the car. That would always send him off. Matt would drive into the night. Either up the coast or over to Hexham. One night he'd even reached the Scottish border.

He was shattered. What was he doing wrong? Did everyone do this?

Finally, Ethan would be asleep for long enough to turn around and come home, and then the surgical extraction would begin. He'd long ago given up taking him out of the carrier, it was now simply a case of transporting him from car to house and attempting to set him down without waking.

One time out of three it would even work. The other times it would be back into the car hoping for another attempt before the sun came up. It was soul-destroying.

With this as the backdrop, it was no surprise that Jane railed against his insistence that he go back and see Joe. Then she'd suggested, begged, he take Ethan again. However, he thought better of it – given that he was no longer sleeping that wouldn't have been a great move. The upshot was that, since saying he was going, he'd definitely not been flavour of the month, and he now stood, waiting for the door to be answered, a broken, shattered and rather irritable version of his former self.

"Oh, hello again." The door had opened and there stood Mary once more in her faded yellow uniform. She looked round him for a baby carrier before failing to hide her disappointment. "He's been talking about you all morning with the other residents. It's not like him – he's been causing quite a stir."

Finally, somebody glad to see me thought Matt.

After a period of silence, Matt had called Joe to tell him when he was coming. The relief in the old man's voice had been plain, and by the sound of it, he was in good spirits.

Mary again led him through the sitting room to the veranda where, as before, Joe sat alone in the corner. But this time he was bright, periodically making notes in the battered, black leather-bound journal that he had always kept with him for as long as Matt could remember.

"Joe, your visitor's here!" Mary half-shouted.

Joe looked up, "Thank-you dear," he said eagerly. "It's so good to see you, Matty. How long do you have?"

"I've most of the day, Joe," he smiled.

"Good. Mary dear, I don't suppose you'd be a treasure and bring us some tea, could you?"

"I'm not supposed to Joe, but since it's you... I'll leave you boys to it."

Matt sat down and lovingly clasped Joe's gnarled hand.

It was indeed good to see him. Quite why he didn't know, but, of this, he was in no doubt.

It was like a wave of calmness had descended over him in the last ten minutes, and the thought of strong hot tea and the possibility of biscuits only heightened the sensation.

"So, Joe," he paused, as he always did, inwardly smiling at the inadvertent rhyme. "Where did we get to?"

"It was like this," said Joe, "Branchford wasn't as green as he looked. He'd cottoned-on that I'd done something, that something had happened, and it didn't take him long to put two-and-two together and work out what that *something* was."

CHAPTER 17

LONDON 1941

Branchford just sat there staring into nothingness. Speechless.

"I had no idea," he muttered finally. "If you just did what I think you just did... then... then... *this is huge.*"

Joseph Howard said nothing.

What could he say? What was done was done. The cat was well and truly out of the bag.

At that instant, he knew that nothing would ever, or *could* ever, be the same again.

But it was still under his control. There was that at least.

Branchford continued to wave his hands excitedly, as if holding some great prize.

"This is amazing Joe. Seeing other worlds is one thing, but you actually touched one, didn't you? You actually saw it, touched it *and chose it*. That's what you meant, isn't it Joe? That's what you meant when you said 'pulled in'. But pulled in what?"

Joe resigned himself to where this was inevitably going to end.

What was the use of trying to hide it anyway, weren't they all on the same side?

"Pulled in a different world," he said. "The worlds I can see, I can't just see them, I can be them, I am them, cause them to be me, be here – be *this*."

He thought for a minute and then continued.

"It's not that simple though," he explained. "Little nudges like this are fine, they're like dreams that fade to nothing in the morning. But bigger stuff... Bigger stuff does things to you, bad things. You'll no doubt know the Sunday-best name for it, but suffice to say it right royally buggers up your head, to say the least."

Branchford looked perplexed, so Joe elaborated.

"Pull in something simple like tossing a coin in the here and now and nothing really changes – there are no roots and branches to rip up, no memories to alter. Pull in yesterday, or worse, further back, and there is a forest of implications to be unwound, and for every one of those implications, there is the contradiction of memories of both realities. Pull in a world from far enough back and this affects the world you walk in, the world you see every day where you can't even tell what happened yesterday, where you can't tell what *real* is. I've seen it happen!"

It was true, he'd seen his own grandfather go that way before he passed away. According to his father, the old man had seen far too many different worlds, had formed far too many contradictory memories not to become completely unhinged.

"*If ever you need a salutary warning Joseph,*" his father had said, "*let it be this moment.*"

Every day, he missed his father's counsel. What he wouldn't give to buy even a little more time with him. To be able to discuss his current situation.

He would have known what to do; he always did.

Joe's father had died of sleeping sickness at the tail end of the pandemic in 1926. Joe had always held himself responsible, since he'd been the one to first come down with it. Even though Joe had been the sickest he'd ever been, his father had refused to leave his side. Ill as he was, those days with his father caring for him, tending him, refusing to leave him, had been some of the best days of his life.

If not for those days, I'd have none of his advice now.

It was true, it was as if his father had known what was to come – *maybe he had* – but if he had, he'd spent their time wisely, filling Joe with as much wisdom as his remaining time allowed.

The tragedy was that, by the time that Joe recovered, his father had already taken ill. Two weeks later he was gone, along with thousands of others.

His mother said she didn't blame him, and her words never gave him reason to think otherwise, but one look into her eyes told a different story.

Desperately, he'd searched in vain for a world where that outcome was different, but it was no use; the point of infection could have been literally anywhere, the virus was rife.

His father's funeral was a simple affair – it had to be, they were not rich, and there was no opportunity for long services. Joseph had tried to speak but found it oppressively difficult.

"*Most of all, my father was a good man,*" he had managed at the service. "*If I could wish for one thing, it would be that I could be as good and as honest a man as my father had been.*"

It was true; his father could have had it all.

"*But that would not be 'right' Joseph. We must always try to do the right thing,*" his father had explained.

He could have had it all.

"Interesting," said Branchford. "So you're saying that you experience both memories, that of where you started from and that of where you end up."

The Professor's words snapped Joe back to the present.

"That's right," said Joe, "and if they're not sympathetic or in harmony with one another, that's when you have problems."

"And what if someone else instigates… this… it?"

"Then it's not so evident, then it's dreamlike. Then where you end up is real and where you came from is more of a fading memory – you're probably feeling that now. Most people don't even notice it. You likely only felt it because your mind had been opened to such ideas, like waking from a dream."

It was true, whatever Branchford thought he had felt, whatever he thought he had known, was now gone. He pressed on nevertheless.

"And have you always been able to do this, Joe?"

He wasn't sure. It was something that had definitely matured with age, but maybe that was just practice. "I don't know – I think it's always been there," he said, finally. "Yes, it's always been there, at some level."

Branchford took a sip of his, what must have now been cold, tea. If he noticed this, he didn't show it, instead, turning over the implications and questions in his mind.

"So what can you do Joe? Could you, say, win the pools, or could you break the bank at Montecarlo?"

"The first, no, the number of possibilities is just too large. The second – maybe roulette, playing black or red."

It was a natural question and one he had asked many years

before. His father's answer had been as he'd expected.

"Joseph, gambling never ends well. For every winner, there's a loser, and you could easily be heaping misery on a family who could least afford it. It's not right Joe. These places would never let these things go anyway. If you won, and won big, do you think they'd leave you alone? They'd be on you like hellhounds, Joe. Like I said – you can do good, but you also have a huge responsibility. Make your choices wisely."

"The thing is, even if I could," Joe said, "it wouldn't mean that I should. It might sound strange, but it would cheapen it, prostitute the gift. Whatever reason *He* has for making me this way, I'm pretty sure it wasn't to be a pit rat. It just wouldn't be right."

It wouldn't be right, but he'd be lying if he'd said he hadn't felt temptation. What would be right, would be to make some good of it? Make a real difference? Make the horrors that he'd heard hushed rumours about not happen? Make the world a better place?

"So how do we put this to use," he asked. "What do we do now?"

"What we do is – we organise, Joseph," came General Envaneer's reply from the doorway. He stepped into the room and addressed the both of them. "With your help, we find others, and we change the world – *one event at a time.*"

CHAPTER 18

"That's where it all began, Matty," said the old man. "From that point onwards, events moved so quickly, it became a blur. The government and military machines were put into motion, with the result becoming the embryonic Commission for Acceptable Outcomes. And they were recruiting. One after another, we visited and reviewed the inpatients at Mill Hill and other locations."

It was always the same process. The two of them would work as a team, Branchford would interview the subjects, concentrating on their psychosis and would repeat coin-tosses with Joe ensuring that the sequence was a never-ending stream of heads.

It was always the same question – *"Tell me about the coin."*

Mostly they'd try to call it out as a parlour trick, saying that the coin had two heads. If they saw through it, they were shortlisted by The Commission. Two months in, however, all things changed.

They were reviewing subject Jacobson, recently returned from the western front. He had been heavily sedated for some weeks since coming home, and his ravings were so severe and pronounced that Branchford had reservations about whether he should be interviewed at all. He seemed to only have two states, distress or utter silence and by all accounts he was slipping further and further away from reality on a daily basis.

"I strongly recommend we skip Jacobson, Sir," he'd said to Envaneer. "All conversation unsettles him – severely, Sir. At best I imagine he'll be unresponsive. At worst, I dread to think. Can we not leave this one?"

Envaneer however, would have none of it. "We'll do what we came to do," he'd said. "No exceptions."

It was with a heavy heart that they'd reviewed him. Branchford's questions were met first with silence and then with pleas.

"Look, just leave me alone," Jacobson said, "if you can't make it stop, can you at least stop your spiel and leave me in peace!"

As instructed, however, Branchford had continued.

"I'm sorry Private, I'm just following orders. I promise, however, it'll be over soon." With that, he'd taken out the coin, the way that he'd always done. "I'm going to toss this coin a number of times, and after each time, I need you to tell me about it. Tell me how it makes you feel."

Silence.

Branchford tossed the coin.

A head.

"How does this make you feel?"

Silence.

Branchford tossed the coin again.

A head.

"How does this make you feel?"

Again silence.

Branchford tossed the coin again.

A tail.

The silent Jacobson forgotten, Branchford looked to Joe for an explanation.

Joseph Howard was equally shocked. *Something had prevented him, something had resisted him. How was that possible?*

"I'm sorry," he fumbled. "I'm not sure why that didn't work. I'll fix it."

Before he could, however, Jacobson looked up from his silence, glaring angrily. "No, you bloody well won't," he said. "You glitched it, and the thing that made you glitch was me. I've enough things going on, in my head, without you two adding to them. *That's* how it makes me feel."

"From that point, the phrase *opposition* entered our vocabulary. We managed to work with Jacobson, help him cope, showed him how to deal with the gift, just as my father had taught me. We showed him how to recognise the triggers and progressively climb out of his hole. Equally, Jacobson showed us how'd he'd opposed us, how he'd seen what we were doing and how he'd stopped us."

This had opened up a whole new world, and Joe had felt like the scales had dropped from his eyes.

If his father had survived, what would he have had to say to him about this, about other fixers and opposing their attempts at grafts? Would he have even known?

By working with Jacobson, Joe was able to detect the activity of other fixers. This could only be detected after what they called the branch point, the point where the two realities ceased to coincide. Tossing a coin, you would have the *trunk* – the reality with no intervention, where a head might have naturally fallen, and you'd also have an alternative branch with other outcomes, head or tail.

What they found was that an action could be detected *and opposed* from the branch point up to the point that the intervention happened. That was the *graft*, the place where the fixer was operating, the point where the trunk ceased to exist, where it was replaced by the alternative. But no matter how many times Jacobson explained it, it still hurt Joe's head.

"So you mean, that I could flip a coin today and based on this, I could decide to either travel to Dover or travel to Salisbury and tomorrow I could decide, say, that this was not acceptable, so on the spur of the moment, I might prefer the other outcome. This would make the branch point the coin toss and the graft point the place where I effected the change the next day."

"Exactly," Jacobson had cajoled, "just a bissel more now, keep going…"

Joe continued, but this was where he usually got unstuck.

"Because the coin toss was the branch point, someone else – *another fixer* – let's say you, could detect that this was happening at any point on the trunk after the branch but before the graft, even *before* I'd decided to do it."

"You've got it," said Jacobson.

This still didn't sit well with Joseph.

How could it be? It would mean that Jacobson, and he, could detect and prevent actions that had not yet happened. Detect decisions that had not yet been made.

But there it was, when they put this to the test it appeared to work in precisely that way; between branch and graft, the opposer could resist the graft the day before, and the fixer could attempt the graft the day after. Stranger still, this could become a tug of war between the two of them, one in the future and one in the past, where ultimately whether a fix was applied or not would depend on the relative strength or opposition being exerted. It could come down to who had the most stamina, who had the stronger will.

If he extrapolated it, it hurt his head, more and more. With a big enough fix, wouldn't that mean that he could potentially detect actions and even lock horns and oppose fixes from someone, not yet even born, from hundreds of years into the future? Everything that he and Jacobson had seen, told them this was the case, but how could that be? What did that mean for free will?

This changed everything – what did it mean?

If his future actions were detectable in the here-and-now, did anyone have control over anything?

CHAPTER 19

Thomas Howard blinked and attempted to open his eyes.

"Good," he heard a man's voice say, "he's beginning to stabilise at last." The voice was not unfamiliar but was one that he struggled to place.

"Can I speak to him?" This time it was Barbara.

"He's making good progress, but I wouldn't suggest it. At least not yet anyway. He's been so delusional since Ethan was born, and you know how many years that's been now. Let his body get used to the inhibitor first before we activate it, and then you can speak with him. He's coming around, but it would be best to keep him under for the minute."

Tom heard the voices drift off into the distance as he managed to finally raise one eyelid.

What had they meant – 'years' since Ethan was born?

Ethan was still young, wasn't he?

Tom's eyes eventually began to focus, and he found himself, once again, restrained to the steel frame of an institution bed. This time he was weak, stiff and sore. To his right was some form of automated drip and various items of monitoring equipment.

Before he could look further, the machinery buzzed and the infusion pump that fed the tubes that were plumbed into his arm administered something which made him fade to grey and slip into the welcoming, soporific arms of unconsciousness.

It was to his surprise that he then blinked and looked through the windscreen at the now green light. The car behind him sounded the horn impatiently.

He was headed to the clinic.

Of course, he was – where else would he be? He remembered that clearly now – Had he dozed off?

He'd half-convinced himself of this when discomfort made him recall the chafing feeling that the restraints had left on his skin. Looking down at his wrists, he was shocked to find them inflamed and angry, with evident marks of restraint.

What if any of this was real?

CHAPTER 20

Over four months The Commission had assembled what they called The Unit. This consisted of privates Howard, Jacobson, Bedford and Young, although Jacobson and Joseph were plainly the main players.

Even after being promoted to Lance Corporal, Joseph Howard's discomfort was evident for all to see. It wasn't so much that he didn't believe in what they were trying to put together – it was something else.

More of a crisis of faith than a lack of confidence. If the future was predestined what point was there in any of this? Was free will itself an illusion?

It was because of this that Branchford had tried to convince Envaneer to bring in external help. Bring in someone who might be able to frame Joseph's misgivings in such a way as to bring some meaning to them and hence find him some peace.

For that, he turned to his *alma mater*, Oxford. He wanted a post doc in either physics or philosophy, someone who was open to ideas and not yet part of the establishment.

Via various separate enquiries the same name kept coming up again and again, a physicist called Tristram Baker who'd done work for the department in the area of the relatively new field of quantum mechanics. Now that Baker had qualified, he wanted to explore his own theories – however, these were controversial, to say the least. Everyone agreed he was brilliant, yet his ideas were not ones that the department could endorse.

As Joe had later come to learn from Baker himself, Envaneer and Branchford had arranged to meet the academic in Oxford to ask him about his ideas.

Baker had been bemused that the *army* was interested in his theories, when his peers patently were not; however, starved for an audience as he was, he was more than happy to play along.

"You may have heard the phrase 'God does not play

dice'," he said, as if giving a lecture. "In 1927 Albert Einstein wrote these words in a letter to Niels Bohr discussing the newly formulated quantum theory. Eight years later Erwin Schrödinger devised his famous quantum thought experiment, *Schrödinger's Cat*, to explore the Copenhagen interpretation of quantum mechanics. The idea was that something could co-exist in two different states at the same time.

"In 1935, Schrödinger had suggested a thought experiment where the reader was asked to imagine that a cat was trapped in a box with a radioactive substance, which over the next hour could either emit a particle from its decay or not; the chance of this happening or not was fifty-fifty. Inside the box, was also a detector that would release a poison gas if the particle were emitted. Because there was an equal chance of either releasing a poison or not, there was also a fifty-percent chance of the cat being killed – or not – within the hour.

"Now here's the thing. Because of this, quantum mechanics says that the cat is neither alive nor dead until the box is opened for measurement. Instead, the situation is all represented by probabilities – like dice. Einstein did not believe in this idea of probabilities and chances, and neither do I. Hence – God does not play dice."

Baker paused before continuing.

"Rather than being driven by probabilities, I believe that quantum effects may be equally explained if, rather than the universe that we think we inhabit, we instead live in a multiverse where every choice is played out in tandem with its alternatives. Normally these realities mutually repel one another, like common poles of a magnet, and these universes occupy an interstitial field. Within the field, there are attracting and repelling interstitial forces in constant flux. I even believe Young's double-slit experiment could be explainable as the interaction between these universes.

"Because these forces are in-between worlds, there is no global clock, no conductor beating time. As such, this repelling or attracting interstitial force would operate outside of what we would usually think of as time, with only the existence of common states across interacting worlds being synchronisation points... and even then..."

Branchford looked at Envaneer and twitched an eyebrow. He wasn't getting all of this, but he was sure of one thing…

He's our man.

Understanding, Envaneer raised a hand to stop him, cleared his throat and addressed Baker.

"I think I want to make you an offer," he said. "But before you answer, I should tell you that may not like its terms. The Army would be willing to support your research, offer you top-notch facilities to rival any university. We have made particular advances strongly connected to what you describe. However, we have been acting operationally… practically, with little or no theoretical underpinning…"

Baker couldn't contain himself.

"What do you mean, 'acting operationally'? What advances?"

"And therein lies the rub," sighed Envaneer, "What we're putting together is possibly one of the most top secret units, one of the most non-standard and ambitious squads ever created. But unless you join us, I can't answer any of your questions. What I can say though is this: join us, and you'll get to explore the kind of ideas that are shunned by those where you are at the minute. I can also assure you that funding won't be an issue. Join us, and you'll get to see some of what you talk about played out in practice. However, on that, I can say no more. Most importantly, join us, and although you *will* do great things, you'll be able to publish nothing, no one will know any of what we do, who you are or what you achieve. As far as the academic community is concerned, you will be a potential that was never realised, a bright light that, as sometimes happens, went dim. No-one will know the name Tristram Baker, but believe me, you will do things that literally change the world, and astonish *even you*."

Tristram Baker sat back to consider his response. The words were on the tip of his tongue, but still he hesitated. Finally, he turned his thoughts into words and began, "My view of physics would suggest that since your offer is intriguing, even if I say no, then somewhere else there is another me that will have said yes."

He paused, waiting for a reaction, but got none.

"Now if I understand what you've alluded to, then as far

as you're concerned, *in all practical terms* I've already agreed."

Baker waited for a reaction. Envaneer smiled, ever so sinisterly, and turned to Branchford.

"I knew he was the right man for the job." Turning back he raised one eyebrow, "I love it when we have a *real* understanding. Welcome aboard."

CHAPTER 21

The addition of Baker completed the first version of the unit, and he rapidly developed a working theoretical basis involving Jacobson's trunk and branch language. It was also Baker that gave the RIFT its name – *more or less*.

"So, when I see the multiple tendrils of other realities, what do I call it them?" Joe had asked, "It's like a window that I need to pull through."

Baker took a breath, "In the model, we're assuming that when you *oppose*, you increase the *repelling interstitial force*, and when you *pull in* you decrease the *repelling interstitial force* between this and another reality. Since we're assuming that there are no shearing effects, then you're not really looking through *anything*. What you're experiencing is a projection relative to the degree of interstitial force for each of the other worlds. This projection is orthogonal to the *direction* of the force; a transection to the line of the force."

Writing on the chalkboard, he read out, "What you experience is the

REPELLING
INTERSTITIAL
FIELD
TRANSECTION

Joe looked at this for a while. "The RIFT," he said.

"Yes. Exactly. The RIFT. I like that."

From that point onwards it was always the RIFT. Ice-broken, Joe continued, exploring...

"Dr Baker," he said, "I need to ask you some questions..."

He'd be lying to say he was comfortable with what this was becoming, but there was an element in particular that bothered him.

When Jacobson had shown that opposition was possible

from two different time points, Joe had been visibly shaken.

"Doctor, if Jacobson and I can oppose one another across time, what the hell does that say about free will? ...If I have a free will, surely that affects the future. ...But the prospect of a future opposer would tend to suggest that future events are predetermined, which suggests that there is no free will."

"That may indeed be true, Joseph," posited Baker, "but I'm not so sure. While everything *could* affect everything, not everything *does* affect everything. Also, the RIFT is effectively outside of time; there are temporal elements to it, but these are more anchor points than anything else. If someone attempted a graft in the future, then initially, with no intervention, the RIFT would be unchanged. Over time, the RIFT would shorten as the repelling forces were weakened – the model suggests that this is progressive. But if you did prevent that future happening then the RIFT would elastically return to its original state and the graft would disappear. What I'm saying is, what you detect is not *the future*, but *a future*. It should be possible to confirm this experimentally, if you and Jacobson are willing.

"However, to me, a more interesting question around free will is one of ethics. Consider this – one in a thousand times, an ordinary man behaves irrationally, potentially lashing out or killing. If you search for, and target, that vanishingly small scenario, and, like a puppetmaster, make it become so... what then of free will? Where does the moral responsibility lie? With you or with the killer?"

"What about choice?" asked Joe, "There's always a choice."

"For a non-fixer, maybe. But what if it were you, and you remember not committing such a crime? You know you've effectively been framed – or have you? After all, the deed would have been done by you. Conversely," continued Baker, "what if a killer commits a cold-blooded murder, and by fixing, you prevent that playing out, but the killer remembers the crime. What punishment does the murderer get then?"

"But what harm has been done?"

"What indeed... is it the intention or the outcome which should drive the moral responsibility? The whole thing's an ethical quagmire. You're right to ask these things though, Joseph."

Joe's head spun.

These questions were for those better than him, he thought. These types of questions were why they had The Commission.

CHAPTER 22

The Reality Commission for Acceptable Outcomes grew from its early beginnings in 1941, its job becoming to formally set the mandate for the fledgling unit. For the time it was progressive, with members drawn from a cross-section of backgrounds, both military and political.

Initially, it set out a liberal framework of ethical principles, which it attempted to abide by. In general, these tenets were underpinned by the idea that the unit should be used to combat evil.

Its members saw their role as steering behaviour towards what they considered *universal good*, and agreed, from the outset, that they would act preventatively rather than aggressively.

Concepts such as good and evil were slippery at best. However, after much discussion, The Commission landed on a working definition of evil as being *an act taken by choice which results in suffering.*

Envaneer's view was, *"If we don't instil these principles now, we'll be creating monsters – Who will guard the guards?"* the phrase '*benign guidance*' driving his vision.

It was against this backdrop that intelligence concerning Nazi intentions filtered through to the group.

In 1940 Envaneer had gained information concerning the Nazi Action T4 euthanasia programme, begun by the SS. Hitler intended to exterminate what the Nazis called 'life unworthy of life'; the afflicted, those who were 'incurably sick', and it was this that The Commission set about steering.

As Envaneer explained it, their goal was an attempt to become the missing moral compass for humanity, to steer and nudge – where possible, to avert.

To do this they sought those within the lower ranks of the SS who they thought might still see reason, they made efforts to seek out those in the Church who might oppose; looked for those who displayed grains of humanity and used this to gain information.

The Catholic Bishop of Münster in Westphalia, Clemens August Graf von Galen, had telegraphed a copy of his sermon calling for a cessation of the T4 programme to Hitler, and it was copies of this that the Royal Flying Corps began dropping among German troops.

As the days passed the unit intercepted radio communications from their sources. The key was to get information promptly, to appraise what they could of the immediate outcomes, to nudge the course of events towards glimmers of charity, towards any reports of dissent from Nazi-dogma – towards the light.

It was difficult, but ever so slowly they felt the tide turn, they noticed from their reports that the weight of opinion began to turn against the policy. Wives questioned their husbands and dissent was sufficient to cause Hitler to disown the policy and castigate leading medical figures instigating it, such as Brandt, as rogue.

They'd made a difference.

In response to the news, Envaneer assembled the Unit's now growing corpus and addressed them.

"Gentlemen, from where we sit in London, we may not feel like we are contributing to the war effort, but from the reports we have coming in, you have done a great service to humanity. Some of you saw some of what could have been, and some of you understand the gravity of what we have achieved. But by doing what you have done, you have saved countless innocent lives and put Hitler and his henchmen on the back foot. To you Sirs, I say this – *Huzzah!*"

CHAPTER 23

As Matthew Howard sat and listened, his grandfather paused, tired. It had been a lot to recount, and he'd barely begun. Finally, Matt broke the silence.

"So, what you're telling me is that in another time and place, you changed the course of history as we know it?"

His grandfather grasped his hand in his and paused before answering, "Not only that Matty, but we stopped the worst of it. The death camps, the wanton extermination. We set in place a course of events that prevented most of it. By the end of the war, as I knew it, Hitler was dead, the German high command had thrown in the towel, and much of what you'd recognise as the Holocaust was something the unit had managed to avert. But it wasn't without sacrifices…"

"What do you mean?" asked Matt.

Joe paused again, struggling to get his words out. "Your grandmother," he finally said.

"Your grandmother didn't make it. As we were working out of the Maudsley, she'd set up as a teacher, and we were living near Denmark Hill. Jacobson and I had been away on a job, and it was only when we returned that I got the news. By then, a week or more had passed and despite my protests, The Commission denied me her."

"What do you mean?" said Matt again.

"What I mean is your grandma Ruth was killed in 1941 by a German bomb."

Matt was stunned. "But how?" he finally said. "Dad wasn't born until 1946. How can that be? If that were true, Dad wouldn't be here. I wouldn't be here…"

"Ethan…"

The blood drained from Matt's face.

"Ethan wouldn't be here," whispered Joe, finishing the sentence that Matt had trailed off.

"And now you start to understand," said Joe. "You must understand that the reality that we currently live in is no less real than the one I left behind, but it is unsanctioned. It is via the deaths of millions of innocents that you have your life."

Matt was rattled.

"Why are you doing this Joe? What are you hoping to achieve?"

It was all well and good to listen to some tale, but this was getting far too close to home.

"You need to stop this Joe." he said, "You need to realise that none of this is real. Fantasise all you like but keep me out of it."

Joe's head sagged. "Just like your father," he said miserably. "I thought you were different. I thought you understood."

"I understand enough," snapped Matt impatiently, "I understand Dad was right." Standing up, he looked at his grandfather. "Joe, I love you, but I don't think I'm equipped to handle this. I'm sorry."

With that, he turned to leave. However, the straps of his coat sent the tea that Mary had brought them earlier crashing to the floor. Deflated Matt looked at the mess of tea and broken china. "Don't worry – I'll clean this up," he grumbled, "but then I need to go."

"Look again," said Joe calmly.

To Matt's amazement, the china that he'd just sent flying was resting on the table unbroken. The floor was clear.

All of a sudden, the alternate memory of turning to leave and not breaking the crockery flooded Matt's mind and the two conflicting events jarred in his head like a song being played out of tune. He staggered dizzily before sitting down heavily, flopping into the seat.

It was all true...

CHAPTER 24

Thomas Howard arrived at the private hospital. Well, they called it a hospital, but as he'd found since his last visit, they only offered a limited set of services for those who could either self-fund or, like Tom, pay via their health insurance. Notebook in hand, Tom had religiously kept records over the preceding week.

Much to Barbara's amusement he'd set off so early he had arrived almost an hour ahead of time so he could settle in, to drink coffee and read the provided newspapers.

"Mr Williamson will be in consulting room number two," the receptionist had informed him. "Although your appointment's not for almost an hour." Acknowledging her, Tom reacquainted himself with where the room was. *Simple*, he thought. The room was directly off the waiting area.

As he waited, an older gentleman with a well-fed paunch and reddening face arrived and called at the reception desk. "Phillip Rountree for John Williamson please," Tom heard him say. "I am a little late."

The man was directed to consulting-room #2, into which he disappeared. Returning his attention to his *Telegraph's* business pages, Tom pored over the paper. After a while, he noticed his coffee was empty and rose to fetch a refill. As he did the consulting room door opened and the man he'd seen earlier re-emerged. "So, John," he said as he left, "you'll keep me apprised about Z1, yes?"

"Absolutely," Tom heard John Williamson say, "he's due here in about..." Williamson broke off at the sight of Thomas Howard. Looking confused and slightly rattled, he looked at his watch. "Oh, hello Mr Howard, what time do you have down for our appointment?"

"Not for a while," said Tom, awkwardly. "I thought I'd take advantage of the facilities," he explained.

"No, that's absolutely fine. That's what they're there for," Williamson said.

CHAPTER 25

Matthew Howard looked at his grandfather, suddenly viewing the old man in a wholly different light.

If what Joe had revealed wasn't fantasy, what did that mean? Could it really be true? Literally be the way he was telling it?

"So," he finally said, "This *rift* that you're on about – what is it? What does it look like? Am *I* able to see it? Show me."

Joe collected his thoughts before beginning.

"The RIFT," he finally said, "isn't something that you see, well not in the way I think you mean anyway."

"The RIFT is the gap between realities, the space between worlds, the *innate barrier* that keeps the different timelines apart. It is the space you occupy when you manage to convince your waking mind to finally witness the truth around you."

Joe paused for a minute to let the words sink in before he continued. He reached out, picked up his cup and took a long sip of his tea. For a minute, he seemed lost in thought, as if formulating a way to express a lifetime of private emotions. "Have you ever seen double?" Joe finally asked.

"What?!"

Matt looked blankly at him, so Joe added, "Just go with me for a minute Matty. Yes or no, have you ever seen double? …Have you ever woken up, first thing on a morning, and just lain there? Have you ever opened your eyes, freed your thoughts and just let your mind wander?"

Joe was obviously trying to say something, but what was it?

The old man leant forward in his chair, and once again grasped Matt's hands. The need to be understood, to impart what knowledge he had, was patently obvious from his face.

But Joe was struggling. Joe's eyes beseeched Matt to somehow comprehend. He scanned Matt's face looking for a glimmer of understanding, but there was nothing.

Matt could see the disappointment apparent in the old man's eyes, the mask of desperate sorrow, staring back at him. *C'mon Joe, help me grasp what you're saying*, he thought.

Trying again, Joe continued, "Have you ever, at the point that you just woke up, looked at something completely inconsequential, like the pattern on the wallpaper; or a cup next to your bed, or the silhouette of a window frame against a grey sky? And in that half-waking state, when your brain is still coming to, have you ever caught yourself seeing two images, one image from each eye, like your mind is not yet weaving them together? If you have, have you ever grabbed those two images and kept them separate? Kept them from combining and simply experienced the feeling of the two different pictures in front of you? Keeping then apart, controlling them, bending the worlds to your will? Or have you ever had a real skinful and tried watching television only to find that you need to close one eye as you can't process what you're seeing as one image?"

Matt still didn't know where this was going, but he nodded anyway. He had done these sort of things – *hadn't everyone?* But where was this going?

"The reason I say this Matty, is that what happens when you're fully awake is that you don't actually see the world for what it is. You don't see the world as the two images. You see the world as a processed and combined view that is neither one thing nor another. Your mind prevents you from seeing a left-view or a right-view, and instead presents you with a sanitised picture that is neither. Matty, *your mind prevents you from seeing what is real*; it takes your vision as input and serves you up a perception of the world which is an invention of its own making. The reason I say this, is that, in a similar sense, you've likely been in the RIFT but not known it. You've likely had multiple disparate reality-views melded together which your brain tried to present as a single coherent world. You've probably seen some confusing stuff where you've thought – *how could that be?* Such as losing your keys, looking where you knew they must be only to find them gone, but then finding them back there minutes later, back where you looked only moments before…

"Elves and gremlins…" said Matt with some degree of

recognition. A distant memory flooding back from a time, with his grandfather, when he was again a child – *long ago and far away.*

"That's right," said Joe. "That's it – *elves and gremlins* – that's what we used to call it when you were a child. You've seen it, but you've never experienced seeing both sides of the coin at the same time. You've put on the green socks but found yourself wearing the blue ones. You've always seen one side or the other. You've never caught the splintered view of reality at the point of waking and forced the many splinters of reality to remain apart."

Matt nodded hesitantly. However, within him, he felt unease driven from the duality he felt inside. On one hand, his rational self wanted to reject what Joe was saying, wanted to call it out for the trick that it must be. At another level, however, he knew that there was more to it than that.

If he were honest with himself, he'd always known that there was something like this, always felt that he didn't quite fit with the world as it presented itself to him. Did this explain his dreams?

Were his dreams even dreams?

If Joe was right, then many things could fall into place – the reason he'd dropped out of college, the reason he was a million miles away from reality.

Unless that was merely an excuse.

Was he really capable of what Joe suggested?

"You can do this Matty, I'm sure of it. It's just practice, just like waking up and stopping yourself from seeing a single world with your eyes. When you're tired, or just waking you can use that to separate what you perceive. When you see the separation you can, with enough focus, keep those views separate. You can force the multiple views apart and perceive them not as a combined whole, but as a set of slightly different worlds, all of which are within your grasp. Rather than just seeing white, you can see the spectrum of different colours. Rather than a mash of information, filtered into a least surprising lowest common denominator, you break down the components, the choices, the various worlds without the veil that your mind generates from its expectations. And when you can do that; when you can see the gaps between worlds, that Matty, that is when you can see the RIFT."

Matt looked into the old man's eyes. Yes – at one level his whole being still rejected what Joe was saying – but at a more fundamental level he knew there was truth to what he was hearing. Certainly, this would explain his lack of focus, why he was so incoherent, why it took him hours to rejoin reality in the morning.

Was Joe really saying that there were multiple, almost infinite, windows onto different worlds, and that he got to pick from a merry-go-round of disconnected, different views?

Were those what his dreams actually were?

"In a sense," Joe said after Matt had asked this. "But they're not windows Matty. Think of them more as doors – doors that close and lock behind you, leaving nothing more tangible than memories of past lives. Memories that will serve to haunt you. Memories which will hound you and make you question your sanity. And somewhere out there Matty, at some point possibly yet to come, they're trying to push the world, as we know it, through one of those doors. Someone is trying to force us through, to a world where Ethan never was."

Ethan – the sound of his son's name shocked him.

Ethan – of course.

The possibility of multiple worlds had enchanted him, had made him almost distracted with a feeling of disbelief – wonder even – but the mention of Ethan caused all that to come crashing down, caused Matt to remember his grandfather's original warning. The thoughts of Ethan caused his pulse to rise, and he felt panic once again well up within him. "But *YOU* can stop them," said Matt, "Can't you?"

Joe sighed deeply and slumped back into his seat. All of a sudden, Joe again looked his age – the vitality that had infused him during their discussion had evaporated.

"I really don't know Matty. Maybe I can, maybe I can't," he said, deflated. "As far as I can tell, the intervention itself is not in the present and not for a long, long while – years even. If it is who I think it is, Matty, then they're waiting for something – some trigger maybe – waiting either to rebuild their organisation or more likely waiting for me to be gone. That's why it's crucial that you learn, Matty. It's vital that you become adept enough to prevent them from succeeding.

After all, compared to me, it would seem time is in their favour.

A chill sense of foreboding filled Matt. *Of course, Joe wouldn't be here for much longer, and then it would be down to him.* He now understood what Joe had said about Tom. *Joe was right – Tom wouldn't understand, and they simply didn't have the time to waste. But if Joe was saying that they could be fighting this battle years from now, what chance did he have?*

"OK, but you can teach me… right? What do I need to do? Where do I start?"

"You need to open your eyes to the wider world," explained Joe. "When you go from here you need to find a way of chiselling at the gaps between realities. Matty, it's different for everyone. You need to find your own way in but you need to do it soon. Keep lots of notes, Matty – if you can, take them as things happen – you'll see why. Every morning I need you to look for the chinks in the armour that your mind is presenting and see round the corners. If you can't do that Matty, then we *really* have no hope."

Hope…

For reasons unknown, the word, once again, rang like a bell through Matt's head.

Hope…

And almost as though another him was speaking, he heard his own voice say, "No – you're wrong. *Hope means everything.*"

And then he wondered – *What did that mean?*

CHAPTER 26

A well caffeinated Thomas Howard sat opposite Williamson, his hands placed in his lap.

"So, Tom. How's this week been?"

It had been OK. The acceptance of the fact that he was working through his issues seemed to have calmed his troubled mind. The unspoken acknowledgement of the process had led him to view his continuing episodes in a far more detached and analytical manner.

"Did you keep a log of your triggers and perceptions?"

He had, but that had been the strangest thing of all – he'd recorded how he'd felt, but much of what he'd recorded had gone missing, almost like he'd dreamt it. But mostly, reaching for his pen appeared to ward off his delusions. But then, had he really captured them all?

"I did, but I don't think I got all of them," he said. "I have a clear memory of what I wrote, but only some of it is in my book... and some of what's in here I only vaguely recognise, even though it's my handwriting."

On different days he could read his journal and be sure it contained slightly different accounts each time. Not different, . as in a progressive continuation, but truly different in an irreconcilable or contradictory way.

"It's like the book is a crossroads of all possible books – a different read every time."

Or was it a different road every time?

"It's like not all of this is real. Like I write in the book, but if there's no evidence of my writing what I remember then is any of it real?"

It wasn't like it was one of those spiral bound notebooks where you could tear out the pages without it being obvious, either.

His train of thought unnerved him.

What if none of what he experienced was real? What if his fleeting visions of the world where he was restrained and institutionalised was the only true reality?

Thomas Howard continued to talk, and Williamson continued to take notes and listen. Eventually, Williamson interjected. "Tom, I think you've made excellent progress this week, but from what you've said, I'd like you to see a colleague of mine in London. He works for an institute that specialises in schizophrenics who believe they see the world in, to use their words, 'a less filtered way than so-called normality'. Their work is cutting-edge, and one of their theories is that schizophrenics actually see elements of the world how it actually is rather than being filtered by expectation. If you're willing to speak to them, the Branchford Institute will pay your travel, and I believe they'd be very interested in talking to you."

CHAPTER 27

Matthew Howard lay on his bed, Jane peacefully asleep beside him. Ethan lay in the cot at the end of their bed. The only sound was from the two of them, Jane and Ethan, each softly breathing.

All quiet on the western front.

Joe's words, from earlier in the week, still rang in his ears and served to keep him awake.

Keep lots of notes, Matty – if you can, take them as things happen – you'll see why...

What had Joe meant?

Abandoning his attempts to sleep, Matt gently crawled to the end of the bed and watched his son, dormant and at peace. As if by request, Ethan stirred, his eyes flicking open, and lay there silently watching.

Don't make a sound, thought Matt, *and he might go back off.* He turned to look at his wife.

Still fast asleep.

He turned back to Ethan.

Eyes half closed. Good, drifting back off.

Ethan's settled state prompted Matt to relax for the first time in days, and he felt himself swaying and drifting off toward very welcome sleep, a soothing wave of calm flooding over him.

At the last point of consciousness, he found himself still facing Ethan. Exhaustion caused the blanket of oblivion to envelop him and, as his eyes began to close, the world around him blurred out of focus.

Welcome sleep thought Matt – *blessed rest.*

Through the haze, a movement caught his attention. *Ethan was awake, eyes open* – Matt's heart sank, instantly tumbling like a house of cards. *So close and yet so far. Ethan would soon be crying.* Rubbing his eyes, Matt silently resigned himself for what was inevitably to come, and inwardly groaned.

At least there was a bottle next to him, sitting in the electric warmer, all ready to go.

No, wait... Ethan was definitely asleep.

Matt blinked again.

Ethan was awake

...and again

...he was asleep

awake

asleep

what the...?

In the distraction created by that thought, Matt's vision blurred, and, at that moment, he could somehow see that Ethan was both asleep and awake at the same time. Lying-still, eyes-open, lying-still, eyes-closed.

That's it, thought Matt. *That's the chink in the armour that Joe had referred to. That's the gap waiting to be chiselled.*

With a sense of wonder, Matt remained motionless and watched. In his mind's eye there were two Ethans, and he could see each of them with equal clarity.

Remember what Joe said he thought. *Keep them apart.*

The asleep-Ethan continued to sleep. However, the awake-Ethan began rousing towards an inevitable cry.

Better pick you up, thought Matt, and moved towards his son. Before he'd even moved, his perception of asleep-Ethan collapsed, and his attention was singular once again.

Was that all there was to it? he thought as he scooped up and cuddled his son. *Was it as simple as interacting with one side or another, as simple as standing at a crossroads and not even putting your foot on one road or another? Was it as simple as purely exerting your will to walk in that particular direction?*

Had he been distracted by Ethan's waking? What if he'd ignored that and instead settled back down and joined the quiet breathing of his sleeping child? Would that have meant that the awake-Ethan would have faded from his view? How could he tell what was reality and what was merely possibility? Did that thought even make sense?

On autopilot, Matt picked up the warming bottle and rocked Ethan back and forth.

Had he even done anything at all, or had he done nothing?

Was any of what he'd experienced real?
Had he even experienced anything at all?

"I did it Joe!" he said down the phone the next day. "I really did it. Well I think I did it anyway. It was like you said – I could see both sides of the coin." Then the doubt came. "Was any of it real though? How can I tell?"

"Real?" chuckled Joe's voice down the line. "What is real? What is imaginary for people like you and me? Is there any difference? What I mean is, who can say what is *truly* real. If everyone sifts their so-called reality through a filter of perception, then what is reality? If there is no history other than your memory, what differentiates your reality from dreams or hallucinations?"

Joe was right. Between him imagining that Ethan was asleep, and there being another universe where there was a set of events where he was actually asleep, there was effectively no difference. A concept of a singular reality was little more than a perspective of a blinkered mind.

"You could drive yourself mad, Matty, with thoughts like that. Take my advice – let it go. Whatever it is, *it just is*. Don't over analyse it. Maybe it was, maybe it wasn't, but you've definitely taken a step into a wider world. I'm glad…"

Matt was far too tired for this. Phone cradled to his ear, Ethan in one hand and a bottle of milk in the other – plumbed into his son's gently guzzling mouth. *This conversation is doing my head in*, he thought, struggling to concentrate.

"How can I tell then, Joe?"

"Now you're asking the right questions. Tomorrow, go buy some dice and a notebook and bring them over the next time you come. Now get some sleep – you sound beat."

Matt took Joe's advice, next day heading off bright and early, propelling Ethan's pushchair into town. Stopping at Woolworths, he bought a pack of dice along with a spiralbound notebook. However on his way home he caught a glimpse of a black leather journal similar to Joe's in Blackwell's window, and bought that as well. "If we're going to do this, Ethan," he said, "we're going to do it in style."

The following weekend, he found himself, once again, sitting with Joe, this time accompanied by Ethan who, for the minute, still slept in his carrier. When he had arrived, Matt had plugged in the bottle warmer he'd brought with him, filled it with water and dropped Ethan's milk powder into it.

All prepared and ready to go.

Finally settled, his attention now turned to Joe, his expectation high – *maybe too high* – he apprehensively waited for the old man to speak.

"Right Matty, what you need to do is start with one die and throw it. However, when you throw it, I need you to always get a six."

Matt took one of the dice out of the cardboard container and turned it over and over in his hands, trying to calm himself as much as he could. The die was wooden and old-fashioned, red with gold markings in its indentations. He smelled the newness and threw the die.

A five.

It was no use. He couldn't see it. What was Joe expecting him to do?

Feeling for him, Joe interjected. "You need to dial back the input, reduce what your eyes are telling you – try almost closing them and squinting."

Matt tried again, this time with his eyes almost closed.

It was ridiculous, he couldn't see the dice at all now.

Slowly Matt crept his eyes open a fraction more.

There they were, multiple dice, sitting like ghosts. Not as many as he knew there should be, but more than one. The dice in his mind's eye occupied similar but different spaces on the table in front of him.

A five, a two and a six.

As he reached for the six the other two dice appeared to melt, and he felt the memory of throwing the six overlay itself in his mind.

"Good," said Joe. "Now do it again."

Matt repeated the process and this time managed to surface four dice, again managing a six.

"Good," repeated Joe. "So how many's that?"

"Two sixes," said Matt. "Or was there a four, first time round?"

The fact that he did not know crept up on him almost unexpectedly. He knew he had thrown two sixes, but distinctly remembered throwing a series of other numbers as well. It wasn't that he couldn't remember, it was that he could remember too much.

"That's the trouble," said Joe. "You've got competing memories. You remember all the realities you touch."

Matt stared blankly at Joe – *a little lamb lost.*

"I want you to use the notebook and want you to write down the numbers you get. Ten rounds, and make them all sixes. If you can't get a six write down what you did get."

Joe sat and watched as round after round Matt forced each throw to result in a six, and at each stage he wrote it down.

SIX SIX SIX

As he repeatedly threw the die it seemed to become more natural, and progressively, he found he had more and more dice to choose from. Each round, he managed to see a higher number of realities. Finally, he put the pen down.

Complete.

"So Matty. How do you think that went?" asked Joe.

Confused, Matt replied, "Good – ten sixes."

"Really?" said Joe. "Look again."

Matt Looked down at his pad.

SIX SIX
FIVE
SIX SIX SIX SIX SIX SIX SIX

The word *FIVE* stared back at him.

How? He distinctly remembered rolling a six each time.

"Let me guess. You're wondering how that happened since you forced a six each time. It's the branch point," said Joe, "and this is *very* important. You thought you were picking, and therefore changing, the outcome of the die-roll you'd just thrown. Mostly you were, but in one case, you went back further. You forced a six by picking a reality where you'd thrown a six, this round, but thrown a five in a previous round. I watched you do it. What you need to do is not only target the outcome, but also feel for where the branch is. Otherwise, you could be changing everything. You need to perceive not only the effects, but the causes as well. Imagine you located a reality where you were significantly richer – but what if that was compensation money for Jane being paralysed? There is always a cause Matty, and as often-as-not its *bad news*. This is why it's crucial to take baby-steps."

As if on cue, Ethan woke and began making a racket. Scooping him up, Matt grabbed the pre-made bottle out of the warmer and, after checking the temperature, popped it into Ethan's eagerly-waiting mouth.

"Try again," said Joe, "and this time watch for the branch point – for the cause, not just the effect."

This time Matt focussed not only on the die but also on the pad, noticing when an outcome would likely change what he'd written. Balancing the feeding Ethan on one arm, he again threw the die, rolling one six after another.

Finished, he put the pen down once again, this time more tired.

Done.

"Better," said Joe. "Well done. But what if I tried to stop you?"

Matt drew in his breath – he knew this had been coming.

OK, bring it on, he thought.

He once again picked up the die and threw it.

The possibilities were now so clear that it was difficult to separate the alternatives from reality – *did that concept even make sense now?*

Picking one of the sixes, he selected it, but found himself bounced out, deflected, rebounded away from it. It was like he was trying to push together the common poles of two magnets.

Although shaken, he'd managed to stay focussed enough to still witness all the realities.

"Good," encouraged Joe, "return to it, but slowly…"

Matt targeted the six and edged his way towards it. He was not rebounded this time, but it was like moving through treacle. For what seemed like hours, he was resisted.

Finally, he gave up. "I can't do it," he said.

"Nonsense," said Joe. "For a first time, I think you're doing just fine."

"I'm exhausted," said Matt.

How am I ever going to do this? he thought. *If, as Joe suggested, 'they' could have considerably more resources to marshal, how could he ever hope to succeed?*

"Is there no other way?" he asked.

"If you come up against them, then this is it," said Joe, "but there may be a way to avoid that altogether."

Before Matt could respond, Mary appeared behind them.

"Since the little one's having such a nice drink, can I get you boys one too?"

Tea would be extremely welcome, thought Matt. His face must have made it obvious, as Mary took his expression as a yes, and busied herself in response.

"Tea would be a good idea," agreed Joe. "You need a break, if only for ten minutes."

Before long, Mary returned with tea, and had, once again, managed to rustle up some biscuits. As soon as the tray arrived, Matt took one, only then realising how hungry he actually was. Reaching for his cup, he drew deeply on the sweet tea and felt calmer almost immediately.

That was good. Just what I needed.

Putting his cup back, he looked at Joe. "What do you mean, 'there may be a way to avoid it'?"

"What I mean is, you don't need to tackle everything directly," explained Joe. "Rather than preparing to win in a direct confrontation, you could potentially avoid it completely by altering the lead-up to when the graft would happen. If we could avoid the set of events that lead to whoever-it-is who is threatening Ethan, then he would be safe."

Joe had discovered this years before…

During the early days of the ACL. Branchford, Baker and he had set up standing orders that every Monday one of the unit should attempt to force a branch onto whichever team member was on the roster. The roster was posted up on each Tuesday, and the exercise was that on the following Monday the team were to force a local change onto the nominee. The alteration needed to have a branch point of either the previous Tuesday or Wednesday, and the nominee's job was to oppose it until the graft-point on Monday was reached.

It was ideal training, in that the target would feel the change building from Tuesday onwards, feel a graft growing over time, and gain practice opposing it.

On this occasion, it was Joe's turn to oppose. And by Wednesday evening he'd pushed back numerous times, but the graft was still there, hanging like a dull headache.

Baker caught up with him out of hours.

"Still struggling with the graft?" he'd said. "Want to make it go away?"

Joe hadn't been impressed, thinking Baker was goading him, yanking his chain; but he listened anyway.

"All you need to do is to give the guys Monday as leave. What you're battling against is an event which hasn't happened yet. If you make it so it never happens the graft should also evaporate – theoretically at least."

"Is that possible?" Joe asked. He knew he could grant the men leave if it were sanctioned by Baker, but was it that simple?

"Why not?" said Baker. "Call it an experiment. The point I'm interested in, is at what point does it actually disappear? What is the trigger? Surely if you decide, right now, to grant them leave, the graft should disappear, even before you've done it. But if the graft has disappeared, then you don't need to grant them leave anymore – in which case the graft won't have disappeared – or is it that it merely weakens? If you're happy to grant the men leave – I'd love to know what happens, and I'd be willing to sign it off."

Joseph shrugged. Fair enough – was it really that simple? On one hand he couldn't get his head round it, On the other hand, it kind of made sense. As Baker explained it, the graft was a weakening of the interstitial field that actually generated a retro-causal effect. However, Baker postulated that a forward causal link could trigger this to either occur or not occur, and this linkage could even be circular.

"It's a recursive dependency," he said, "but what I want to know is, how does it act?"

"Fair enough," said Joe. "You sign it off and you've got yourself a deal."

"Already done," Baker said, handing him the typed foolscap sheet. "All it needs is for you to action it."

Joseph could feel the decision building in his mind, and as he did, he felt the graft ebb and flow.

"Leave it with me, I'll do it tomorrow."

Decision made but the graft remained.

"Interesting," mused Baker. "It obviously needs to be actioned and not simply intended…"

The next day Joseph had called the men to order. They'd recently completed a major operation, so the pretence was not too farfetched.

"Gentlemen. In recognition of your recent operational successes, General Envaneer has sanctioned time from now until Tuesday as extra-ordinary leave for the company. Well done men! Report back 6am Tuesday. Very well done. Dismissed."

To his amazement, the graft completely evaporated, there and then. Reporting back to Baker, his astonishment was clear.

"See, there's definitely more than one way to skin a cat," Baker said.

"How does that work? The only reason I gave them the day off was because they were attempting to graft me, but by giving them the day off, they never attempted the graft, so why did I give them the day off?"

Surely this was a paradox. He thought the universe should complain… or something, shouldn't it?

Baker could see his unease, "Don't think about it like that Joe, in such black and white terms. You're thinking like they were grafting you from tomorrow and because of that, you prevented that from ever happening, leaving you to ask, why did I do that… The way I'd prefer to think about it is that you were heading down a path where they were due to graft you. However you switched tracks like a train on a set of points. They're still there trying to graft you, just not in the reality that we both currently occupy – you're not heading down that track anymore, but that track is still there. It's like catching a ball, you move to catch it well before it is even thrown. If at the last minute it isn't thrown, why did you move? Rather than a ball, if it were a grenade, you could take action to prevent it being thrown, couldn't you? What are you basing that on, if not actionable symptoms of a future event? Don't think about it as the intervention being the cause of the graft. Instead think of it as the branch leading to a set of circumstances that results in an intervention. And as you've just proven, change the circumstances and you divert the branch."

"That's completely different," said Joe.

"Is it?" Baker had replied.

"So what are you trying to tell me?" Matt said over his now un-drunk tea.

"What I'm saying Matty, is that whoever is creating this graft, is doing so maybe twenty years from now. What I'm thinking is, rather than oppose them directly for the next twenty years, maybe you can change the here-and-now just enough to avert the events that lead up to it – get inside and avoid the graft in the first place. Bump your train onto a different track."

Matt's mind was suddenly alive.

Could it really be that simple?

"OK," he said, "How do we do that?"

"That's where we need to figure it out Matty, put our thinking caps on. In *my* reality, it was my interaction with Envaneer and then Branchford that put the wheels in motion; created the ACL. Now, if little to none of that happened, then there must be something else, some other event that kicks things off. There must be something else that triggers things. Without me, Branchford would never have managed to create the ACL – well not in the same way anyway. Someone with the gift must be helping them – we need to find them and nudge them just enough…"

"But how on earth does that help?" said Matt. "Didn't you say Branchford was already an old man when you met him? Surely he wouldn't still be around – would he?"

"No. He'd be long gone, but we need to start somewhere. If

he left behind a trace – if there's a record…"

Joe was probably right. It might be a wild goose chase, but finding out what became of Professor Arthur Branchford was as good a start as any.

Looking over at Ethan as he slept, Matt realised that he could now see what Joe had been telling him all along. He could see the graft affecting Ethan, ominously hanging there. Matthew Howard looked at his son and despaired. Ethan was fading, translucent in comparison to the things around him. He felt helpless, yet responsible – after all, he was Ethan's father.

Whatever the answer, he needed to find some options. If someone with the gift was triggering this, he needed to find out who they were.

CHAPTER 28

Thomas Howard arrived at Waterloo station and briskly exited the train. London was another world to him, and he wasn't exactly sure that he liked it.

The majority of people plodded by, faces grim and weary, the exception being the suited and booted management types who seemed to stride purposefully, expecting the crowds to part like the Red Sea. Tom did neither – a confused and startled rabbit might be a better description of him.

Welcome to the smoke.

He'd arrived early that morning and was due to see Director Rountree at a place called the Branchford Institute at 11am. As ever, Tom was early, and he found the door to the institute in more than enough time. It was an austere building from another era and, rather surprisingly, did not have a public reception. It was strangely not unfamiliar and Tom had the feeling that he'd been here before. This was not a strong sensation, but what he understood others describe as *déjà vu.*

What kind of place is this? He thought as he pressed the buzzer.

"Yes?"

"Tom Howard to see Professor Rountree."

Rountree – the name had a strange sound to it, as he realised that until now he'd only ever read it.

The lock buzzed open and Tom entered, unaware that, in fact, he was being watched closely – with a mop of unwashed hair and dark glasses, the stranger wore a battered trench coat and boots only fit for growing plants out of; his seemingly hungover and homeless appearance so out of place that it afforded him an invisibility than only denial and intentional avoidance could provide. From across the square, he sat on the bench that lay obliquely opposite, and quietly observed.

CHAPTER 29

Matthew Howard arrived at King's Cross station. He'd taken the Leeds train from Newcastle that morning. Although planning to get to London as early as possible, the prices had caused him to blanch. Instead, he'd left Newcastle at 7:29 and was now drawing up at King's Cross just before 11:00. Leaving the train, he asked the guard where he might get a tube to Covent Garden.

"Round the corner mate, and down the stairs," he said, indicating to where Matt could now see the familiar circle logo of the London Underground. "You'll want to take the Piccadilly line."

Twenty minutes later, Matt found himself in Covent Garden, London A-Z in hand, planning his onward route.

As he scanned the streets, the proximity of where he was headed and the sheer number of people made him begin to question himself for the first time that day.

What I am doing? he thought. Did he even have a plan other than reconnaissance? He could hardly knock on the door and ask *'Are you the zygotic embryo of a secret organisation that in two-decades time will seek to erase my son?'* But if not that, what was he even doing here?

Rather than dwell further on these thoughts, Matt concentrated on the fact that he was here, and that he needed to turn up something useful. *To make some progress at least.*

With that thought in the front of his mind, he made his way by foot from Covent Garden to finally find himself in a grassy square surrounded by a set of similar looking buildings. Passing a heavy panelled door, he spotted an array of buzzers next to a black plaque that simply read *The Branchford Institute.*

It was a Georgian building, so unimposing and seemingly hidden that he had nearly missed it.

OK, so at least I know where you are, he thought with an element of dread that caused him to keep on walking. He was aware of his panic levels rising and his heart pounding in his chest.

He needed to get away – to regroup and gather his thoughts.

He kept going, out of the square and down the street. It was not until he arrived at a Starbucks that he finally stopped.

"White coffee please," he muttered, almost distractedly.

The girl behind the counter looked at him with disdain and rolled her eyes, before pointing at the board and launching into the same routine that she'd no doubt followed hundreds of times.

"Oh – What? Sorry – yes, Americano with room for milk, then," he replied, still distracted.

Why was everything so complicated? Since when did coffee have to be Crappuccino?

Coffee in hand, he made his way back to the square opposite the institute and sat himself down on the bench some distance away that afforded a view of the entrance. For cover, he took a battered book from his rucksack and, in between sips of coffee, leafed through it.

At least it's a nice day.

Over the course of the next three hours, literally, nothing happened. No one arrived, and no one left. He wasn't sure what he'd expected, but he knew this wasn't it. His earlier panic now abated, he gave a depressed sigh.

What was he doing here?

****

Thomas Howard sat in the waiting room within the Institute. It was smaller than he'd thought it would be, given its grand title. After a short while, he was met by the man that he'd seen at the clinic, talking to Williamson.

"Tom," he said, "Thanks for coming, my name's Phillip Rountree, so glad you could make it. Please, come through."

A further sensation of *déjà vu* jangled within his head. It was as if he recognised Rountree – *No, that wasn't the right word*. He knew he'd seen him at the clinic, but there was something else. It was as if he'd seen him in a different setting – *but where?*

Then, as soon as it had come, the feeling was gone, and

Thomas Howard found himself dumbly standing motionless in the waiting room. He followed Rountree towards what looked like a Victorian consulting room. *Something Freud might have had in Vienna*, he thought.

Books lined the walls ceiling to floor in glass-fronted cases, and by the window – a battered psychiatrist's *chaise lounge*.

Tom made his way towards the couch. However, Rountree quickly interjected. "Don't bother with that," he said, "unless you want to rick your back. I only got it for show. It's probably full of fleas, to be honest." Instead he indicated towards a leather-upholstered captain's seat, "Please, sit here," he said, taking a seat himself.

"First things first, I ought to explain who we are and what we do here. This institute was set up by the late Arthur Branchford as, in his words, a means to treat *high-functioning schizophrenics* who lucidly describe other worlds."

Was that him? Tom thought. The label certainly depressed him, but maybe it was appropriate; perhaps it was right.

"Arthur was convinced that schizophrenics had a window onto another reality and was determined to help them. He developed one test that I'd like to start you with, and that's to test your perception and your predisposition to interpret the world, or to effectively view it in the raw."

Rountree drew down the blind and illuminated a set of spotlights. In the corner of the room stood what looked like an old-fashioned gramophone with a comic-tragic mask sitting on top of it.

"Is this where you're going to put your BAFTA?" joked Tom nervously.

"Eh? – Oh yes, quite. Very droll," said Rountree sounding confused. Setting the mask slowly spinning, Rountree looked at him, "So, Tom, tell me. What do you see? Do you see the inside of the mask? Do you always see an outward face? Or do you see something else?"

****

Matt sat on the bench and pretended to read his book. He scanned each page and turned them one after another. After each couple of pages, he held up the empty coffee cup and pretended to drink.

This was stupid, what was he doing here? It was nearly three o'clock, and no one had come or gone.

A voice behind him suddenly made him jump.

"Let me guess – the only reason someone would sit here for three hours sipping an empty cup, is the same reason I would. You're in my seat by the way."

Matt's heart raced, and as he fumbled for an answer he turned to look behind him.

"I'm sorry? I don't know what…"

"Sure, you don't," the man replied, cutting him off. As Matt now saw, the man was in his mid-thirties with wild, shoulder-length hair and, like some throwback from the 80's, was dressed in combat boots and a battered old trench-coat. He wore shades and an overly confident, almost all-knowing smirk.

He theatrically circled the bench before crash-landing heavily next to a bewildered Matt. Raising his glasses to the top of his head, his eyes stared out wildly like he was some kind of manic pirate. "Next you're going to tell me your name's not Howard and you're not a fixer…"

CHAPTER 30

Matthew Howard's heart raced as he sat, frozen to the spot.

How did this stranger know him? Know about him? Know about the gift?

Apprehensively, Matt looked the man in the face.

He didn't look like he belonged to the establishment – certainly not as Joe had explained it. He didn't look like anything that Matt had expected to encounter.

He didn't look like anything...

Who, or what, was he?

"Who... Who are you?" he said finally. "And how do you know my name?"

Annoyingly, the stranger insisted on smirking, rather than answering, and continued to examine Matt.

"See..." he said wagging a finger, animated and grinning madly, "See... I knew it was you. I told myself it was you, but then I thought – *No, it can't be, not here.* But here you are. And here I am, the two of us... together."

The man, openly excited, gesticulated wildly as he spoke and waved his hands like some flamboyant clown. Suddenly serious, as if remembering Matt was there at all, he ceased his flourishes and lowered his hands.

"Don't worry," he said hoarsely, almost whispering, before furtively looking round, "I'm not with them. I'm not one of them."

Matt just looked at him but said nothing.

"And, as for how I know your name – I recognised your face. Well not *your face* exactly, that would be *too weird*," his hands were off dancing once again. "I recognised Joseph Howard's face. The fact that you're here now, like me, means that we need to talk. But not here – *not like this.* Come on, since you've been drinking the same empty cup for three hours why don't you refresh it and buy me a coffee?"

Not knowing quite what to say, Matt just nodded and followed the stranger back into the heart of the city.

By virtue of no longer being in the square, Matt completely failed to see his father leave some minutes later by the door Matt had been watching, oblivious to his son even being in the vicinity.

"So... who are you then?" Matt said as he queued in yet another Starbucks, this one further away and only a little larger than a front room. The tone of his voice was one of pure annoyance.

"All in good time..." came the reply, the stranger focusing instead on the intricate job at hand. Coffee preparation seemed to take precedence over anything Matt could say and, as the bizarre ceremony involving milk & sugar unfolded before him, Matt felt his patience fading. Finally complete, the stranger perched himself at the bar that faced the window before nudging the stool next to him, saying, "Take a seat."

Matt sat. Infuriatingly, the man ignored him once again and took a long draw on his beverage, "Oh, That's good..."

The man, either ignorant or unconcerned with Matt's ire, looked at him almost curiously before beginning, "To answer your question, the name's Jacobson."

The stranger's eyes burrowed into Matt looking for a reaction, his head rocking, chimp-like, left to right, examining Matt's face from multiple vantage points.

Jacobson, thought Matt. The name was indeed familiar. Joe had mentioned a Jacobson in the ACL – the tortured prodigy that had introduced Joe to the concept and act of opposition.

"I see you recognise the name. That's good – a good start. So, who was Joe to you? Father? Uncle? Grandfather?"

"Grandfather," replied Matt "Joe's my grandfather."

"Well, back in the day, *if that's the right phrase*, your grandfather knew my father, and given that you're here, you'll know what they were involved with, and you know how that ended up. Like I suppose Joe did, my father found himself here but, unlike most, he remembered where he had come from – people thought him deranged but he told me the stories, and I listened. He was a keen artist, and he used to sketch pictures and put faces to names so that he wouldn't forget them. That's how I recognised you, how I knew you." Pausing he took another drink of his coffee, "Is any of this making sense?"

"More than you can imagine," said Matt. "So, can you...

you know, do what Joe and Jacobson could do?" Matt wiggled the fingers on both hands.

"A little... and only recently. You?"

"Likewise – in the last month. So," said Matt finally, "what are you here for? Why here? Why now?"

"An excellent question my young friend, and one I might ask of you. Why indeed... *Why now*, because according to my dad, the *mad-meshuggener* that he is, something big is going to go down. Not for a while yet, but as things go, something huge, spanning over twenty years in the making. I can feel it too, like electricity, like a charge building-up. *Why here*, because, according to my father, this is where the ACL began – with Branchford – and we know how that ended up. Like a lot of people, he lost everything he cared about in that one. If they're starting up again..."

Matt breathed between his teeth, whistling slightly.

Everything that Jacobson was saying confirmed what Joe had told him. But Jacobson appeared to be unhinged, only slightly in touch with reality. Every instinct within him told him to stand-up and walk out of there. But then it wasn't just about him, there was his son. Ethan...

"I have a son," said Matt. "According to Joe, in the graft that is building, my son... he's not there, he doesn't exist. I need to know who they are and why they–" He broke off, taking a sip of his coffee while he gathered his thoughts. "No," he growled. "I don't need to know *who* they are. I don't even need to know the *why* of anything. I just need to stop them any way I can. I can't lose my son."

Jacobson nodded slowly.

"I can relate to that more than you know."

Raising his coffee cup, he gently touching it to Matt's.

"L'Chaim, to *life* my friend!"

Taking a long draw on his drink, he stared out into the street.

Matt's gaze followed his, and for a while, the two of them sat there in silence, watching the world go by.

Outside, the weather had turned, and it had begun to drizzle. The traffic passed the window, and Matt watched hundreds of people flowing in every direction.

All of them think this is the only reality, that this is all there is, he thought. *None of them knows how fragile any of this is.*

All of them leading their petty lives as if they can really change things.

Finally, Jacobson spoke. "My father told me the real problems began when they started believing their own press. They believed that there wasn't anything that could not, or should not, be fixed. If there are no consequences, then there are no morals and ultimately no limits. If you operate with impunity, who are you responsible to?"

What was the phrase that Joe used? Who will guard the guards?

"This can't be something left to clandestine organisations to execute on a whim," said Jacobson. "In the reality where we are now, trepidation, or at least a common sense view of risk, kept Churchill from attacking Russia, kept it all from going completely Pete Tong. Without consequences, there's nothing to keep people reined in, nothing to stop them taking world changing decisions. Nothing to stop another fuck-up like last time. Life's not a video game where you get to replay a level any number of ways until you win. I'm not going to let that happen. Not again!"

Matt was not following him.

What was Jacobson referring to?

He needed to speak to Joe. It was evident that Jacobson assumed he knew far more than he did, but he also knew that he needed to say something. "The road to hell is paved with good intentions."

Jacobson nodded. "True... But that, what they did, that was *downright evil*! They treated humanity, not as free-thinking individuals but as objects to be manipulated, with the ends justifying any means. With a power like ours, either it stays hidden like it has for generations, or everyone knows about it, and society keeps it in check." As he spoke, his attention seemed to drift further away from Matt to the world passing by outside.

"That kind of power needs to be with the people. It can't be with *The Man*," he added, to no one and to everyone.

Matt realised that Jacobson was making him very nervous; very nervous indeed. Gone was the levity he'd seen earlier, replaced by an almost religious fervour.

I definitely need to speak with Joe.

I've not so much found an ally, as discovered someone with a shared foe, he thought as he also stared out of the window. *If I've got his number, he'd rail against an organised government but would quite happily let the word burn in the name of some hippy-ideal.*

"So, what's the answer?" he asked.

"Concerted action," said Jacobson, his attention snapping back to Matt. "We need to know who they are and what they know. We need to know if they're *a front*, if they're planning something big, we need information. We need to bug them."

Matt thought that Jacobson could be planning to walk into the lion's den, and, indeed, his meddling could make things worse, as much as make them better – but what other leads were there? Jacobson's very existence here proved there was substance to Joseph's claim, and it wasn't as if he was prepared to sit back and do nothing.

I can't pretend I'm comfortable with this, he thought, *but what choice do I have?*

"OK…" he said. "What do you need from me?"

CHAPTER 31

Thomas Howard rode the train back from London, his mind revisiting his earlier exchange with Rountree.

"This institute was set up as a means to treat high-functioning schizophrenics who lucidly describe other-worlds."

"Arthur Branchford was convinced that schizophrenics had a window onto another reality."

Looking out of the window he fought the disbelief that he'd felt since then.

Rountree seemed to suggest his episodes were not delusions, but actually a result of seeing the world for how it actually was – fractured and multi-faceted. The notion had rattled him to the core. But, *worse than that*, what they appeared to be saying was that until speaking to him, these ideas had been mere conjecture. For over sixty-years the institute had plodded on, operating to the late-Arthur Branchford's request that the work continued in the hope that patient-zero, someone who could lift the veil, would eventually be found.

If that were the case, then did that mean that his visions of being institutionalised and restrained were actually real?

Could that really be happening in some other world?

If that were true, did that also mean that rather than being crazy, Joe was possibly one of the few people that could see the world for what it was?

Surely it was just a theory – and until he had some proof it was one he was going to keep to himself.

Worst of all, Tom knew one thing for absolute certainty...

If it were true, and if she ever found out, Barbara was definitely not going to like this...

She was not going to like it one little bit.

CHAPTER 32

Matthew Howard grasped the black leather-bound notebook which he'd purchased as a gift for Joe and looked out of the window of the east coast carriage as the train sped him back north. The journal was like the one he'd recently bought for himself, but classier. He'd found it in Liberty when he'd gone to try to find Jane a gift to assuage his unexplained absence.

He'd failed miserably on that front, but at least he was sure that Joe would like the notebook, and as he looked out at the passing scenery he took comfort from the soft feel of the leather's nap against his skin. All in all, it'd been a productive but thoroughly strange day.

He'd agreed to meet Jacobson again at the end of the month when they'd take *concerted action* – as Jacobson had put it. *Against my better judgement*, thought Matt. But what else should he have said? If he'd refused Jacobson, where would he have stood then? What would have been his next move?

He looked again, out of the train window, at the tableaux of images which flashed in front of his eyes, and struggled to take it all in. His mind was already elsewhere, revisiting the earlier conversation.

"I'm going to get in, plant equipment, and get out. The trick is going to be not being discovered, and that's where I need your help, Howard."

Matt had said nothing and had merely raised an eyebrow.

What was Jacobson expecting him to do? It was like he was planning a heist with a grotesque version of the Cadbury Milk Tray man.

"I need you to monitor the institute, look out for mistakes, and nudge the outcome towards us remaining undiscovered."

"I'm not sure…" he had said.

Could it be that simple? It sounded straightforward…

"When would it be?"

"I still need to do some prep, so we'd be talking the end of the month – Saturday night through to early-doors Sunday morning."

Matt had paused waiting for his brain to generate cogent protests, and got nothing.

"OK," he had finally heard his voice say uneasily, "I'll be there."

What was he getting himself into?

Some days later he sat opposite Joe, sipping strong tea, on West Verity's glazed Veranda.

"So, Jacobson made it," nodded Joe. "I'm glad – he remembers, and he has a son. A chip off the old block from what you've said."

"He was really disconnected, but really concerned at the same time," said Matt. "He referred to what you two were involved with, and how that ended up. What did he mean? Why is he so passionate? Why does he care so much?"

Joseph Howard sighed deeply, obviously uncomfortable with the topic but pressed on. "OK Matty," he sighed heavily. "I'll tell you."

CHAPTER 33

It was in May '45, shortly after celebrating Victory in Europe, that Envaneer, Branchford and Joseph were called to Churchill's War-rooms. They were soon to find out that, rather than being in high-spirits, Churchill's thoughts were clouded with concern.

"It's the Russians," Envaneer said to them beforehand as they waited to be seen, "He thinks they can't be trusted – he's probably right."

The way things had turned out had undoubtedly surprised the British High Command. There had been a tacit assumption that after the war, Great Britain and the United States would be dominant, and Russia would be on her knees. That was so far from the truth that now faced them as to pour scorn on the fact that it had ever been forecast in the first place.

Like others, Joe had seen the reports and heard the rumours – rather than liberation, territories were progressively being annexed by the Russians. But even if such a land grab was happening, surely that was still liberation from Nazi control, wasn't it? There had been solidarity against a common enemy, but when that common enemy is neutralised, do an enemy's enemies still remain friends? Only a fool or a dreamer would think so.

"So, where do we come in?" Joseph had asked.

"Where we come in," explained Envaneer, "is that we are able to give him options. We provide him with a safety net to steel his resolve. By offering him a back-out plan, we're able to let him take the decision that England needs him to take – we're able to offer him *Operation Overstrike*."

The plan was simple, they would create a pre-determined branch point around the specific decision to pre-emptively attack Stalin's Russian forces. The conventional armies, along with the recently co-opted German forces, were to descend on the Russian troops and within three months, one way or another, it would all be over.

By making the branch point explicit and specific, they had their back-out plan. Come the worst; come a disastrous end, they could, at least, overstrike the attack on the Russians, like reminting a damaged coin; remake it so it never happened, to make it so that the *point-decision* was reversed.

It was far beyond anything they'd ever attempted, and Joseph had blanched at the prospect of such an initiative. He'd had real doubts.

"You do know that if you impose a graft over that length of time, that it'll effectively be the end of the ACL? They likely wouldn't survive a graft of that magnitude. If they did, they'd be to take away. *WE'D BE TO TAKE AWAY!* Arthur, a shift on that scale could make basket-cases of all of us."

It was true, those involved with the operations would endure months of conflicting memories, they wouldn't know what was real and what was no-longer real, what was actual and what was virtual, what was material and what was imaginary, what had occurred and what were purely potentialities of what-might-have-been. It was enough to literally drive anyone insane.

"In this war we all have to make sacrifices Joseph," said Envaneer.

"But the war's over, isn't it?" said Joe. "We won! Didn't we?"

"Don't be so naive," said Envaneer, rolling up a sleeve to reveal a tattoo – *Si vis pacem, para bellum* (If you want peace, prepare for war). "We're always at war Joseph, we always will be. It never ends, but it will change. But from now on it will be a case of a war fought in the shadows."

Joseph sighed.

It was ever the same. Some were born to command, and some were born to fight and to die. Like many others through history, he was about to be cast aside for some idealistic view of the greater good. Well, so be it, what did he have to lose anyway? Though more likely the ACL was about to be sacrificed on the altar of Envaneer's pride and vanity.

Maybe it was being present in Churchill's oak-panelled corridors of power which emboldened him, but Joe felt it his duty to raise concerns.

"As long as we're not over promising…" said Joseph. "If what you're proposing is truly in the country's best interests I'll follow you into the gates of hell, however if this is some political…"

Envaneer stiffened, turned and cut him off. "Captain Howard, may I remind you *where you are* and *to whom you are talking.*"

Joseph Howard steeled himself for the chastisement that was to follow, but before Envaneer could continue, or before Joseph could respond, the doors opened and they were summoned to the PM.

"What was he like?" asked Matt. "Was he, *you know*, like they say?"

"From what I can remember, he was tired mostly," said Joe, "but yes, he was a commanding presence. He'd been briefed about the ACL of course. He knew all about the unit."

His plan assumed a surprise attack on the Soviets in Germany in order to "impose the will of the Western Allies" on the Russians.

In '45 he'd found the Americans weren't going to liberate Berlin as they'd previously indicated, and instead, they were happy to abandon it to the Russians. Churchill was madder than hell – furious! In his view, the Americans had gone back on the promise that they wouldn't let post-war Europe be segmented into Russian states. Only a few months earlier, the heads of state had reached agreement at the Yalta Conference on that very point.

Churchill's view was that pressure needed to be kept on the Russians to make them respect the Yalta agreement, to guarantee the future shape of Europe; but the Americans would have none of it, and things should have stopped there. But the existence of the ACL drove Churchill on, emboldened him, made him rash. Because of the ACL – because of us – he attacked the Russians without the American's help. It was near suicide, and it quickly went from bad to worse. Britain endured a long and sustained bombing campaign, far worse than the Blitz, this time being pounded by Russian rockets, newer and more powerful weapons.

"Churchill became increasingly reclusive, and the nation's focus was instead rallied unexpectedly by a newly elected MP, Lady Grace Derbyshire. When Churchill eventually withdrew from public life she rose in popularity and stepped into the breach. In our darkest hours, her radio broadcasts brought hope to the nation. The country loved her and called her *Mother*, as a term of endearment.

"When Churchill was unexpectedly killed in a rocket attack in '47, she had become, against all the odds, the natural choice to replace him. Way before Margaret Thatcher, Golda Meir or Indira Gandhi, we had a female prime minister, and she was certainly a force to be reckoned with.

"Mother knew about the unit, and she understood what Churchill's rationale was; however, she still thought it madness and fought tooth and nail to engage with the Russians in conventional terms. But, by the autumn of 1948, it was painfully evident that we'd lost. Thousands were already dead. Soviet troops were running amok in the streets. It was complete carnage, Matty.

"The plan was to jump to the graft which had branched at the point of the decision to attack Russia. That was deemed sufficiently safe and would not undo all we'd previously achieved. You see Matty, at this point, *in that reality*, Hitler had been reined in; he was still as evil, but he had not gone unchecked. We were taking a pasting from Stalin and the Russians and were at the point of defeat, but humanity had not gone through its darkest hour. Prior to what we'd thought of as the end of the war, we'd managed to avert the worst of the Holocaust.

"We knew it was all over in '48. We were beaten, and, given that we'd brought it on ourselves, no one was going to come to our aid this time. The unit had struggled to hold onto the graft – the memory was fading and it was only myself who could see it at all.

"I was summoned again to the War Rooms for a final briefing. I was asked to fix us to the '45 branch; invoke *Operation Overstrike* to back us out. However, when it came to it, the Russians managed to stop me. I was opposed – and opposed aggressively. The cabinet bunker was overrun, I was shot and lost the branch. They fatally wounded me, Matt.

They'd won.

"In the seconds that followed, I grabbed desperately at anything I could. The '45 branch I was clinging onto was long gone. All I had left was the branch in which I was sure that your grandmother had survived the bombings of '41. I was fading fast, and as I clung to that thought, I pulled."

Joe paused, taking a draw on his tea. His eyes darkened and his brow furrowed as he continued.

"And in that moment, I lived. You got to live, the ACL, and therefore, the botched attempt at taking on Stalin's Russia, never was. That was the positive – the upside. The problem was that in this world, Hitler and his acolytes went far, far further than in the reality I'd just come from. Maybe the ACL had stopped him, maybe it was just chance, but the horror that met me after I branched, was inconsolable. Because of what I'd just done, the ACL had ceased to ever have existed. And without the intervention of the ACL, the Holocaust came about, meaning millions of innocents were led to their vicious and brutal deaths. So when Jacobson speaks about *what I was involved with, and how it ended*, he's referring to the fact that he would have been flipped into another reality, where all that he'd fought-for the past five years, and all that he'd cared about, had been blown away in an instant. He'd been flipped into a reality where evil had been left to fester. Unchecked by the ACL, millions had suffered and died in worse than awful circumstances. Who knows how that would have affected him, or what he lost."

Joe recalled it all like it was yesterday. The memories of waking with Ruth flooded back to him, and suddenly, he was back there, remembering Mother, the Russians and how it had ended in an instant. The horrific certainty. He knew that by his unmaking the ACL he had become responsible for the torture and death of literally millions of innocents. He remembered, not only how it had ended, but also how his new life had begun.

CHAPTER 34

Joseph Howard blinked through the dimness, as the orange glow of the crackling hearth lit the room. The gentle snapping of the meagre coals interrupting the peace of the tiny, otherwise silent space.

He was alive – But where was he?

He felt the sudden warmth from the open fire on the right side of his face, but on the other side…

Something else…

Something soft…

"Don't worry Tommy," he heard a familiar voice say; a voice he hadn't heard in a long, *long* time.

…but a voice he'd also heard only moments before.

"Daddy's going to be just fine; he just needs a little time alone; you run-along and play. Daddy's just having one of his *Walter Mitty* moments; *aren't you Daddy?*"

His eyes finally focused on Ruth; *his Ruth*, but a Ruth that looked years older, and both tired and concerned. Her right hand tenderly touching his face – *soft*, her left hand gently but firmly grasping his.

He was in unfamiliar surroundings, disoriented – *where was he? But this was his and Ruth's home, the cottage they'd bought together all those years before. It had always been so… but it had never been so… Ruth was dead and gone. He'd grieved for years.*

There was something else, something was wrong, very wrong. He could feel it, like electricity, in the very air around him.

Manoeuvring herself protectively in front of the small child that now stood still, frozen behind her, Ruth continued, this time more sternly, "Tommy darling, I *SAID* go play in your room."

Was it that Ruth was scared of him?

Joe watched transfixed, as the *somehow-alien-yet-somehow-familiar* child toddled out of sight and Ruth's concentration seemed to focus in on him. Distraction now removed, the fear in her eyes abated, finally melting away.

"Be still. Calm yourself dearest Joe, still your mind my darling – this will pass." Her soothing words now hung melodiously in the air like a long-forgotten lullaby.

Tears welling in his eyes, he croaked, "I thought I'd never see you again?"

"But Joe, I'm right here, I'm not going anywhere."

Before he could say more, a tidal wave of seven years *alter-vu* memory began unpacking in his head one memory falling into place after another, like toppling-dominoes.

The child. Tommy was his son – of course he was.

Their son...

Something else... He was somehow broken inside... Is that what Ruth feared?

Germany – Auschwitz – VJ Day – Potsdam – Attlee – Cold War...

Without the ACL's intervention, they had been no disastrous campaign against Stalin's Russia, Ruth was alive and well, and they were parents – he was a father. However, the unspeakable atrocities he'd spent years helping to avert had all come to pass – and far, far worse.

What had he just done?

Joe recalled it all like it was yesterday. He remembered the instant, the horrific certainty, the point at which he knew that by unmaking the ACL he had become responsible for the torture and death of literally millions of innocents.

Possibly not morally responsible – that lay with others. But certainly causal and actual responsibility, nevertheless.

The child, Tommy, was their son. The shock that Ruth was *alive*, and they had a son – but with Ruth, there had been something else...

She couldn't cope with him like this.

Like what?

It was too much...

Through the hotchpotch of elation, confusion and despair,

his mind, and all that he was, collapsed, torn asunder by the torrent of guilt that drenched him to the bone. Wrenching free from Ruth's embrace, beyond distraught, beyond consoling, he screamed inside and then outwardly cried. Claw-like, his hands ripped and tore at his hair.

Unable to control himself, he wept. "All those souls", he rasped between tears. "I've killed them! Tortured them, blighted generations; wiped them from the face of the earth. I've killed them all! WHAT RIGHT HAVE I?" he screamed. "Who am I to say who lives and who dies? Oh dear God."

Involuntarily, and repeatedly, he retched though his stomach was empty.

What had he done? Who was he to decide?

Undeterred, Ruth continued to fight against Joe's protests and deflections. Slowly but surely, his distress and sobbing diminished. Holding his head to her shoulder, she finally began to bring him some calm.

Inwardly, she was a tumult of emotion. His episodes had been progressively increasing in intensity, but this was far worse than anything so far. She'd previously vowed to keep his condition secret, keep it in the family, *keep mum.*

The thought of Joe being in one of those horrid places, one of those asylums that *dealt* with this sort of thing, chilled her, but *this... this was something else. This was yet another level again...* and of course, there was Tommy to consider. There was always Tommy to consider.

How would they survive should Joe get even worse? She had given up teaching when Tommy had arrived, so Joe's electrical work was their only income.

"Hush my darling," she soothed, "everything's all right. Everything's going to be just fine."

"You don't know what they'll do," raved Joe, momentarily jerking away from her, "There will be consequences." *They had said that. If there were any justice in the world, how could there not be?*

Dear god, thought Ruth, *where do you travel when you leave me? What kind of demons do you flee?* One part of her wished she knew – another was glad she didn't. But for now, as she held him once again, it was enough that she loved him. She *had* always loved him. She *would* always love him.

Whoever, or whatever, haunted him, they couldn't have him. Wouldn't have him. She would see to that.

"My *sweet, sweet* darling," she said trying to calm him, "whatever happens, we'll get through it; as Scarlet would say, *after all, tomorrow is another day.*"

It was an attempt to lighten the mood, a reference from their youth, but here in the dim glow of the crackling coals, as she gently rocked the grown man that was yet her husband, she realised it was more than apt.

I'll think of some way to get him back.

After all... tomorrow IS another day.

Joseph Howard clung to his wife desperately; he'd got her back, but how many tomorrows did they have? How many would they have?

The Commission would never let this go, never tolerate this outcome. Eventually they'd find him. Eventually, they'd come for him. It couldn't end well.

As vivid as they were, the images and memories slowly faded and, once again, Joe found himself in the room with his grandson.

Matt looked into the old man's face as he sat in silence – worlds away. What Joe had told him was an enormous amount to take in. He could quite plainly see that, although it was a lifetime ago, a piece of Joe had died that day – ironically not through being fatally wounded, but instead by the grim realisation at what he'd brought to bear on the world.

"That graft would have turned the world upside down for any number of folks," Joe finally said, "and that is going to have led to a large number of disturbed and extremely angry people."

"Angry enough to want revenge?"

"With the families of far more than six million souls to pick from, the odds support it... but I don't know Matty," he sighed wearily, "but if not that, then what?"

"So, you think I need to support Jacobson, even if he seems less than connected to reality?"

"Like I say... I don't know Matty, but if not that, then what? What I do know is that his father was a good man."

Joseph was right. If not that, then what? He had no choice.

CHAPTER 35

Thomas Howard had spent the previous two weeks attempting to work out how to speak to his wife about the Branchford Institute. He sat in silence staring at the letter that had arrived that morning.

They wanted him to return to London, on a regular basis, as soon as he was able – could it possibly be that what he was experiencing was actually real?

Barbara was never going to accept that, but this was ready cash, and with his work drying up, she'd accept that easily enough. But Barbara was out and he sat at their kitchen table, coffee in hand reading the letter again and again. The Branchford Institute wanted him to work with them to further their research. Stranger still, they were willing to pay a not inconsiderable sum of money to do so.

It seemed too good to be true.

What was the catch?

Pushing the nagging doubts out of his mind, he reached for his pen and signed where the letter indicated.

For the sum of money they were talking he would be happy to help them. After all, what did he have to lose?

CHAPTER 36

Matthew Howard looked out of the window of the intercity as it sped southward along the east coast mainline. Half-asleep, he distracted himself by watching the myriad of actions and reactions within the train.

Over the last weeks, he'd practised his gift, and now he watched in wonder at the random gamut of behaviour on display. He watched silently, as the occupants of the half-filled carriage played out their lives. He watched as the exponential number of events simultaneously occurred or failed to happen. He watched in silence, as the passengers variously either did or didn't: drink-or-spill their coffee, forget-or-recall their luggage, or play-out a countless number of other miscible choices. It was unsettling; the more he perceived, the less he identified with the strangers in the carriage.

If he could herd them in any which way he pleased, were they little more than sheep? Lambs to the slaughter?

The direction of his thoughts shocked him.

Was he any different to them? Surely not, but then again...

He shook his head, and the multiple images snapped into one. Taking a sip of his coffee, he focussed his mind on Jacobson.

What did he really know about the man? Could he be trusted? What was he getting himself into?

****

Jacobson had suggested that they meet in Soho, at a pub called the Intrepid Fox. Although it was more than well past its glory days, when it had played its part in music folklore, the pub's constant stream of punk and goth subcultures meant that anyone looking to tail them would likely stand out a mile, or at least find it incredibly difficult to overhear anything they said.

Matt found the shabby pub in Wardour Street, surrounded

by a rag-tag mostly black-wearing sect, a collection of guy-linered adolescents all desperately trying to be different-and-original in exactly the same way. *Too cool for school.* He remembered it well.

Matt wandered through the door, and immediately felt at home. He'd not been here before, but the sounds, smells and motifs were like old friends. The jukebox was cranking out Motörhead's 'Ace of Spades', and in the corner he saw Jacobson mouthing to the lyrics, utterly oblivious to his entrance.

"Hey!" shouted Matt, as he stood in front of Jacobson.

Like before, Jacobson only gave him a portion of his attention, and held up an index finger indicating for Matt to wait... in the palm of his raised hand Matt noticed a half-eaten banana. Jacobson continued to mouth the lyrics until he reached the guitar break.

"I love this song," he shouted.

"Sure...Whatever," replied Matt, sitting down next to him. "How are things?"

Jacobson, who looked like he'd had a few, only shrugged. He sat there in the same trench coat and garb that he had previously worn and seemed overfilled with enthusiasm.

"Did you know, that, bananas," he slurred, indicating the one in his hand as an illustration, "are one of the world's most interesting things. For instance, did you know that when you buy foam banana sweets they don't taste like bananas?" He sat there looking at Matt.

Did he actually expect an answer?

"But, here's the thing. Actually, they do. Fake banana flavour is based on the Gros-Michel banana, which pretty much went extinct in the early 20th century. This..." he raved, "this ... is a Cavendish ... named after ... someone called Cavendish ... probably. A completely different taste."

He'd definitely had a few.

"Banana trees walk too," he said. "I'll tell you another time. And they're slightly radioactive. And they're sterile – all clones. So I reckon in 50 years they'll have all died out. That's why I eat them while I can. You should too... Here..."

Matthew Howard sat and looked in disbelief at Jacobson, who was rummaging in a carrier bag, presumably trying to find him a banana.

Had he really come nearly 300 miles for this?

"LOOK!" muttered Matt, his anger rising, "As strange as this may sound, I didn't come all the way down here to talk about frickin' bananas!

"What's wrong with you?

"What the hell are you on?"

In an instant the weight of the last few weeks seemed to come crashing down on Matt.

It was hopeless! Pointless! His son was at risk of erasure from reality itself and the best, and the only plan he had involved talking to a drunken loon about bananas. How could it possibly end in anything but disaster?

"Look, please can we focus on what I'm here to do?"

Jacobson, genuinely surprised by Matt's outburst, stuffed what remained of the banana into his mouth and mumbled a reply. "Yeph we haph no bannannath!" Seeing not a shred of amusement on Matt's face, he gulped it down and finally changed his tune. "Okay, okay, but if you'd had literally nothing to eat all day Thursday, then you'd be starving too. Anyway, down to business."

From under the table Jacobson pulled out a battered leather-satchel and tapped it proudly.

"In here, I have a couple of devices that I managed to procure from, well let's just call him an acquaintance. These are the state-of-the-art in digital surveillance."

Jacobson passed over the satchel to Matt who peered inside.

His heart sank. "Baby monitors… You're kidding me, right?"

"Think about it though," Jacobson said. "Digital clarity with a receiver that's designed to be portable."

Matt was speechless. *It was either stupid or brilliant. Maybe both – that was Jacobson all over.*

"Okay – for the minute, let's say that this isn't the most ludicrous idea that's ever been hatched. What next?"

CHAPTER 37

Thomas Howard lay conscious, eyes-closed, on the now-familiar institution bed. Through slits, he feigned sleep, but still he perceived the scene round him. Careful not to move, his mind once again aware of his restraint. The same cream bed. The same buzzing machinery to his side.

To his surprise, however, Rountree was there, wearing hospital-whites. "Tell Stevenson that Howard has progressed enough to bring his inhibitor online," he heard Rountree say. "Hunter will want an update too."

CHAPTER 38

It was 12:45am on Sunday morning. Jacobson had run through his plan many times but was reiterating it once again.

"OK, here's what's going to happen: We call 999 from the call-box down the street, saying that we've just seen some students pushing fireworks through the letterboxes along this road. I'm assuming that they'll call a key-holder to check this out, and then we'll take it from there."

"Who's making the call?" said Matt.

"I thought you could," replied Jacobson.

"Can *you* not?"

"I'd say I've a recognisable accent. Yours is almost RP."

It was true, Jacobson's thick accent made his voice extremely recognisable, where his own accent was middle of the road.

Reluctantly Matt acquiesced, and five minutes later he found himself making the call

…

"Hello – yes,"

…

"Fire, I think."

…

"Look never mind that! This is urgent. I've just seen a bunch of students pushing fireworks into letterboxes. Some institute opposite the square and some other buildings too…"

…

"Yes. That's where I'm calling from."

Hanging up, he turned to Jacobson.

"They're coming."

****

A crowd of students had gathered around the fire engine. Most of them were half-cut, and all of them were pestering the fire crew with questions. Matt and Jacobson stood back from the crowd and let them ask away.

"We've had a report of fireworks being pushed through letterboxes, so are asking the owners to check."

Presently, a small, academic-looking, grey haired man arrived, less-than-pleased to be there. He opened up the door to the institute and was followed in by one of the fire officers. After a while, they returned to outside the building where they continued to talk.

"OK," whispered Jacobson, "what we need is for him to forget to lock up, or to become distracted. Wish me luck, or more accurately create me some luck."

Matt nodded and tried to hide his nervousness. While the grey-haired man was pre-occupied, Jacobson mingled into the crowd that was making their way down the street toward where the fire-crew stood talking to the attendant. Matthew Howard watched as Jacobson deftly tripped one of the group to send him sprawling to the street.

The attendant's attention was diverted – *what now?* All the attendant wanted was to get back to bed, and Matt's attention was completely focused on him.

Matt felt his heart pound inside his chest. His mind's eye saw multiple possibilities stretch out in front of him.

Some where the attendant was alerted to Jacobson.

Some where the attendant was oblivious to him.

Some where the attendant went to the aid of the student.

Picking one which appeared to have Jacobson ignored, Matt tracked his rag-tag friend's progress behind the concerned group, and watched as he slipped, unobserved, into the building.

Although Matt had selected the reality where Jacobson was unobserved, there was little Matt could do to calm his mind. The seconds seemed to drag by, and all he could do was wait.

What would Jacobson even find inside?

If they were responsible for Ethan, would an intervention so close to the institute go undetected?

The thought unravelled in his mind and tumbled like a house of cards. His mouth dried to flour as his blood pounded in his head.

Not the time for doubt. Not now...

Struggling to focus, he saw Jacobson re-emerge. With Matt's help, he passed similarly under the radar and slipped out again.

"Any issues?" he asked when he rejoined Matt.

With a mixture of relief and dread Matt shook his head, "Nope."

"Good – with any luck now we'll get to find out who our mystery man is."

Matt was suddenly distracted by what Jacobson had just said.

What mystery man?

"How do you mean?"

"On the day we first met, there was a visitor to Branchford. Well, he's becoming quite a regular, but I don't know who he is…"

Jacobson paused and regarded Matt.

"Come to think of it, he looks a little like *you* actually."

It was an exhausted Matt that lurched himself back on the train at ten o'clock that Sunday morning.

Jacobson had walked with him the two-or-so miles to King's Cross and waited with him at the McDonalds round the corner until the trains started running.

"It wasn't like this when I was young," he said, pawing his food. "You were lucky to get a sausage roll. Hey, do you want to hear something crazy? The great British stalwart, the ploughman's lunch, didn't exist before the '50's…"

But Matt had had enough. He stood up silently, waved Jacobson away and wandered off into the station. Collapsing into his seat, he set the alarm on his phone, and almost immediately, fell into a post-jentacular slumber.

He was somehow aware, that he was dreaming, revisiting the events of the day, and before he knew it, he was back once again at the Branchford Institute. In the definite way one knows things in dreams, he knew it was the night before. The streets were deserted, and the institute stood before him, its door wide-open.

It was still the Georgian building that it had ever been, but it now loomed huge in front of him. Ominous, its angles bent and distorted, as if viewed through a convex lens.

Matt stood in the middle of the silent and empty road and felt tiny. The open door seemed to taunt him as much as it drew him in. Stepping across the threshold, he found himself faced with a vast expanse of checkerboard flooring that disappeared into darkness before even reaching the walls.

Feeling smaller still, and uncomfortable, he turned, attempting to bolt; before he could exit, the massive front door slammed shut, echoing like thunder in the cavernous space.

And then he heard it.

It wasn't so much a growl as it was a low rumbling – something was waking, something sinister, something that he felt inside his chest.

A pair of eyes flicked open and glinted in the darkness. Matthew Howard recognised the sickening, fetid smell of death.

What had he done?

Ethan…

CHAPTER 39

"So?"

It was just one word, but it said everything that needed to be said. In that one word, Joseph Howard rested his hopes and his fears, and so much more.

"Yes." came Matt's reply.

"Yes?"

"Yes, it's done."

They had managed to plant bugs, of sorts, and Jacobson was monitoring them.

"Good," said Joe, "Now we wait and hopefully get a little clarity."

Since his last trip to London, Matt had been in low spirits.

Yes, they'd achieved what they'd wanted to, but was it really progress? Was any of this achieving anything? Or if it was, were they waking something from the shadows, something that had lain asleep for decades?

Something dark...

Would they regret it? He just didn't know; only time would tell.

Both he and Jacobson had purchased phones – pay-as-you-go mobiles – to stay in touch, but without any records to relate the phones to either themselves or each other. *Burner-phones*, Jacobson had called them.

"I'm due to speak with Jacobson at the end of the week," Matt said, "Then maybe we'll know something."

Reaching into his bag, Matt pulled out the leather-bound notebook which he'd bought on his previous trip to London.

"I saw this and thought of you, Joe. Not this time but the time before – I forgot to give it to you."

Joseph Howard took the notebook from Matt and felt the hide on the outside of it.

It was indeed like the one he'd had forever, but new.

"Thank you, Matt – A new chapter eh?" he said.

He turned the book over and over in his hands and smelled

the hide. He liked it, since it was from Matt, but also liked it since, in a changing world, it was a link back to his past. To *something real* – to a simpler time.

"I'm *so* proud of you Matty, you know that, don't you?"

He opened the book and picked up a pen to write. However, instead, he dropped the pen in shock.

As he looked to the first page he could see two versions of the book, one was blank, as expected, but one had faint spider-like writing which he could clearly make out to read:

STOP   FIXING   ETHAN

Stop Fixing Ethan!

Joseph could feel the energy emanating from the book.

Someone was trying to warn him off. Well, it was not going to work.

Matt saw it too.

Joe's head swam as he felt his heart beat faster than it had in a long time. Instinctively he opposed it, pushed back against it.

If the ACL thought they could threaten him, they had another think coming.

Joe didn't stop to think how they could have brought to bear a graft of such sophistication; he merely resisted it with all his might.

Matt watched as Joe gasped for breath and sweat formed on his brow. The exertion on his grandfather's face was plain.

Had he brought this upon Joe? Was this his doing?

Joe's eyes bulged and Matt watched as, forgetting to breathe, his grandfather's face reddened further and further. But slowly, he felt and saw the ominous message in the book begin to recede. It was fading, going…

Gasping, Joe began to breathe more normally.

"I thought I was going to lose you there for a minute, Joe," said Matt.

The text was now almost gone and continued to fade.

"This is extremely bad news Matt. They're on to us."

As if in response to his statement Matt and Joe felt a surge from the book and the text began reasserting itself.

Whoever it was, they were certainly determined.

Steeling himself once more, Joe dug deep and pushed back

with all his might. His face reddened, purple with effort and the veins on his head became grotesque with prominence. Joe rasped angrily, eyes burning into the book.

"YOU. WILL. NOT. HAVE. HIM!"

For what felt like minutes, the stalemate held. Matt watched, frozen with morbid fascination as slowly the text once again began to fade. When it was almost gone, he felt a surge of energy as Joe seemed to oppose the graft with such ferocity as to ensure that this time the door remained closed.

And with that, it was over.

The book was clear, the page was empty, and all that surrounded them was the silence of the bemused residents who populated West Verity.

Although he'd managed to oppose the graft, Joseph Howard felt worse than he'd ever felt, more drained than he'd ever known – he strangely felt cold, lost and alone. His head swam with dizziness and his vision blurred. "Matty, I'm …"

Like a machine seizing up, Matt watched as his grandfather stopped abruptly and the features on his face sagged. In that instant, all that was Joseph Howard vanished.

Whatever it was that Joe was about to say, neither he nor Matthew Howard would ever know.

CHAPTER 40

"He had a good innings, Matty," said his mother.

Distraught, he waved away her words, clenched his fists and railed against her. "You don't understand. None of you do, and it's nothing I can explain."

They were in Tom and Barbara's kitchen. The floodgates had broken and his despair was plain for all to see.

Standing up, he spat, "I'm going to get obscenely drunk."

The next day, he was far more sanguine.

"We need to talk about arrangements," he said. "We should give him a send-off to be remembered."

Although Joe had lived for another two days, he had never woken up. It had been no use, and Joseph Howard passed away, surrounded by Tom, Barbara, Jane and Matt.

At least I had been with him, thought Matt.

At the time, he knew he should have cried, but the tears would not come.

He was still far too angry. Had he and Jacobson brought this on themselves? Had they woken something? He shook the thoughts away. *That was crazy – just a bad dream.*

****

Joe's funeral was to be a week later, with a wake at a pub near Tom and Barbara's house. As soon as he felt able, he called Jacobson to give him the news about Joe.

"They pushed him over the edge," he said, "Now or in the future – either way, they did for him and I'm not going to let that go!"

Jacobson fell silent. "I'm sorry Matt, I know he meant a lot to you." After a pause, he added, "Do you mind if I bring my dad to the funeral. I'm sure he'd like to go."

"OK, but no weird stuff. OK? From either of you."

"Okay, Okay."

"Anyways," Matt muttered crossly, "What have you found?"

Jacobson sighed, "Not a lot. The line is clear, but there is very little happening. We haven't seen mystery man again, but from what I can tell they think he's someone with latent abilities to see other worlds. They call him *Subject Z1*. Ironically, they've reported that he's just had a death in his family too. What are the odds? But that aside, they're scratching at the surface, they're nowhere. To be honest, I'm wondering if we're wasting our time there."

"It's the only lead we have though," said Matt. "There has to be something that triggers things. Anyway, I'll speak to you next week."

It would be good to see Jacobson, someone who understood the situation at least. It was a surprise that Jacobson's father was still alive. But why would he not be? Why had he thought otherwise?

Matt wondered if having Jacobson and his father at Joe's funeral was a mistake, but it was agreed now, and there was little he could do to change that. *It would be what it would be.*

****

The funeral of Joseph William Howard was on a dark and miserable day in November. The rain lashed down in sheets, and the sky was the kind of grey that leeched the very colour out of the world. It was as if God were showing his solidarity by confirming that there was absolutely nothing good about the day, nothing good at all.

The service was small and quiet. Neither Matt nor Tom could bring themselves to speak, so, instead, it fell to the priest to give a well-meaning but ultimately bland review of Joe's life.

Jacobson, looking almost respectable, had quietly joined the back of the service, pushing a wheelchair occupied by an old man who Matt assumed was Jacobson's father. Keeping a low profile, Jacobson indicated to Matt that he'd speak to him at the pub afterwards and slipped out of the back of the chapel as quietly as he'd arrived.

Matt stayed behind to thank people for coming and to say the kind of things one ends up saying at funerals. Finally, Ethan in arms, he left Tom and Barbara to make his way with Jane to the wake.

Joseph Howard's send-off was held in a back room of the Coach and Horses hotel, and both Jacobsons had been there a while by the time Matt arrived. Neither of them had wasted any time.

"I hadn't seen him in over fifty years," slurred the old man. "I thought him gone already, like the rest of them, but he was a good man. Everything I cared about went that day, and when I finally find Joseph's alive, after all these years, it's too late already."

His son scowled and grimaced at him. "Don't start Dad – not here."

"How did you know him?" asked Jane.

"Well, I could tell you," the old man said, wagging a finger at Jane, and then with a wry smile, "but I'd have to kill you." He wasn't exactly steaming, but it wouldn't be long before he was.

"Suffice to say, we both served together in the war. Joseph was my commanding officer. The stories I could tell you would make your hair curl, my dear. But that was before it all went to hell."

"I didn't realise Joe was in the forces," said Jane, turning to her husband.

"Well, he was, and he wasn't," interjected Matt. "Long story."

Jane looked her husband up and down. Matt was struggling with the day. She could tell that. He was amiable but completely disconnected. *He just wants it to be over*, she thought. *Maybe a few drinks will do him good.*

Reaching over she took Ethan from Matt, and in doing so realised he needed changing. "Matt, I'm going to go sort this little man out."

"How much does she know?" Jacobson asked after she left.

"Nothing," hissed Matt, "and I want to keep it that way."

Jacobson said nothing but raised his hands in a defensive gesture.

By now the back room had started to fill up. However, apart from a few faces that Matt had recognised from West Verity, none were familiar.

"I heard what happened to Joseph," the old man said to Matt. "I'm sorry. He didn't deserve to go like that... he was better than that. But I guess he went down fighting."

That he did, thought Matt, *that he did indeed.*

"I understand that you think that whoever did for him was way in the future…"

"That's what it felt like," replied Matt. "It was distant – although I'm no expert."

"That'd make sense," the younger Jacobson said. "If it is Branchford, where they're at now, they've got no capability, and to be honest, I don't think they know *what* they've got."

"Don't underestimate them!" said the old man. "It took them no time at all to organise last time. If they've got a fixer to kick it all off, then it won't be long before…"

"I don't believe it!" gasped his son, suddenly cutting him off and staring at the doorway.

Matt turned but saw only his own father, who had finally arrived.

"What is it? What's wrong?"

Jacobson was stunned for a second but then said in hushed tones. "That man. The one who's just arrived. Who is he?"

Matt looked again. "My dad – why?"

"Because that means you may want to ask your dad what he's been doing at the Branchford Institute."

Matt looked at him, completely at a loss, and then stared back at his father.

"He's the one who's been going there regularly. He's their subject… Matt, your dad's their fixer!"

Matthew Howard stared in disbelief at his father and then at Jacobson. A crash of emotion flooded his thoughts and caused his head to spin. "That's not funny," he finally said. "Tell me you're winding me up…"

"I swear Matt – he's subject zero. He's their Z1."

Matt desperately fought against the alcohol in his system that prevented him from thinking clearly.

If that were true, what the hell was his dad playing at? They needed to talk, but not here. Why did this have to be here? Why today? Why like this?

CHAPTER 41

Thomas Howard was drenched to the bone. In the short time it had taken him to walk from the car to the pub the heavens had opened and he now stood dripping wet. Shaking himself off he removed the cap he invariably wore. He spotted Matt and raised a hand in greeting.

Matt simply glared back.

Odd, thought Tom, but then again it was a less than usual day.

Arriving at the bar, Tom ordered drinks for himself and Barbara. Like the other drinks, they were put on his tab. Looking up he saw that Matt had now joined him. "Helluva day, eh Matty?"

"You could say that again," said Matt angrily.

"For all I've said over the years, I'm really going to miss him, you know?"

"Well, maybe you should have told him that when you had the chance," scolded Matt, before taking another swig of his drink.

Tom was taken aback by his son's demeanour. "Steady on Matthew, we're all hurting you know."

Matthew Howard struggled for words.

Where should he start?

Where COULD he start?

"Dad, what have you been getting yourself into? Why?"

His father looked at him blankly.

He really has no idea. How could he not? How could that be?

"What are you talking about Matt?"

"Branchford; Dad! Branchford! Don't try to deny it. What's that all about?"

Tom Howard looked at his son with an utter lack of comprehension. "Matt, this is neither the time nor the place. Why? What's your mother been saying to you?"

"Mum? What's Mum got to do with it? Nothing. Look, this isn't about her, this is about you and them. What is it that you've been doing with... *them*, and why?"

Tom Howard screwed his eyes up and shook his head in confusion.

"What?!"

"Look, Dad, Joe didn't just have a stroke because he was old. He had a stroke because he was trying to oppose someone forcing something on him. And more than likely that *someone* was able to try to do that because of whatever you're doing at the Branchford Institute."

Tom just stared at him blankly.

"Matty, What the hell are you on about? I'm attending a clinic in London that is helping me with some issues that I'm having, which, *if you don't mind me saying*, are none of your business. What has that got to do with anything?"

Matt was now aware that the surrounding noise had abated, and although their words could not be heard, many, if not most, eyes were now focused on the two of them and the rising tone of their conversation. As a result, he lowered his voice. "They're not a clinic, Dad," he hissed. "Don't be so naive! They're a front. I know about them, not from Mum, but from the fact that that's who Joe was involved with in the war. According to Joe, they were part of a government agency that specialised in manipulating reality, and resisting them was exactly what killed him!"

From Tom's reaction, it was patently obvious that, whatever he was involved in, or whatever he was doing, he was not culpable in any of it. Matt had known him long enough to read him like a book, and he could see from his eyes that his father was at a loss. That was his father through-and-through, well-meaning but ultimately flawed.

For God's sake Dad – what have you bumbled into?

"Look, Dad, we need to talk – when everyone clears-out, there are some things I need to tell you. Stuff you need to know. For now, though, let's have a drink and remember him."

Tom was shaken, but nodded nonetheless. The speed at which he finished his drink only served to emphasise his discomfort. Side by side, they ordered another, and drank in stony silence, which was how Barbara found them when she arrived moments after.

Two hours later, many of the mourners had left, and much of the crowd had dispersed. Jane and Barbara were looking after Ethan and making their preparations to pack-up. This left only the Jacobsons at their table and the Howard men at the bar.

"Okay," said Barbara, fondly touching Matt and Tom's shoulders in turn, "I'll see you two when you get home. Don't stay too long. OK?"

And with that, they were gone, leaving only the four men, all in one way or another staring at each other across the room. The air seemed thick and pregnant with expectation, the silence dragging-on for what seemed like minutes as Matt returned to the table with his father. Jacobson looked up but said nothing. Finally, Tom took the initiative.

"So, tell me, Matthew," Tom sighed as he sat down heavily, "tell me who these two gents are. Tell me what I've supposed to have done and tell me about Joe. Tell me it all."

CHAPTER 42

Three hours had passed since he'd sat down, and a collection of empty glasses now filled the table.

Dead soldiers.

The four of them sat, equally-spaced but distant, around the table – standoffish, distrustfully leaning away from each other, as if being repelled by the blast radius created by the empty glasses.

Tom slumped forward, placed his palms on his temples, and reflected on what he'd just heard. A wave of realisation flooded over him. For as long as he could remember, he'd denied his father's outbursts, refused to listen when Joe had tried to raise such topics – but coupled with what he'd been discussing at Branchford, fantastical as it seemed, he could dismiss it no longer.

Remorse hit him and hit him hard. It kicked him in the stomach and left him bleeding. It took the wind from him and turned his insides upside-down, made him feel like he would retch. He tried to disbelieve, but he could not.

Something was coming, something big. He knew it. He could feel it in the air. But for now, all he knew was that, in many ways, it was all too late. Joe was gone, and any chance of telling Joe that he was now beginning to understand what, for all those years, he had tried to teach him, had gone too. Forever.

But could it actually be real? If it were, what did 'real' even mean anymore? If nothing were detectable, if nothing left a trace. Dreams and imaginings? Obviously, it had been real to Joe – but what did that even mean?

He was both angry and confused. Truth be told, he didn't know what to feel.

But, like them, he knew that something was coming.

Something big.

And he also felt it round Ethan…

He'd always felt it around Ethan…

One way or another they were all feeling the same as him. All feeling the rising tide, like electricity on the wind.

"I can feel it building too," he said.

All of them were the same. There was a storm coming and, other than the link with Ethan, none of them was any the wiser about where it was coming from, when it would strike, or who was behind it.

It is just there.

But what he couldn't believe was the connection and significance that Matt, and the rest of them, seemed to place on the Branchford Institute.

As to his involvement with Branchford, he'd told the three of them everything, laid it all out, and thankfully they'd accepted what'd he'd said. If Tom had stopped to think, he would've been amazed at the distance that he'd come. He'd gone from denial to belief in the space of a few weeks. Branchford had opened his eyes to a much wider world.

But all that was left now was an overarching feeling of regret. All those years he'd written Joe off as crazy when he'd been one of the only ones who'd seen the world for what it was.

All those missed opportunities.

But was Branchford really to blame? He couldn't believe that.

"I'm not sure you're right about the institute," he said. "They don't come across as some clandestine group."

A sigh erupted to his right. "Maybe not now, but it's what they could become we're talking about – not what they are now." This was Jacobson, "Isn't that right, Dad?"

Wheezing, the old man acknowledged his son before leaning over in his wheelchair and taking another pull on his drink. "That's right," he said, fighting for breath. "Joseph and I did what we thought was right because we were there to try to guide things. Without us, who knows what that would have become. Joseph was a good man, and he knew we tried to make a difference for the better. In the short term anyway, before it went to… feh!"

"But isn't that the answer then?" exclaimed Tom. "Isn't the answer for us to guide them? And if necessary, stop them? Then we'll see… Then we'll know. If nothing else, it's probably better to have them in the tent than outside it, if you know what I mean."

Matt looked at Jacobson. His father had a point. If Branchford were the driving force of any future ACL they'd be at the helm. They could steer things.

"After all," said Tom, "There's no fate but what we make…"

Matt rolled his eyes. "You watch too many movies."

CHAPTER 43

Thomas Howard stood, once again, in front of the Branchford Institute. It was one thing to arrive there as a patient – *this was something else.*

After Joe's funeral, the conversation had continued to roll on well into the night. They'd all agreed that Tom should continue to attend and that he should ultimately determine the institute's goal.

Continue to attend, he thought, remembering how he'd signed his life away – *as if he had a choice.*

As ever, he pressed the buzzer and waited. It would be a lie to say he was not nervous. *Now that he knew Matt's fears, things were different. But it was more, much more than that.*

As the night had worn on, Matt and Jacobson had demonstrated beyond doubt that they could nudge reality, that they could open windows onto different worlds and that he could see them too. The before, the after and the in-between – he could see everything. It was as if Branchford had opened the door, but it had been Matt who had shown him the way through it.

A lot of things suddenly made sense. The bridge. Ethan… everything. And, in his own way, he was filled with a strange mix of emotions. In one sense, he felt calmer, more comfortable in his own skin than he'd ever felt before, but in another sense he felt the same tide of anxiety that Matt felt about Ethan.

He saw it now when he looked at his grandson, or more accurately, he perceived it and understood it now. But still, the question remained; who was driving this, what did they want with Ethan and why?

It sickened him and panicked him in equal measure.

But what could he do? He certainly wasn't convinced by Joe's theory that it was all driven from the Branchford Institute.

But then Rountree had begun appearing in his visions, so

maybe Joe had been onto something after all. The thought of Joe made his stomach turn over and over and generated another pang of still so very raw emotion. Once again, the regret he'd felt earlier returned, reminding him that he'd never made this journey when Joe was still alive.

How he wished he could talk to him again, if only just once.

Oh Dad, why couldn't I have listened to you sooner?

But before he could ruminate further, his thoughts were interrupted by a squawk on the intercom. "Tom Howard," he replied curtly, still distracted. The door buzzed and steeling himself once again, he crossed the threshold to let himself in.

OK Tom, he thought, *I hope you know what you're getting yourself into...*

Eli Phillip Rountree emerged to greet him, clasping his hand in between his own, and, as before, he ushered Tom through to the consulting room. "Can I get you a coffee?"

Tom was about to shake his head but then changed his mind.

Why not? Perhaps it would calm him...

"Yes, that would be nice – thank you."

It didn't take long for Rountree to return, and, after handing Tom his drink, to settle into his seat. "So, where did we get to Tom?" he said opening his notebook. "Ah, here we are, you were explaining how sometimes you feel like none of this was real."

Tom sat, hands clasped in front of him. He turned his head to the right and stared into middle distance.

It was true; none of this *was* real. Certainly, not in the way that Rountree meant. But then again, no one could really perceive the world as it truly was. He could see that now; the fact that he perceived it differently from the average man on the Clapham omnibus, different from most, was neither here nor there. Even for him, it was still a case of just scratching the surface. Ironically, what he perceived, for all his protestations of unreality, might actually be closer to the truth than most normal people would ever know.

Normal... that was a joke. *In the land of the blind, the one-eyed man is king.*

Tom squirmed as he shifted in his seat.

Time for a different tack.

"Can I ask you some questions?" he said.

Rountree paused, a little too long before attempting to look natural. "Sure – fire away," he replied.

"I don't really know how best to say this, so I'll just get on and say it. Well... ask it – well... I have more than one question." Tom pulled out the notebook of his own. *This was going badly.*

"Well, three really..."

He took a sip of his coffee before continuing.

"You see... What I want to know is... Firstly, where is all this going?" He paused, his index finger touching his little finger, as he counted out the points, and then the digits of his left hand. "Secondly, am I the only patient you have? And lastly, are you funded by either the army or the government?"

If Rountree were surprised, he didn't show it, he just looked at Tom for a long time before speaking.

"Are you finished?" he said finally.

Tom nodded meekly and attempted to hide behind his coffee cup.

"Okay, since you ask, I'll be straight with you Tom. To your first question. As I explained during our first meeting, the institute is predominately a research organisation which attempts to explain and prove some of the theories of the late Arthur Branchford. So, in a sense, it's going in the direction that he laid out. They follow his lead, or they don't get paid.

"To your second question. Yes Tom, you *are* the only patient that they currently have. This organisation has been looking for someone like you for over fifty years. So you're extremely important to them. Your third question is probably the hardest to give a simple answer to. The institute is not directly funded by the government or the armed forces, but they have been funded by them in the past, and as a result of that previous arrangement, they do have links to them, and *do however* have a duty of disclosure in that regard."

Tom sat there, letting Rountree's words flow over him.

"What does *a duty of disclosure* mean?"

"What it means, is that at the end of each month, they need to disclose the institute's activities, the research and their outlook for the near-term."

Tom considered what Rountree had said.

"And what has been reported so far?"

"Very little really. They've got high hopes for you, Tom, and that has come out strongly, but formally there's been very little more."

Tom sat back and thought.

They had talked about this that night at Joe's funeral. What their approach should be. They needed to assert control, but not overtly, not too obviously, but control nevertheless. That was what had been decided.

Tom sat in silence, considering what he'd heard, something about Rountree's phrasing bothered him, something was not right; something that he couldn't put his finger on.

"I don't like the idea of government involvement, but I get it. It is what it is… but this isn't just about academic research is it?"

"No Tom, it isn't. If what Branchford's theories suggest is true, then you would prove very useful to us."

As Rountree spoke, Tom realised what had unsettled him – Rountree had referred to Branchford as *they*, but now he used *they* no longer.

You would prove very useful to *us*…

"You think what I see is real, don't you?"

Rountree nodded.

This is where I have to tread carefully.

"I understand that I'm starting to open a Pandora's box with what we've already discussed. It's evident that something is going on, but I want some assurances about what this will lead to, and I want to be kept informed."

Rountree looked at him, confused.

"I don't follow, Tom. What are you telling me? What are you trying to say?"

"What I'm trying to say is that, contractually, I get that I've made my bed and am signed up to work with you over the next few weeks. I also know that you've seen the glimmer of something – something that you're going to pass on. So, I want to give you a choice – we can either proceed as we have been doing, with this being a curiosity at best, and at the end of what I've signed up for, we go our separate ways. That would mean that you've found something, but it would take forever to develop…"

Tom paused, letting the words hang in the air. "Or alternatively, we accelerate this and take it to the next level.

But for that I want to see the bigger picture. Unless I get to see where this is going, all of this will effectively stop here and now."

For the first time, Rountree looked taken aback.

Good, thought Tom, *he's on the back foot.*

It was a risky move, he knew that, but what they needed was information – they had nothing.

"And if I can do this Tom, what is the prize? What do we get in return?"

"We open this up," he replied. "We take it as far as it will go. We use whatever this is, to do some good. We make a difference."

Tom had discussed this with the others at Joe's wake. With the situation with Ethan, all of them had agreed that if they were going to change things, they needed to get in there and influence matters. Rather than let events play out as they would have done, they needed to be-in – *on the ground floor.* The four had agreed that the principle of keeping friends close but enemies closer applied. As Tom himself had said, *I don't trust them, but it would be better to have them in the tent than outside it.*

"But aren't we handing them the keys to the castle?" the younger Jacobson had said.

"You know what's coming," Matt had said, "each of us can feel it building. Each of us can feel the energy that's coming. After what happened to Joe, we can't just stand by and let things play out. I'm not going to let an organisation come into being that ultimately erases my son. Not if I can help it."

"We have to get in there, we must intervene," had come the reply of the older Jacobson. "My family was taken away from me. I don't know who did that – if I can't find who did it, at least I can try to help prevent it happening to Joe's family too."

"So what do we do?" Tom had asked.

"What we do is we take control. We get involved. If an ACL is to exist, we create it and steer it and make it ours. We change things progressively from the inside out. We take the initiative. We approach Branchford with a proposition. *We make them an offer they can't refuse.*"

Tom sighed, "Why do I think that I'm likely to be the messenger in all of this?"

And, days later, here he was nervously delivering what he hoped was being taken as an ultimatum.

"Tom," Rountree said, "I can't help noticing that this is a long way away from where we started only a few weeks ago. What's happened? Who else have you been talking to?"

Tom paused, realising that he'd done it. *He'd hooked him. Now to reel him in...*

"Let's just say that you'd be very interested meeting them. And under the right circumstances, I'd be happy to discuss that further... but there'd be certain conditions."

Rountree looked, and Tom struggled to hold his gaze. Finally, he spoke, "OK, I'm listening. What conditions?"

Tom reached into the inside pocket of his jacket and withdrew a piece of paper. He unfolded it and continued. "Five points," he said, counting them off on his left hand.

"One. This can't be in the shadows, can't be purely military. A board would need to be established to oversee anything further.

"Two. A set of principles would be formed, similar to a Hippocratic oath, to set boundaries on this.

"Three. My family would be kept safe. Under no circumstances would they be put at risk.

"Four. Anything that this leads to, we get to see the *why*. We get visibility of the bigger picture; before and after.

"Five. We get a seat at the table on any and all decisions."

To Tom's surprise Rountree left him and withdrew with a view to discussing his demands. After about thirty minutes he returned.

"Alright, here's the thing Tom. In principle, they'd be able to do what you say, but they need something more than what you've given us so far... They need something big. Give them that, and you're on. Give them that, and you've got yourself a deal."

CHAPTER 44

Matthew Howard lay in bed, attempting to sleep.

Tom had told him that their message had been delivered.

So now, they were committed. This would be it... No going back.

Swinging his legs out of bed, he padded to the bathroom, trying not to disturb Jane. Not wanting to make himself wake-up further, he left the light off, slipped down his pyjama pants and sat down. The steady flow of urine seemed to have a calming effect on him and, as he rubbed his stubbled cheek with his left hand he felt himself dozing. With some surprise, like in his previous dream, he was back at the Branchford Institute.

The streets were once again deserted and, like before, the institute stood before him, its door wide open.

Standing up from the toilet, he was still in his bathroom, but he was in the street also – but now fully clothed. He found the sensation of being in two places at once curious, but it was not something that overly bothered him.

Focusing on the Georgian building, he felt himself being fast-forwarded to its interior. And then, once again, he heard it. The pair of eyes were there in the darkness, but this time he saw what they belonged to.

It was human, but not human.

In his dream-state, he could not recognise its form, but he knew it of old. It was the oppressor, it was the whip hand, it was the personification of evil.

But worse, *its* eyes were *his* eyes.

It was *him*.

He could no longer see it, because he *was* it, he was *all-powerful* and as large as a building. A great lumbering beast, dictating over a world where freedom had died.

All around him, people ran like ants.

He was evil. He was the devil. He crushed them under his boot and whipped them bloody. He watched himself do this, but it was without emotion, and seemingly without free will.

A sea of writhing bodies, they moved as one, a frightened mass, scattering to flee from him. For some it was no use, he trampled them underfoot and felt their soft bodies burst. One after another they were reduced to pulp, until he found it difficult to move, hampered and clogged by a bloody swamp of shit and gore.

He was responsible. He knew it was a dream, but why was he doing this? He was their weapon, but it was not by his will.

And then he saw her.

In their midst – *Jane, battered and bruised, on her knees, bleeding and pouring with tears.*

She raised her head and looked at him with a glare filled with hatred and betrayal.

It broke his heart.

CHAPTER 45

"So, Gentlemen, what can you tell us?"

It was four weeks later, and Tom and Matt were in an unknown location, sitting opposite an austere looking man in a white shirt and a no nonsense suit. He'd entered the room, sat down without introduction and had matter-of-factly said only that.

They had arrived at the Branchford Institute hours earlier that day, but rather than being met by Rountree, they'd instead been greeted by a thin, stern-looking woman who'd shown them into Rountree's office, saying only, "You'll be collected in due course. Please wait here."

Outside, the November morning had dragged on and, conscious of the high likelihood of their being monitored, both Tom and Matt sat in silence. Matt looked round the room and then looked at his father.

What were they doing here? What was he getting himself and his father into? Matt again looked round the room, for the first time really taking in the detail of the study. *What secrets could these walls tell?* he wondered, before turning to look again at his father. Tom was less than comfortable and was fidgeting badly.

Come on Dad, keep it together he thought before, once again, turning to the walls of the study. Finally, in an attempt to kill time, he began trying to count the many books that lined the walls. It was pointless; he regularly became distracted and kept losing track of where he'd reached, but at least it served to occupy his mind.

After what seemed like an age, the woman returned. Matt glanced at his watch – o*nly half an hour had passed.*

"How long are we likely to be?" asked Tom, clearly agitated.

"Please be patient," she replied, her thin lips revealing nothing, "I can get you some refreshment if that would help…"

Matt glanced at his father, and they both shrugged – *why not? They were likely in for a long wait.*

Plied with coffee, they continued to sit in silence until well after darkness had fallen.

The last four weeks had gone quickly. Not long after speaking with Rountree, they'd each received a call telling them to come to the Branchford Institute at the end of the month. The calls had been short, terse and to the point, with no opportunity to engage in any kind of dialogue. Neither Tom nor Matt liked the way things were playing out – today was no different.

"Gentlemen, if you could follow me…" the woman said when she eventually returned to retrieve them. She led them out of the front of the institute, where a car with darkened windows was waiting. The car, a recent Jaguar, in other circumstances would have had a certain degree of prestige to it, but today it just looked ominous and sat there, seething tension.

"Where are we going?" asked Tom, the nervousness still obvious in his voice.

"If you could get in the car please," came her curt response.

Although comfortable, the back of the car was little more than a gilded cage with a limited view of the driver and outside world. As the woman from the institute closed the heavy doors, it was clear that the light in the car was artificial.

Sealed in.

The car drove through the night for what seemed like hours. However on checking his watch, Matt found it was scarcely over forty-six minutes. Where they were, he had no idea, the darkened windows of the car had put paid to that.

When the car finally pulled up, they stepped out in front of an imposing Georgian building, rectangular and imperial, floodlit and set within its own grounds. Once inside they were shown to a utilitarian room that looked for all the world like a police station interview room, and it was there the unknown man had asked the question.

"So, Gentlemen, what can you tell us?"

Matthew Howard sat in silence, but as if reading from a script, Tom calmly raised a hand and mouthed – *just wait.*

Matt sat and looked into the man's eyes. In other worlds he

and Tom were engaged in an almost infinite number of conversations. In some, the man gave away more. In some, he gave away less. Different strategies were employed, almost on the spur of the moment. In one, he revealed his name was Stevenson. In another, he did not say his name but revealed his role was one of a unit focused on anti-terrorist intelligence. In one, he'd asked if he would have been able to prevent the 7/7 tube and bus attacks in London earlier that year. In another, he ranted about this being a waste of his time.

In this reality, however, he patiently sat and waited.

So, what can you tell us?

Matt took a breath before beginning. "I can tell you that your name's Stevenson and your focus is intelligence around potential terrorist attacks. I can tell you that you don't believe this for a second and think it's a waste of time. I can tell you that you're wondering if we could have done anything to prevent the attacks on London this summer."

Stevenson's face blanched – he obviously wasn't expecting what he'd just heard.

"Alright. You've got my attention. Well, could you?"

Could they have done something to have prevented that? To be honest, Matt didn't know. With the right information, being in the right place at the right time. Maybe...

Matt looked at the man's face and saw that he was still clearly shaken.

"Possibly... It depends, nothing is ever certain. What we can see are different worlds, where different events play out in different ways. Often this means we can get glimpses of *what-might-be* by what happens elsewhere. Under those circumstances, then, as I say, possibly..."

The four of them, Matt, Tom and the Jacobsons, had all agreed that fixing was something that, for now, should be left unmentioned, better to keep that in reserve. Keep their powder dry.

Stevenson looked at his notes, this was suddenly not the subject to be discussed, and he was entirely unprepared for that. Flustered, he said, "It says here you have a number of demands which would need to be met in order for you to help us."

One by one they went through the list that Tom had given Rountree.

"You'll have to sign the official secrets act," he said. "It's often said, once you're in, you're in for life. You *do* understand what I'm saying?"

Tom gulped, but Matt just shrugged. *In for a penny...*

"You'll also need to be whiter than white. If you think that our background checks are likely to unearth anything, you'd be wise to tell us now."

Matt put his hand on the table in front of him. "Look, I get all that. We have the opportunity to do something worthwhile, put things right in multiple ways."

Stevenson leant back in his chair and seemed to consider what they'd said.

"So how do I know that this is on the level? How do I know that this is not some scheme to infiltrate or discredit us? What you've done so far is little more than parlour trick. I'm going to need more than that if you want us to believe that there's something in this."

"What do you suggest?" asked Matt.

"I suggest a test," Stevenson replied. "If what you say is right, we should see it played out to our benefit.

"If that *is* the case, then you've got yourselves a deal. You can stay here. We have everything we need. We'll start in the morning."

CHAPTER 46

The next morning, Matt and Tom began the day at 6am with breakfast in a large dining hall in the centre of the building.

They'd been housed in what Stevenson had termed the east wing of wherever it was they were, and were conspicuously aware of the men that were posted outside of their doors.

Tom had protested that his wife, Barbara, would fret. However, this was met with blank stares and what-do-you-want-me-to-do-about-it shrugs. At 7am they rejoined each other and were shown into what they called the situation-room. Matt was tired, but Tom looked wretched.

"Does Jane know where you are?" he asked.

Matt ever so slightly shook his head. "No, she doesn't."

"Barbara neither… they're going to be beside themselves, Matty."

It was true. However, there was little they could do now. Matt was determined to push these thoughts out of his mind.

"It'll be OK Dad."

The situation room surprised him – for a state-of-the-art facility it was relatively low tech. There was a large video-con on one wall, but the main thrust of the work looked to still be old school backed up by modern technology.

It wasn't long before Stevenson joined them. "You two, come with me," he barked. Any trace of uncertainty or trepidation, that might have been there the night before had now gone. "Gentlemen, we have a situation. Last night's plan to test you is now out of the window. Something has come up. Something real. Something that could show what you can do, maybe make that difference you mentioned."

Stevenson led them out of the situation room and across the building. Through the large window, they could see what looked like an interrogation room containing a bored looking young man, absently staring at the floor in a seemingly unconcerned manner. Inside the viewing-gallery, various monitors also lined the walls.

"Don't worry he can't see or hear you. The man in there is part of a group we've been watching. We had a man on the inside, but last night Billy Boy over there clocked him and hospitalised him. We had to pull him out, but the others don't know he's gone. We don't know what they're planning, but we know when they realise he's gone they'll either be panicked into action or they'll melt like shadows. So, we need to know what they're planning and we need to know it now. Time to sink or swim..."

Matt and Tom watched through the glass as the man was interviewed. Matt slowed his breathing and half closed his eyes.

C'mon, see through the here and now. Open it up and see the worlds beyond our own.

The one-way glass brought to mind a prism of splintered realities, a continuum from *what is*, to multiple *what might have been's* or *what might be's*.

The questioning was going nowhere. The man sat in stony silence, claiming that *it was no more than just a fracas and that they had no right to hold him.* The other man that had been in the room with him left, trying not to show his exasperation. Entering the observation room, he sat down heavily.

"So what now?" he snapped. "I'm all out. All we know from *our* man is that he thought that they were planning something against a landmark, a tourist location, but that was just from a throwaway comment. It could be anything anywhere..."

"What would you do if you knew where it was?" asked Matt.

The man said nothing and just looked at Stevenson, who nodded, causing the man to open up.

"We'd let him know that one of his accomplices was being held and he'd revealed the target. We'd offer him a deal if he co-operated."

"But you'd only be able to do that if you were certain of where?"

"Exactly. We'd need him to believe we had a path to everything and if he didn't help us others would."

"Alright." said Matt, "That is what I want you to do. On your laptop, make a list of all possible targets, no matter how obscure, and number each of them. Then what I need you to do is use these." From out of his pocket he pulled a set of dice.

The man looked at Stevenson, "Sir, you can't seriously expect me to…"

"Just do it," said Stevenson firmly "What else do we have?"

"OK. What I need you to do is this – whichever location the dice says, that's what you need to go with. No changing… even if it's your weirdest longshot. Treat it as being one-hundred percent true. After all, from what you've said, it's likely to be in there."

The man once again looked at Stevenson.

"Sir?"

"Just as he says."

It appeared getting to the list was simple, it was a spreadsheet they'd already drawn-up. It was huge and had everywhere Matt had ever heard of, plus a number of places he hadn't. Matt instructed them to give each of the locations a four-digit code, using only digits 1 to 6. These began at 1111 and approached 6666. He then asked that the dice be rolled to determine which site to concentrate on. He knew he could have no involvement in this process, and the list was taken away without him ever witnessing the outcome.

"You'd better be right about this…" cautioned Stevenson. "To say this is a long shot…"

Matt calmly raised his hand to silence him, and once again slowed his breathing.

It was a waiting game. Like catching a fish.

The man in the interview room seemed relaxed – *too relaxed*. He obviously suspected that they were scratching for information and was attempting to play the innocent. Matt watched as different paths began to fan out in front of him. In some the man sat in silence. In some he drummed on the metal table with his index fingers. In one he paced and called for attention.

Good – he was already seeing a number of worlds. Seeing the RIFT.

Matt watched motionlessly as, one by one, different versions of Stevenson's associate progressively entered the room like overlapping echoes. Each multiple version of their man confronting the suspect.

Matt was impressed. For the main part, his demeanour and

approach were consistent. *Training* mused Matt.

"I thought you'd be glad to know that you'll be leaving here soon."

The man replied with bravado – "I knew you had nothing. How could you? I'm innocent."

His interrogator smiled, "Oh I wouldn't say that. I'd say that we have everything we need. You're not going home – you're just leaving *here*. We have one of your associates, and he's told us everything."

The man spat. "You can't scare me. You've got nothing mate. Nothing!"

"To the contrary, we now know exactly what you and your so-called friends are planning on doing at St. Paul's Cathedral, and as you've not cooperated in the way that your colleague has, there's very little I can do for you."

The man laughed in his face and shook his head in disbelief. "What are you talking about St. Paul's – you've got nothing…"

In thousands of worlds it was the same but in one the mention of the church of St. Martin-in-the-Fields caused the man to blanch. In that reality, he started talking and talking fast in an attempt to cut a deal.

"It's St. Martin-in-the-fields," explained Matt, "They're planting a bomb to go off at the evening service on Tuesday."

Stevenson relayed this to the room where the man still feigned laughter.

"No you're right, it's St. Martin-in-the-fields on Tuesday, not St. Paul's, what was I thinking… anyway, you're no longer needed and, as I say, there is very little I can do for you – especially since you're unwilling to help."

The man's laughter stopped immediately. He was suddenly serious.

"What are you offering?" he finally said.

Stevenson couldn't say that he understood everything he just witnessed, but he was still impressed. So much so, that he appeared to be letting his guard down. The following afternoon he was absolutely gushing.

"Your five points," he remarked, reading from the folder in front of him.

"One. This can't be in the shadows, can't be purely military. A board would need to be established to oversee anything further.

"Two. A set of principles would be formed, similar to a Hippocratic oath, to bind this.

"Three. Your family would be kept safe. Under no circumstances would they be put at risk.

"Four. Anything that this leads to, you get to see the *why*. Get visibility of the bigger picture; before and after.

"Five. You get a seat at the table on any and all decisions.

"From what we've seen today, these conditions are acceptable. However we have some conditions of our own. You will not speak of anything you see or hear pertaining to these matters, here or anywhere else. Internally, you will be given the title of Special Advisors to Her Majesty's Government. Let's just say you will be handsomely rewarded, but for the sake of security, you must be completely open with us, and I can't stress this too strongly – *completely open.* In due course you will be given cover stories and you must become fully versed in these – they must be the truth that the rest of the world sees. These covers will be the only contract you will have, and you will have nothing that shows the work we do or the conversations we have.

"Finally, you will submit to a scientific analysis of what it is you do. This will be non-intrusive, but it may be lengthy. If you can live with these terms, then I think this may be the beginning of a fruitful partnership..."

CHAPTER 47

"What the hell do you mean you can't tell me? I'm *your* wife and *his* mother!"

Jane Howard looked at Barbara as she launched into both Tom and Matt. Jane had never seen her look so ill. Haggard with worry and incandescent with rage.

She looks dreadful.

"You and Matty go off for the day and come back two days later, and all you can say is 'I can't tell you!' You expect me to put the kettle on and say what? *Well, at least you're here now?* It doesn't work like that. What do you expect me to think? What's going on?"

Jane sat at the kitchen table and watched as Barbara continued her verbal assault for the next fifteen minutes before finally running out of steam.

In the silence that followed Jane murmured, "Do I need to worry, Matty?" Gently she touched his hand across the kitchen table. "Do I need to worry that you're involved in something that's going to lead to me getting a call from the police to say that you've been arrested... or worse? If you can't tell us, can you at least tell us that?"

Matt took his wife's hands in his own to comfort her. "I wish I could tell you, but even if I could, you wouldn't believe me. But believe me when I tell you that everything that we're involved with is legal and above board." Continuing, he looked over at his mother. "There is something that Dad and I have to do for the good of the family, and I need you both to trust us on this. I wish we could say more, but we can't."

"So, was this a one-off, or is this likely to happen again?" asked his mother, her irritation abundantly evident for all to see.

Neither Tom nor Matt spoke. The implication was clear.

"Well, that's just great..." Barbara spat, "Just great!"

CHAPTER 48

Six months had passed, and things had moved fast. Stevenson had built a structure round the two of them and, true to his word, an embryo of an oversight board had been established.

The members of the board were shortlisted and approached covertly. It was an awkward conversation for obvious reasons, but it was mainly couched in language pertaining to providing special advice to sensitive government departments.

The original board consisted of six members from different backgrounds – a politician, a technologist, an intellectual, a soldier, an industrialist and a judge.

The politician was required to be in the confidence of, and have the ear of, the prime minister. They would represent the prevailing political wind. The technologist was there to represent the view of the engineering and scientific community. The intellectual was to represent philosophy, rationalism and ethics, and to attempt to ensure lessons from the past were respected and mistakes not repeated. The armed forces were required to represent Military Intelligence. The industrialist was to provide an economic perspective to the board. The judge was there to represent the law.

They were to act as a benign oligarchy that governed the use of *other-world* information. They acted by committee around a core set of principles. Each was partnered by a deputy should they be unavailable, and each had an equal vote. Tom and Matt were similarly partnered, and their vote took the quorum to seven.

At Matt's request, they were called The Commission for Acceptable Outcomes and were set up as a Government-Organised Non Governmental Organisation, a GONGO, to manage how information was channelled, and by implication, to manage interaction with the RIFT.

As it had been with Joe, the new Commission established principles round the combat of evil.

The first session was chaotic, to say the least. Most of the representatives were bemused and only semi-informed as to the nature of what lay in store.

The board members had first filed into a briefing room at the location to which Matt and Tom had been taken. Other than purely being called *The Manor* this building and its history remained nameless. The board was greeted by Stevenson, with Rountree also in tow.

The fourteen of them had been shown into the room by aides and seated round an expansive, oval wood and frosted-glass table. Each had a delegate badge with their role but no name. Stevenson's badge read *Military*, Rountree's badge read *Science & Technology*, Matt and Tom's badges simply read *Channeller*.

What do they expect me to do? he thought. *Dig canals?*

The aides withdrew, and the doors were closed. Stevenson stood and greeted them. "Welcome, all of you, to the beginning of something unique, something powerful, something historic. Each of you has been selected as experts representing the views of the respective area on your badges, and you've already been given clearance. Needless to say, I don't need to remind you that this commission is strictly top secret.

"If all agree, we will be operating under a variation of Chatham House Rules. That is, as participants, you can make use of the information gained, but you must not divulge where the information came from. In addition, however, you may not reveal any of the circumstances under which this information was gained. Crucially you must not reveal, nor discuss, the nature nor the existence of this board nor anything that might imply the work, or even the existence, of this programme or this commission.

"Finally, your private lives will effectively end here. In the interest of security, there can be no secrets within this room. This commission requires and demands complete openness."

The industrialist sighed, and using both hands he slowly and gently put down his pen in front of him.

"Look, we're all used to operating under strict confidentiality, and we read the rather cryptic brief which was circulated, but unless you tell us what this is all about, we're going to struggle here…"

It was true; entry into The Commission had been by personal recommendation only, and although each of those present had been given a briefing pack, this only alluded to what was to come – and it had been intentionally woolly and vague.

Around the table, there were murmurs of agreement.

Stevenson held up his hands in acquiescence. Nodding, he said, "You're quite right of course. Well, let me keep you in suspense no longer. The reason that you're here is simple. As you may be aware, many people believe that there are multiple separate realities, spawned by an infinite set of possibilities, created by the many different choices and outcomes that make up our lives. Until now, this so-called *many worlds* view of reality has just been theory, but here in this room, we have two men who make that theory real. Next to you are what we are calling *channellers*. They can see into these *other worlds* and use information from these to steer our own."

Stevenson waited until the murmur which ran around the room abated. Turning to the giant video screen on the wall, he clicked a pointer causing it to spring to life.

"Late last year we were able to channel the view from these other worlds to prevent a terrorist attack in Trafalgar Square. We were able to determine that the target of the attack was the evening service at St. Martin-in-the-Fields."

As Stevenson spoke, still images of the events last November flashed up on the screen. The slideshow continued, eventually culminating in scenes of the arrest of various men that neither Matt nor Tom recognised.

"We were able to arrest the group planning the attack before it got off the ground. You may have seen this on the news. However the details were kept hush-hush. The reason we were able to do this was because we could see other realities played out – we could look into the minds of these individuals from the choices that they might have taken. Or more accurately through the choices that they *did* make in different worlds. So why, might you ask, are you here? What has this got to do with you and what is the role of this board?"

Stevenson let his words hang in the air as he scanned the faces in the room. He had their full attention.

"The purpose of this Commission is to be the voice of reason for this new-found ability. This could be the brink of a new horizon, and it needs to be handled responsibly. In this room, we not only have the protagonists – *the channellers* – we also have leaders in the fields of science and technology, economics and industry, politics and government, education and philosophy, the military and the law. Together, this commission will form a think tank, a body of experts providing advice and ideas on how information from other worlds can, or should, be used. We will, no doubt, make mistakes, but, in time, we'll become more adept. In time we'll amaze ourselves with what becomes possible. Therefore, it is crucial that we lay the foundations now, set guiding principles in place to avoid this ability from being used to the detriment of society. This is a tiny step, the start of a journey. Today we're able to see different worlds – we must remain humble – eventually, who knows... But in order to do that, we can have no side-agendas, no secrets, no private interests. There is far too much at stake... I must warn you now that any variation from these principles will be met with consequences most severe."

If there had been any doubt previously as to Stevenson's seriousness, there was absolutely none now.

The inaugural summit of The Commission for Acceptable Outcomes agreed almost unanimously that they should proceed with caution. All decided that it would be hubris to believe that grave mistakes would not be made in the early days, and therefore actions should be targeted at least initially on the *great evils,* rather than, say, financial gain.

The views of Leighton-Jones, the industrialist, were, at first, against this restraint, arguing instead that it had always been the case that all was fair in love and business. However, this resolve weakened when confronted with the prospect of a market in free-fall with rampant suspicion of insider-trading becoming rife. It was one thing for sovereign intelligence agencies to have privileged information; supporting that stance within a free-market economy was another.

CHAPTER 49

"What have we achieved? What have we changed?"

Matthew Howard looked at his father, the tears wanting to well up in his eyes. They had brought about The Commission in much the way that they had wanted. It had all gone as well as they could have expected. It had been disorganised, yes but they'd got to a consensus, and it was positive. So why then when he looked into the RIFT did he feel like absolutely nothing had changed?

What were they missing?

What was HE missing?

The minus-Ethan graft still sat there, stubborn as a hangover resolutely refusing to go away.

Whoever it was who was trying to enact that graft was still there. Or more accurately – whoever it would be who would try to enact that graft was still due to do so.

Matt threw his hand in the air in exasperation. "Six months in and we're no further forward. We still don't know who's behind this."

From what he'd seen of The Commission, something would have to radically change to make him think they were responsible.

At this rate, Ethan would run out of time and cease to be, without ever knowing who was targeting him.

"We need more information Matt," said Tom. "We need Stevenson's lot to help us figure out how to determine who's behind this. Otherwise we're just busy fools."

But that would mean revealing an awful lot more than they'd felt comfortable doing. Revealing that there was a lot more than simple viewing.

His father was likely to be right; he usually was.

But that didn't mean he had to like it.

CHAPTER 50

"I need your help, Eli. We need to talk."

Eli Phillip Rountree had received a call – Matthew Howard had asked to meet him somewhere outside of the Branchford Institute, somewhere neutral.

Matt arrived alone, looking troubled.

"I need to speak to you about research," he had said. "Stevenson mentioned that there would be a research track set up. I need to be on it."

Matt was extremely nervous, far more than usual, and Rountree, finding the agitation contagious, struggled to maintain his calm.

"What's going on Matt? What's this about?"

Matthew Howard was not in a good way. Rountree looked into his eyes.

Desperation...

"Call it a crisis of faith, Eli, but I need to know what this is all about. I need to understand the *why* of all this. Do you believe that things happen for a reason? If so, what is that reason? I need to know; I need answers."

Attempting to maintain a picture of calm, Rountree had let Matt know that the research track he'd spoken of previously was indeed beginning to come together. He'd initially seen this as passive observation, but if Matt wanted to engage with them directly then he didn't have a problem with that. Not as far as he was concerned. That said, something still nagged at him, something that he couldn't put his finger on.

Did he really, all of a sudden, have an interest in research? Or was Matt Howard playing him? Either way, Rountree was sure that he was going to have to watch Matt carefully.

CHAPTER 51

Matthew Howard joined the research arm of The Commission. Other than him, the team consisted of three core members.

They were an intentionally oddball group consisting of a computer scientist called Grant, a psychiatrist called Fellowes and, much to Matt's surprise, a physicist called Baker.

They were well-meaning but laughably inept – floundering about haplessly. If there were a connection to the Baker of Joe's day, it wasn't apparent and clearly not something Matt could bring up.

If only I could open their eyes to what I could do, he thought. *But how much is too much?* He didn't know.

He instead focussed on telling them as much as he could about the RIFT in a passive sense. They, for the most part, focussed on attempting to diagnose him as schizophrenic, trying to give him a label, trying to classify him and parcel him up in a neat box.

"Tell me about what you see when you experience these other worlds," Fellowes would ask as she continued to write. "Describe them to us."

Matt found that language continually failed him. As his grandfather had often said, *'see'* was definitely not the right word, but if there was a right word he couldn't find it.

"It is complete, as immersive as it gets," he told her. It wasn't that he saw another reality. Instead, it was that the walls between this world, and all others, seemed to fade away into nothingness. It was as if he were skimming some weird Goldilocks-zone, *not too shallow, not too deep*, but *just-right*.

It was Grant who Matt understood least of all. Slender-build with dreadlocks, his real interest was quantum computing and how he could apply some of what Matt could do to his field. Over coffee, Grant tried to explain the principle of what his research was ultimately trying to do.

"It's like this," he said, "traditional, or classical, computers can basically only do one thing at a time. Sure, you can chain a boatload of regular computers together to make some kind of so-called supercomputer, but that won't really help with some problems. Take encryption, even the fastest supercomputer would still take months to crack a very strongly encrypted message. A quantum computer, however, can effectively try all possible factors in parallel and cut through encryption in an instant."

"But why would you need a quantum computer for that?" asked Baker. "Isn't what Matt here did with St. Martin-in-the-Fields not computationally equivalent to that? The trick would be achieving sufficient randomness, pushing sufficient *true entropy* into a system and let it run on that input. In most universes, it will fail, but with enough randomness, surely it will succeed in at least one. So rather than a quantum computer, you would have a *many-worlds computer*; effectively a supercomputer made up of an almost infinite number of regular computers, one in each reality."

"But computers are far too predictable," said Fellowes, "would that work?"

"Good point," agreed Grant, "that would certainly be the case if you had a pseudo-random number generator, the trick would be to use a truly random number generator, some hardware-based device. If you managed to generate truly random events at the quantum level, surely, in an infinite universe, those would span all possible inputs and, pushing them through a Monte Carlo algorithm, would make what you're talking about possible."

Matt had thought he had been following, but the last piece had lost him completely.

"Monte Carlo...?" he asked.

"Named in reference to the Grand Casino in Monte Carlo," Grant explained, "A Monte Carlo approach is one which uses random inputs to try to simulate some output where the exact mechanism is unknown. Normally the longer you leave it, the better it gets, but it flattens out, meaning that past a certain point the answer is *good enough*. Take trying to figure out the area of a circle, if you didn't know how to do it. Generate a few thousand random points in a containing square and by seeing if they are in or outside of the circle you'll get a pretty good estimate of what the area is. That's standard Monte Carlo. I guess what we're talking here is a lot closer to *parallel trial and error* with near perfect parallelism. Kind of like the idea of infinite monkeys with typewriters hammering away – sooner or later one will write Shakespeare. Personally, I never liked that thought experiment, as there wouldn't be sufficient fair entropy in the system, but as an image I guess it serves its purpose…"

"So, what *are* you saying?" asked Matt.

"I'm saying that, if we could run a parallel trial and error decryption with enough randomness, in one world it would work. If we could use you to identify the winning answer, we could, in theory, cut through just about any level of encryption."

"You're scaring me now," said Baker nervously.

Barely able to contain his excitement Grant just said, "We've got to try this."

CHAPTER 52

A few weeks later, Grant and Baker had rigged up something they wanted to have Matt test. They'd sourced, or made, various entropy generators applying operating principles such as low-level harvesting of quantum mechanical *shot-noise* signals, but also attempted to use the rate of nuclear decay and beam-splitting.

Rather than test complex processes such as decryption, they attempted the far simpler task of identifying an arbitrary number, by randomly generating all possible numbers in parallel. The idea was that each universe would have generated its own number and somewhere, at least one would match. Grant's idea was that an exact match would trigger a beacon for Matt to focus in on. The beacon, in this case, was some code which sounded a klaxon and caused the illumination of an otherwise blank screen. The screen was to be illuminated by the numbers in question.

Setting the target number, Grant hammered in a random sequence of keys and hit return. As expected, the screen remained blank as the computer running in their universe failed to exactly match the entered number.

Matt tried to relax into the moment and focus through the RIFT. He concentrated on the computer screen in front of him and attempted to let his mind wander.

Eventually, he managed to locate what he was looking for, a screen which was not blank. Struggling to focus he attempted to read the number. Before he could, however, he noticed more screens, each with numbers. All were large, as far as could see – not any two the same. "It's no use," he groaned, "I can see them, but there are hundreds of hits, all different."

"I don't get it," said Grant, "how can he be finding different answers?"

Baker clicked his fingers. "Of course, it's not different answers, just multiple answers to multiple questions, each one is correct in its own way in its own universe. Grant, the issue is how you came up with the target number, that was a random event in itself, like the monkeys and Shakespeare – but we were the monkey. As a result, I think what you're seeing is the not only the entropy in the random number generator, but also the inherent random effect of how you're picking the number in the first place. The reason you see hundreds of different results as answers is that the way you're picking the number is, in itself, generating hundreds of different variations."

"So, what do we do?"

"If we had an encrypted message, we would have already had an established event – *a fixed point*. We need to give Matt a similarly established event. Grant – determine a number and write it down. Don't change it but don't let Matt see this. Give this a small amount of time before starting."

Following Baker's instructions, Grant recorded the target by writing it down. Looking up he realised all were looking at him expectantly. "What?" he said.

"Well if you need to give it a little while, I was assuming you'd get down to the mess and get us all a coffee…"

****

Leighton-Jones, the industrialist, sat quietly in the tea room of the Charing Cross Hotel. The server he'd spoken to earlier came and went, bringing him a coffee – Jamaica Blue Mountain. Slowly sipping, he savoured the flavour, waiting for his eleven o'clock appointment.

At the stroke of eleven, Hunter, the politician from The Commission arrived, taking a seat and ordering a hot tea. "I have a twelve o'clock with the PM at number ten, so I can only stay twenty minutes; I was glad when I got your call. I agree, with you – The Commission is not moving fast enough, we could do so much more to leverage what we have, to make Britain Great again. But to do that, we need a different approach. We need a disaster they didn't foresee. We need to take control…"

"To Great Britain," said Leighton-Jones raising his cup.

"To Great Britain," replied Hunter. "Now and forever."

****

Grant returned bearing a tray of drinks. Setting them down he looked at the others, "Are we good then?"

"I think so," said Matt, taking a slurp of his drink and settling in for a second attempt.

It was different this time, there was still variation around him, but he'd hoped it was variation in how Grant was entering the target, rather than as before, variation in the target number itself. Once again he blurred his world-view and scanned the jittering computer screen.

It was much harder this time; all screens as far as he could see were blank. It was like searching for a needle in a haystack.

It was no use.

Shaking his head, he said, "I'm sorry, there's nothing there."

"That's OK, don't panic yet," said Grant, "We've got more than one random number generator. Have another go."

One by one, they repeated the same process with one piece of hardware after another, until finally Matt got a hit, found a computer screen blinking bright red with a number in the centre of it. Matt looked at it through the haze of an almost infinite set of realities.

He could not do anything to interact with it. He knew for certain he must not read it out loud. Try as he might, he attempted to commit to memory, but given the length of the number, it was difficult to the point of being nearly impossible.

"OK, I think I've got it." As Matt spoke, the other reality-views collapsed from around him and he was left, once again, with the three of them staring at a blank screen.

Grabbing a pen, Matt scrawled digits down as fast as he could.

3 7 3 4 6 4 8 3 9 8 2 0 1

Grant checked the digits. "Pretty damn close but, no."

"OK, rerun it," said Matt.

Once again Matt immersed himself, and once again he managed to find the hit. This time however he was able to see where his error was, find his mistake.

3 7 3 4 6 4 8 3 9 8 5 0 1

"Yeah man!" nodded Grant – a hint of Jamaican accent surfacing in his excitement.

"This is going to be huge!" said Baker.

CHAPTER 53

In less than a week they'd managed to feed information into decryption attempts using the entropy generator they'd found to work sufficiently well across different realities. It was still hard work, as Matt had to memorise what was effectively a string of gibberish to decipher messages.

What they'd done was to create a mechanism to rapidly decrypt arbitrary cypher-text. Matt didn't see the content of the messages, he didn't have to, and he didn't want to.

"This is going to change everything," said Leighton-Jones, the industrialist, when The Commission next met. "Nothing is going to be the same again – this means effectively, nothing is secret. There is no electronic signature that can't be duplicated. No code that can't be broken."

"If that's true, this is serious," cautioned Stevenson. "What if other groups could do this? We need control."

"What do you mean... control?" asked Haider, the intellectual.

"I mean that Baker, Grant and Fellowes have been able to cheaply rig hardware to allow Howard here to cut through any encryption code like butter. This isn't some supercomputer we're talking about – this is basically a low-end PC with a bunch of readily available gizmotronics plugged into the back of it. If they had access to someone like Matt, *kids at school* could do this. If the wrong people had access to Matt, God alone knows what could be done."

"If what you say is possible, then things have shifted to another level."

"We need to know who has the potential to do this."

And so, on the back of this discovery, The Commission covertly supported the broader sharing of information between governmental departments. This was helped by the passing of the 2007 Serious Crime Act, introduced via the Home Office by Baroness Scotland of Asthal.

Once this framework was in place, they followed this up by

tackling and targeting secondary measures to allow governmental departments to arbitrarily access medical records and personal data. To avert concern from civil liberty groups, they intentionally focused this on compelling scenarios.

Stevenson had explained this at the time.

"If we raise this directly, saying we need access to medical records, the lefties are never going to go for that, they'd have a fit, start talking about *a police state.*"

Haider suggested that they shouldn't refer to accessing medical records but should instead refer to it as linking datasets that the government already had. *Who could object to that?* He pointed out that people generally believe that government can exchange data between its departments for administration purposes and are surprised to find that it cannot. He went on, "Removing barriers to sharing or linking datasets can help to design and implement evidence-based policy – for example, to tackle social mobility, assist economic growth and prevent crime. It's the linking of data that we already have," he said. "The trick is to keep it low-key. To concentrate on examples of what mishaps could have been avoided if such sharing were commonplace. Cite the pensioner who under medical advice had been told not to drive, the nursery worker who knows she's HIV, the business owner who pays no tax but whose bank records imply regular trips to expensive restaurants.

"We would mention all sorts of controls that sound robust but insert a get-out clause, such as *unless required for security purposes,* that would effectively render the controls ineffective. It would be innocuous and, if we get it right, it will sail under the radar. When it is passed we will have access to the mental health data to target all records of schizophrenic behaviour."

"But how will that help?" asked Matt, "That wouldn't have picked me up, I've never been diagnosed as such."

"One thing at a time," replied Stevenson. "Once we have access to all mental health records we need to separately push for compulsory mental health profiling. Base this upon us striving for the greater common good, and with sufficient cognitive-bias it will go through on the nod – become the new norm. The key is to make it palatable."

Haider nodded, *"Beauty is truth, truth beauty – that is all you need to know."*

Matt raised his eyebrows – *Really*! Haider's reference was lost on him and looked round the room. *I need to push on for the sake of my family*, he thought, struggling to convince himself, *I need to get to the bottom of this, for Ethan...*

But what was he creating?

What was it turning into?

Who shall guard the guards?

CHAPTER 54

Matthew Howard looked at Ethan attempting to blow out the candles on his fifth birthday cake. It was 2009, and his son had not long since started school.

Like the other parents, he stood around at the soft-play gym which they'd booked, coffee in hand. However, unlike them, Matt looked on with a mixture of pride and dread.

In the past months, The Commission had steered the government towards their planned data-sharing legislation and had passed special measures which effectively gave them access to *any* and *all* medical records – but as far as his concerns with Ethan, little had changed.

Much to the displeasure of his mother, Matt continued to work, and be secretively involved in things neither she, nor his wife, Jane, was allowed to be privy to, and, as a result, it was really only family events, such as this, that drew them together.

Over the recent months, Matt had on a weekly basis worked through a small set of encrypted communiqués which he, Grant and Baker managed to routinely decipher. By means of this and other activities they'd managed to keep the wolf from the door in terms of intelligence, managed to avert a number of terrorist-incidents, and managed to stay broadly one step ahead of what The Commission referred to as *groups of interest*.

However, much to his chagrin, none of what he'd progressed seemed to have altered the situation with his son. Matt felt the weight of this knowledge exhausting and it affected his waking moments, sucking the joy out of his world.

Would it have been better to be ignorant? Only time would tell, but he would be lying if he did not pine for the time before, rather than the joyless state in which he now found himself.

Like a washed-up town after the circus had moved on, he

felt empty with only memories of what had gone before. He was in mourning for his son before he'd even gone. He was wishing his life away on a daily basis – it couldn't go on like this.

Time... he thought, *I'm wasting all of it.*

Standing beside him, his father watched his son playing with the other children from infant school. The normality of it all jarred with them both. There was nothing to distinguish Ethan's smiling face from that of the others, but then again, there was everything to distinguish him. Watching him now brought the future home, and Matt felt the grip of long-standing panic weigh heavy on his chest.

The graft still hung there as before, but if size and shape could be used as a metaphor, it was larger and more definite than before. It loomed large like an approaching storm, like creeping death. As before, and as always, He felt a wave of nausea ride over him.

It could go to hell, he scowled.

"Nothing's changed, Dad," he sighed, "I can't believe that The Commission is responsible for the graft affecting Ethan. How could they be? They've not the capability, the inclination or the motive. But if not them then who or what?"

It had been a while since Matt and Tom had last spoken. After beginning The Commission, Stevenson had agreed that Tom should be kept informed, but that Matt be the *primary channeller*. In the months that had followed Matt had simply dug in. As if progression of The Commission's aims would somehow solve all of his problems. It was classic transference, he realised that, but that didn't mean he could prevent himself.

"I don't know what to suggest Matty," said Tom. "Has the research group thrown any light on matters at all?"

Matt sighed. The answer was, sadly, no. The group had covered a lot of ground, but this had been predominately in the field of applications; mainly cryptography rather than theory or anything that could be used to locate, or even give a clue as to the identity of Ethan's would-be assailant.

"Around code-breaking, yes. We're helping the country, *I'm sure*, but anything else, anything that could help Ethan... not so much."

The challenge was that group, and the wider commission,

still regarded the RIFT as a passive window onto different worlds. If Matt were to get them to help him determine what was happening with Ethan, he needed them to understand that there was more to the RIFT than this. *But it had been so long, how could he reasonably bring it up now?*

"To get anywhere, I probably need Baker's help. But I need him at another level, I need him to appreciate and understand *grafts*, *opposition*, and need him to figure out how to find who's behind this. I need him to up his game."

"This Baker, do you trust him?" asked Tom.

It wasn't that he didn't trust Baker; he thought that he probably did. It was the wider group. Their almost Stasi-like reaction to the encryption application had made him extremely uneasy, to say the least. How far would they go, could they go?

"Him personally? Sure. It's everyone else. They make me nervous. Everything's right, but everything's wrong at the same time. This thing with mandatory mental-health profiling – it's not right."

"I get you, Matt," said Tom, "Who shall guard the guards – right? But if the graft is not driven by The Commission, would their actions, however uncomfortable they seem, not put you in a fundamentally better position than you are now? If we're after finding the needle in a haystack then surely, having a list of where all the needles are kept would be invaluable, whatever the price."

"OK, but–" Matt struggled for words. "Do you not think it's a case of the road to hell being paved with good intentions?"

"I don't know Matty, I really don't. We have a gift, you and I, but for all we can see and for all we can do, what we can't see is the future. That door is definitely closed to us. Like anyone, all we can do is make the best choices with the information we have. You and I can see this thing, whatever it is, coming for Ethan, but for all our efforts and for all our gifts, we're still none the wiser as to who, when or why any of this is. I feel helpless, and it's driving me mad."

Matt nodded. His father was right; they were chasing ghosts, and he was sick of it. He then looked across at Ethan, completely oblivious, playing contentedly with his friends.

So innocent. Without so much as a care in the world. How

could he deny that? He looked at the smile on Jane's face, looked at the love in her eyes and listened to the light and the laughter in the voice of his son. Why did she put up with him? With the secrecy, with the time away? He didn't know. She didn't like it, she had made that abundantly clear, but she trusted him implicitly.

In that instant, he knew. It was that simple, no further consideration or discussion was required. There was no way he could abandon Ethan to the vagaries of fate. Not when there was the slightest chance that he could do something, anything, about it.

If they were ever to resolve this, he was going to have to confront Baker, and maybe the rest of them.

CHAPTER 55

When Matt returned to the Manor, The Commission had made further progress toward their goal of introducing compulsory mental health profiling. Haider had authored a whitepaper on the case for *mandatory diagnosis* of psychological conditions. In it he cogently argued that there were many professions – teachers, police, the armed forces – that were detrimentally affected by such mental conditions, and it was in the public interest to actively monitor these groups. It was an example of *salami tactics* at their worst.

On review, Stevenson had quipped that, without sufficient psychopaths, the British army would never have accomplished ten percent of what it had over the years, and so it might be the case that the condition was not always detrimental.

"You can't say that! There'll be hell-to-pay," exclaimed Phillips, the political advisor standing in for Hunter. "Everyone knows you need a percentage of *individuals* in the military that, in other walks of life, would be incarcerated. Everyone knows you need, let's call them, specialists that you simply wind up and let loose on the enemy. But no one's going to admit that in public, and certainly not in the guise of a government whitepaper."

Haider steered clear of these areas and instead expertly brought-in concerns over parenting, management and topics so broad that one would struggle to exclude anyone from the proposed regime.

And so it was, to Matt's growing unease, that a few weeks later, in early 2010, these proposals received their first reading in the House of Commons.

"I'm nervous about where this is all going," said Matt.

Baker, who'd been absently looking through the window, looked up. "Eh?"

"I said, I'm nervous about where this is all going," repeated Matt.

"How do you mean?"

"I mean that everything that is going on is a form of creeping normality, but over time this normality becomes a death by a thousand cuts. A grain of sand means nothing, but a grain every day can become a mountain. These changes that Haider's forcing through – I don't like them."

Baker shrugged.

"That's life Matt. The little guys get shat on. It's always been that way, and it'll always be that way."

"But we're the ones making it worse Greg," insisted Matt, "We're giving them the ammunition…"

Yesterday's radical was becoming today's routine.

"Let's say with my gift, we find that we can leverage something… *so crucial*… something… *so powerful* that it could change everything. I don't mean like the crypto thing. That was big, sure, but I mean huge… What then?"

Matt was aware that he'd left the question hanging like a ripe apple asking to be picked, like a flower waiting to be plucked, like a thorn waiting to scratch and draw blood.

Baker wasn't stupid – even at the hypothetical level the implication was clear. He just sat there letting the words click into place, ever so slightly rocking backwards and forwards in his seat. Eventually, he spoke. "We are all conscientious men, Matt," he said nervously, "and I'm certainly no exception. I'd like to consider us friends – my loyalties are first with truth and science."

Matt paused, words on the tip of his tongue.

It sounded plausible, but was Greg Baker merely feeding him lines, giving him what he wanted to hear. How could he be sure? How could he know?

"How can we ever know?" said Baker, as if reading his mind.

CHAPTER 56

Matthew Howard looked across the table at Baker. It was two days later, and his mind was made up. He was going to come clean. "Greg, I need your help," he said, "but this needs to stay between us, at least initially."

Matt had insisted that when they talked, it be away from the Manor. They'd chosen the nearby pub, close enough to avoid suspicion, distant enough to provide for some privacy. It was midday and the lunchtime crowd had started to build up.

Thankfully, the staff from The Manor did not usually frequent the Horse & Groom, and looking round he didn't recognise the few patrons at the bar, who paid the two of them scant interest.

After ordering two pints they had settled into a booth made from old church pews beside a wide, lead-lined casement window. Through the dim half-light, Matt's face was illuminated by the glow of the open hearth.

"OK," said Baker, "enough of the cloak-and-dagger act, what's on your mind? What's so important that you can't discuss it at work?"

"Like I said the other day," explained Matt, "I need your help, Greg. There's something that I've told none of you. Not you. Not Grant... not Fellowes – no one."

"Okay," said Baker.

Matt paused.

Where should he start? Where could he start?

It was impossible.

Taking a sip of his pint, he began.

"I can't just *see* other places, Greg, I'm there. I can actually control them. I can pick and choose between them as simply as that. I can see all possible realities, all at once, and select between them, some of which branch out into the future, some branch at a point in the past, but I can pick between them. But the thing is, when I flow through to a particular path, that path not only has its own present and future, but also has its own past. And any other past that might have existed, is effectively gone – removed.

"It's like I'm changing the past but *not* changing the past. It's more like separate realities exist where alternative courses of events are generated by alternative sets of cause and effect. And, flowing into a reality which exhibits an effect triggers a set of causes that must have led to it."

If Matt expected a verbal reaction from Baker, it was not yet forthcoming. The physicist simply blinked and furrowed his brow in concentration.

Matt pressed on, "When this happens Greg, all previous causes are thrown to the wind and are gone. But that's the problem – there are others that can do this too, and each of us can feel when the others change reality. We can feel the door closing on the reality we're in, like a bubble contracting. The problem is that ever since my son was born, I've felt such a bubble contracting – someone is trying to force this world into a different reality where my son has literally never existed."

Baker sat there, stunned, attempting to take in what he was hearing. "I think I need a drink," he said, drawing slowly on the glass in front of him. "If what you say is true, you could do practically *anything*. What could you possibly need from *me*?"

Matt raised his hand in front of him – open, in a gesture of his cycling thoughts.

How could he make Baker understand?

"I've got all this power Greg, sometimes to the point that it scares me, but ultimately I'm helpless. I don't know who's trying to erase Ethan. I know it's not for many years, but I have no way of telling who it is or why. That's where I need your help. I don't even know where to start. All I know about this gift is what I learned from my grandfather. He was onto something I'm sure, but whoever it is that is after Ethan, they tried to warn him off. He managed to resist, but it killed him. I need to understand what this is so that I can determine and understand who's doing it, and why. At the minute I'm being driven mad by this – I go to bed every night knowing I'm a day closer to the day where all of this is gone, but I don't have the faintest idea where to even begin. I need to understand this. I need someone who can look at this analytically and help me figure out who is doing this, or who is *going to be* doing this. I need you to build a model of what all of this is so that between us we can figure out who's behind it. I need some mechanism to do... something."

Baker stared pathetically at him like a rabbit in front of a set of headlights.

Matt could tell that he'd saturated the poor man's understanding and he needed to give him a little time for it to sink in, for it to gel. Baker sat there, eyes glazed, as if in another world. Finally, his attention seemed to snap back to his surroundings.

"Blimey, you don't ask for much do you, Matt," he said. "Of course, I'll do what I can to help you. After all, I like a challenge."

CHAPTER 57

Over the course of the next six months, Matt and Baker began working covertly on understanding Matt's gift. Progressively Baker was able to develop what he called his reality theory. Unbeknownst to him, Matt was still shaping his thoughts, leading him, prompting him, guiding him in the right direction. It was no real surprise, that a few weeks in, Baker's theories contained concepts which, years before, Joe had mentioned. With more of Matt's gentle prompting, Baker described his model in terms of multiple universes kept separate and held apart by repelling interstitial forces. Baker took it further however, describing each universe being like reality-bubbles which occupied what he referred to as something called a higher-dimensional manifold. Similar universes were in some sense close to one another and dissimilar universes were in the same sense far away from each other. Similar universes repelled one another like common poles of a magnet. Baker theorised that what Matt was doing was somehow overcoming this interstitial force, effectively hot-wiring one universe to another and so causing the target universe to trample the other universe out of existence.

"So we're destroying universes?" said Matt.

"That's the net effect," he told Matt, "but it's the wrong way to think about it. We think we live in a world of certainty, in a world of definite outcomes, but what you've shown is that we don't live along a straight line of causation, that we live within a tree of possibilities with masses of uncertainty. The RIFT is the gap from one branch to the next. And when you jump from one branch to the other all uncertainty collapses, and rather than a tree you're left with a single path from a common root to where you jumped to. And once you've done it, wherever you've come from is gone."

Matt tried to understand what Baker was telling him, but it

was far too abstract. As if sensing his frustration, Baker attempted to explain once again.

"Try this," he said. "Throw the die three times then make it so you throw three sixes…"

Even though it was a parlour trick, Baker never got bored of Matt throwing dice; it was somehow magical. When he began to theorise and understand the underlying cause, it only seemed to intensify his wonder. From Baker's perspective, the dice had always been sixes – but after Matt had finished, he said, "Now, rather than throwing it once again, make it so you always threw four-fives…"

Matt searched the RIFT but there was nothing remotely there, it was like he'd wiped the slate clean.

"You can't. Right?" asked Baker "once you jump you *make-definite* that portion of reality and that denies further manipulation. Sure, you can go much further back, but that then throws everything up in the air, you can make something not happen but under those circumstances, selecting what does happen instead is nigh-on impossible. If only I could find some way to detect when it occurs," he said, "or to detect *something* at least. I'm making progress Matt, but I'm only one man. To understand this, we need more eyes on it. Can't we share this with Grant and Fellowes?"

Matt was unsure. It wasn't that he didn't trust them, it was more that he didn't want this to be public knowledge. However, over the course of a number of weeks, Baker's progress seemed to slow, and if what he was saying were true, there would be no way back should the word be changed so that Ethan had never existed.

Matt was sure that the source of his unease was, in part, the impact that the last two-and-a-half years had had on what he thought of as society. In that time The Commission had pushed through a number of measures none of which were ground-breaking in themselves but which, in concert, represented a constant erosion – a wearing-away at common values, and possibly morals. Where was it going to end?

However, before he could continue along this train of thought, Matt's Blackberry buzzed, demanding his attention. Unlocking it he read:

From: Stevenson – Mandatory Commission meeting 14:00 today – come immediately.

Matt looked at his watch – *five minutes*... The Commission met regularly, but this was not the regular scheduled meeting, something was up...

Matt looked up at Baker. "Got to go," he said, "something's come up. Let's catch up on this later this week – OK?"

With that, Matt left the lab to Baker's nods and hurried down the passage towards the conference suite. The Manor was an eclectic building, almost like a hospital in its architecture; a hotchpotch of styles ranging from Victorian to modern – the corridor he now hurried down was parquet-floored and had dark green enamelled tiles that caused his footsteps to ring out.

What could be so urgent? he wondered. *Had The Commission found out, or had Baker let on?* The sound of his footsteps increased his panic. Was it his footsteps he could hear, or was it his heart?

Matt reached the thick-set oak door that was the conference suite and taking a deep breath, stepped inside.

To his surprise within the conference room were three faces he'd not seen in the same room since Joe's funeral – Both Jacobsons and Tom. But worse, were the military police that stepped forward as the doors closed behind him.

Shit!

They knew.

CHAPTER 58

What is this? thought Matt, flicking between Jacobson and his father, who sheepishly attempted to avoid his gaze. The Manor's main conference room housed an enormous oval table with a space in the centre making it look like a large, oblate ring. Matt stood transfixed, stunned by the appearance of the other fixers.

Did they know? If they did, how much did they know? And how?

At the head of the table, if such a thing made sense, sat Stevenson, flanked by Rountree and Haider. "Come in Howard," said Stevenson. "Sit down please."

Matthew Howard looked around the table – *other than Stevenson, did anyone know what this was about?* Matt Howard looked again at his father for an indication of what was so urgent to warrant a mandatory meeting, but Tom once again just avoided looking him in the eye.

In the years since forming, there had been emergency sessions, but a meeting like this was unprecedented.

And what were the Jacobsons doing here?

As the doors closed behind him, Stevenson flicked on a monitor to reveal a single word.

OPENNESS

Standing, he began. "Openness," he said, seemingly pausing for effect, "is something that this Commission was built on." Glancing at his notes, he continued, "Each of us when joining agreed that there would be no side-agendas, no secrets, no private interests, and you were warned that any variation from this would not be without severe consequences."

Matt did not like how this was going, he did not like it at all.

The fact that his father was here. The fact the Jacobsons were also present. Was he on trial? Were they to be witnesses for the prosecution?

He could feel his heart pounding in his chest. Beads of

sweat began forming on his forehead. *Keep it together, Matt,* he thought, continuing to focus on Stevenson.

"Some of us in this room," he said, "have not been so open. Some of us have sought to pursue their own ambitions, sought to pursue their own political agenda, which is why I have called you here today. This must be dealt with and dealt with now."

Why wouldn't his father look at him?

"A key tenet of this commission is that 'we are one'. Without that unity, we cannot succeed. This commission can do great things, has done great things, which is why it saddens me to be saying this. I can only ask that they now have the decency to stand up and come forth. To not force me to name them…"

It was over. Matt knew that much, *Stevenson had obviously got to Tom and the others. There would be little use denying it. Had Baker reported him?* He didn't suppose it mattered – he knew he'd gone against them.

"You're all fools! You don't know what potential you've got!" Suddenly Matt realised that military police had been edging towards not him but towards both Leighton-Jones and Hunter. It was the industrialist who had made the outburst at the point of one of the MPs planting a firm hand on his shoulder.

"You're pussy-footing about when we could be changing the world," he ranted. "Do you not see the opportunity? We could overtake China and the US economically – we could ruin them commercially and militarily. We could make Britain *Great* again."

"Enough!" boomed Stevenson, "These two men, for all their self-righteous indignation, conspired to displace this commission, to discredit it, and take it over from the inside out. Their objective was to mount a number of false flag incidents aimed at wrong-footing us, showing us up, setting us up to fail! Their plan was then to take control of Matt and Tom here by duress…"

Matt was stunned by what he was hearing.

"Take them away," barked Stevenson, "take them away now."

The two men were led out of the conference room scowling as they went.

"I'm sorry about that, gentlemen," Stevenson said, "but I think it essential to do these sort of things, as difficult as they are, not as clandestine affairs in private but instead to shine a light wherever it is needed." Turning now to look at the Jacobsons, he continued, "On a separate topic, I have some thankfully better news. Six months ago these two gentlemen were identified as 'interesting' by our data aggregation and mining work, and they have since been working with Rountree. "Father and son, they both have innate channelling ability, and they have agreed to join us. However, there is something more."

Stevenson looked at Rountree, who now stood up and addressed the room.

"That's right," he began. "As remarkable as it may seem, our observations of these two gentlemen appear to suggest that it is not only possible to *see* other worlds but actually to interact with them…"

CHAPTER 59

Matthew Howard looked at his father and then to the two new channellers.

He was aghast.

What were they thinking? How did they even come onto The Commission's radar?

Around the table, there was an uproar of questions.

"What did he mean by 'interact'?"

"What can they do?"

"Can they teach this to our channellers?"

"All in good time," quietened Rountree. "In due course, there will be a report covering these points, but for now I'm leaving them in the capable hands of Tom, Matt and the research team."

Jacobson looked at Matt and shrugged his eyebrows.

Heigh-ho.

Matt spent the rest of the afternoon with the research group, playing ignorant and questioning the new arrivals. The channellers feigned unfamiliarity with one another and also with the 'new' concept of 'interacting with realities'.

"What does this interaction do to you?" Fellowes, the psychiatrist, asked. "I mean, is it even the same you?"

The older Jacobson looked up from his wheelchair, "You don't know the half of it my dear," he said. "It can range from something-or-nothing, to tearing you apart. It can be like you're multiple people all fighting in one head, and every time you experience an interaction, it gets worse."

"In one sense you're you, but in another sense, you're not you." said his son, "the wider the gap, the worse it is. Imagine living the last ten years of your life differently. Now imagine mixing those two sets of memories from two different lifetimes together, not in a measured way, but just smashing them together – cut and shut."

The older Jacobson, frail with age, once again began speaking. "It's horrendous – people who you know died are alive, and vice versa. That happened to me in '48. It's enough to take you over the edge."

Alright, thought Matt. *That's enough* – what were the Jacobsons trying to do?

"…and what would I feel if you did this?" asked Fellowes.

"Probably nothing," said the younger Jacobson, "unless to some extent you've got the gift."

"So how did they find you?" Matt said finally.

The younger Jacobson sighed heavily and looked him in the eye. "Certainly, not by choice," he said. "Some computer thing flagged both of us up. They said we were persons of interest based on profiling. Something about datasets. To be honest, I didn't really understand… One thing *was* clear however, and that was this guy, Stevenson. He was definitely of the mindset that we were either with them or against them, or more accurately with *him* or against *him*. We didn't ask for details, but we soon got what he meant. They arrived one morning and bundled us into the back of a car, citing HM special regulations this and extra-ordinary powers that. It was like…"

His father reached out and weakly grabbed his hand – "It is what it is…" he chided. "Don't go making things worse. We're here to assist, let's concentrate rather than giving an appraisal, shall we?"

And with that, the focus turned back to the situation in the room and what could be done with this interaction. Over the day, Jacobson's mood mellowed. However, the edge never seemed to completely disappear. The conversation with the seven of them continued into the evening. The older Jacobson dozing and his son demonstrating how he affected simple things like coin tosses or die rolls.

To the surprise of Fellowes and Grant, both Tom and Matt were fast learners and, seemingly, in no time, were able to pick the technique up.

Baker was less impressed. If truth be told, he smelled a rat, but the convenience of the arrival of the two new members of the team was something he wasn't going to sniff at.

"So, you know what this means?" Grant offered rhetorically at breakfast the next day. "It means that the multiverse is no longer *read-only*, it's *read-write*."

"Well," said Baker, "if you fire up your encryption-cracker, you don't have to somehow memorise the key, you could just as likely jump to the version of reality where the code is already decrypted."

"If that's true…" the computer scientist's voice trailed off as he became lost in thought.

"…we've got to try this," Grant said. Running ahead of them, "Follow me."

When they got to the lab, Grant was already firing up his workstation, configuring the entropy generator and starting up the encryption program. "Like before, Matt," he instructed, "only this time. Become the reality – don't just read it."

Matthew Howard steeled himself for the charade ahead. *It was grotesque, but what choice did he have?*

As before, Grant's approach was that a non-match would be silent, whereas an exact match would trigger a beacon for Matt to focus in on. The difference this time was that the *beacon*, and therefore the *hit* should manifest in this reality.

Submitting a file of cypher text, Grant set the machine away.

As he'd done many times before, Matt relaxed into the moment and focussed through the RIFT to where the hit was – where a screen which was not blank resided.

Straightforwardly, he reached out for the computer, and the reality-stream jumped.

From Grant's perspective no sooner had he fed the computer the code that it generated the result – an instant positive hit.

"That's amazing," he grinned. "Tell me you did it and this wasn't some weird one-in-a-million chance?"

Matthew Howard gave an almost imperceptible sigh.

"No," he said, "I did it."

CHAPTER 60

Eli Phillip Rountree put the report down on the table. He must have read it about fifty times but it still made his head spin. Looking round the room at the other faces of the assembled commission members, he attempted to work out whether each of them understood the report's implications.

Grant had presented the research group's finding to The Commission and was currently fielding questions. When the questioning finally began to peter out, Rountree asked his own.

"Grant, on page 37, you say that encryption can be routinely broken by transitioning to the reality which randomly selected the correct decryption key."

It was true, again and again, the experiment worked in precisely the way they had predicted.

"That's impressive. However, what I want to know is what the limits to this are. Rather than locating keys and decrypting messages using a random number generator, can we not consume the natural entropy all around us?"

Blank faces

Rountree continued, "Rather than attempt to decode a message, can we not get the technology to alert us to the fact that, in a particular universe, the message has been decoded – or for that matter, anything else has happened?"

It was so simple, it was beautiful, and in a moment he saw it all. In an infinitely complex multiverse where everything that could happen did happen it was just a question of creating the sieve to filter out the desired outcome. Anything could be charmed into existence, and the use of technology meant that the definition of success could be arbitrarily complex. As long as the effect could be sufficiently well described, the cause would fall into place.

A winning lottery ticket…

"If this works, we've just created Aladdin's lamp," Rountree said finally, "I only hope to God we have the presence of mind to use it responsibly."

Stevenson was clearly shocked.

"What do you mean Aladdin's lamp?" he said.

"What I mean is, if every combination of events happens in parallel in different realities then, for any given *wish*, there is a reality which matches that. If we can make it so technology can detect that and draw a channeller's attention to it, then effectively you have a wish-factory."

"Is that true Sir?" asked Baker, "surely it is limited to the set of realities where we've already set up the technology?"

"You're right Baker," agreed Rountree, "but even so, the possibilities are still effectively huge."

Matt wasn't sure that he understood, "Are you saying it can only detect things that have been previously thought-of?"

"In effect, yes," said Baker, "you need to set the seeker program away before the event, as otherwise, the program can't detect it."

Matt felt something on the edge of his mind struggling to take shape – "I understand that," he began, "but what if you have two seekers?"

"How do you mean?" said Baker.

"Well, what if you had a seeker that randomly sought out a reality – or if you like – *all* realities, and then you had another seeker that sought out the correct seeker program. Would that not get you round the problem?"

Matt looked at the stunned silence around the room. Finally, Baker broke through.

"So, if I understand you, what you're saying is that you can't set a seeker-program running to find a reality where, say, I'm dead because in your timeline I'm alive and therefore it would only run in universes where I'm alive. However, you could have previously, in the past, set a random seeker running, that seeks anything and everything, in parallel, and then you use another seeker to find the particular version of the random seeker that is seeking a universe in which I'm no longer alive. You then graft to that universe, where in effect that program has been running for a while, has always been running... and use that to piggyback... It doesn't solve everything, but yes it should extend things quite a bit... However, I'm not sure I like my own example."

Matt's head was spinning. *Why did it need to be so complicated?*

Stevenson, who had remained silent all of this time, finally spoke. "So, what you're saying is, that whilst you can't do anything, such as follow this Aladdin's lamp thing, you can arbitrarily do anything from the point that you set out to consider doing it. And what's more, you don't need to identify the 'what', you just need to ensure there is a 'what' and determine the 'what' later, putting in place the computer program to locate the universe where the correct location program has been running?"

"That's right," said Baker, but once you've used it, you've used it. It's a one-shot, a one-use system."

But couldn't they just run lots of these side by side? thought Matt.

As if reading his mind, Baker continued, "You're probably thinking, *could we run multiple seeker instances*, well you could, however locating a universe would likely nail it down."

Matt disagreed – "That would only be true if you ran them all together. If you ran them one after another, then assuming you locate them in the order that you ran them and jumped to universes where you had run them, it should work – like Russian dolls."

Stevenson held his hand up, "Gentlemen, enough. It sounds like you're making progress, but we need the utility of this. Grant – you need to tell me what we need to productionise this and run it as a programme."

CHAPTER 61

"So, we need to 'productionise' a wish factory," sighed Grant. "No pressure then – has anyone got the number of our North Pole office?"

Following the meeting, they'd adjourned to the mess hall on the topmost floor of the Manor. Fellowes smirked at Grant's comment before looking at Matt – "Matt, if *you* could wish for anything, what would it be?"

The question took Matt by surprise and caught him off guard. "If I could wish for anything... If I could wish for anything, I would wish that this, so-called gift, didn't exist. I don't just mean for me, but for anyone. It's a curse."

It was true, and it was like they'd begun by spinning a plate on the top of a cane. Now it was more a case of keeping things moving than concentrating on the reason for any of it. It had become all-consuming – when was the last time he'd spent quality time with Jane? With Ethan? He was pissing it all away. And for what?

"You're not wrong, son," nodded Jacobson's father. "It's brought me nothing but misery. In '45 I had it all. I had both children and an extended family – it was all good. In '48 they were gone in a heartbeat. Obliterated. The Russians had overrun us, there was a plan to reset things to 1945, but that never happened, instead it went back a lot, lot, further, and that changed everything."

Tears welled up in the old man's eyes. As he spoke, he grabbed the arms of his wheelchair.

"My family, my children, my wife, my parents, all gone – all of them. But worse, much worse than that was how they went. Either in Nazi death-camps or denied their very existence. One moment they were there, in some cases in the next room, the next moment they had either been dead for years or never even existed in the first place. So yes," he said looking at Matt, "I agree with you, I wish for none of this. But failing that, I hope and wish that whoever it was that sent them to their fate is burning in hell, along with everything they ever cared about."

Matt felt his heart quicken and the chill of the blood draining from his face. He felt suddenly sick with fear and realisation.

It was not The Commission who would ultimately target Ethan. It was Jacobson. How had he not seen it earlier?

The look in Tom's eyes told him that his father was thinking the same thing, and thankfully the others were too focussed on the old man to see his, or his father's, discomfort. He looked down and avoided the eyes of the others.

Jacobson had the means, the motive and the opportunity. From the existence of the graft, he reasoned that it was only a matter of time before Jacobson found out the truth; discovered that it was Joe who had been responsible for the graft that had shaped these events.

Then what?

"I've always been a disappointment to you, haven't I?" the younger Jacobson snapped. "I'm sorry that I'm not as good as them, but I didn't ask to be born any more than you asked for them to go. But I'm sick of hearing this Dad!"

"You don't know what you're talking about!" his father spat back. "You should show some respect."

"Why? You've never shown me any. And to whom? Ghosts who passed before I ever was… Anyway, I've had enough of this. We're going."

With that, he stood up, roughly grabbed the handles of his father's wheelchair and began pushing him out of the mess hall.

"Come on then," sighed Baker, and one by one they followed the old man.

Jacobson reached the elevator at the end of the floor and pushed the button to call the lift.

"Good luck," said Grant. "That lift is temperamental as hell." You may be better off using the one at the other end, you know – the one we came up in."

"That's typical…" muttered the elder Jacobson from his chair.

The elevator doors slowly opened, but instead of there being a lift-car there was an empty shaft.

Matt looked at Tom and raised an eyebrow.

"See what I mean?" said Grant. "It's buggered. If this were a civilian facility, it would be condemned."

"Well that's just great!" complained Jacobson, before continuing to berate his son.

Tom looked at the old man as he spewed venom.

If he ever found out about Joe, what would he be capable of? He had to know. Looking past the open lift shaft, Tom Howard looked into the RIFT and felt the possibilities open up around him. In most of them, the Jacobsons got more argumentative – but then the different realities bifurcated sharply. In some the younger Jacobson stormed off, but most had them shouting at each other till they were red in the face. Almost with morbid fascination, his attention seemed to be drawn to where the agitation between them was most severe. It was out on an extremely unlikely backwater branch of the RIFT. However, the ferocity of the vitriol that they displayed towards one another drew him in, like a moth to a flame.

"You're a disgrace!" shouted the old man over his shoulder to his son who still held the handles of his wheelchair, knuckles white with the force with which he now gripped them.

"Are you ever going to let this go?" bawled his son. "Nothing I do is ever going to be enough for you..."

"Nothing you do *is* good enough..." railed his father.

"Well if that's the case..."

Tom watched transfixed, as he realised that *that reality's Jacobson* had depressed the brake-lever with his foot and was pushing his father forward, toward the open lift shaft.

"No!" shouted Tom, and grabbed at the younger Jacobson, too late to stop him giving his father an almighty shove towards the open gaping chasm.

With Tom's interaction all other possible realities collapsed and Jacobson's actions stopped being *mere possibilities*. Instead, they were made real. In horror, Tom and the others watched as the old man was sent screaming down the lift shaft. His screams were only silenced by a sickeningly dull thud.

"What the...! Jacobson. What did you just do?" gasped Grant.

Fellowes ran, smashed the alarm with the heel of her hand

and grabbed the emergency phone which hung on the wall.

Jacobson ripped at his hair in torment and bellowed in despair. Slowly he raised his head to look up, eyes boring into Tom.

"What did you just do to me?!" he snarled, in a voice that sounded like death. Steadily, he advanced towards Tom, like a snake waiting to strike. Tom, backed away, tripping over his feet.

"Jacobson, he was trying to stop you," said Baker.

"Shut it!" Jacobson hissed, continuing to close in.

"Get away from my father!" rasped Matt, moving to block his path.

But before Jacobson could respond, a group of staff, armed-to-the-teeth, entered the landing. Looking down, Jacobson discovered the tranquilliser dart that had appeared in his side. He then staggered and keeled over.

CHAPTER 62

"So – who's going to be the first to tell me what the hell just happened?"

Matthew Howard sat before Stevenson. Beside him were the other witnesses to the old man's death. In the hours that had followed, Jacobson had been hauled to the infirmary and Stevenson had instructed that he should be kept sedated, at least until they could determine what had happened.

Grant spoke first. "Jacobson was having a blazing row with his father, the lift doors opened, and it looked like an opportunity presented itself to him. Jacobson just snapped. Tom here, tried to stop him but he wasn't quick enough. Jacobson said something like 'Nothing I do will ever be enough for you...' and then he did it."

Matthew Howard was in shock, not because of the recent events with Jacobson, but because those events had made precisely zero-difference to the graft, which still hung there.

Whatever nascent theory he'd had about the old man had evidently been unfounded.

Unless he'd been targeting the wrong Jacobson...

"This puts us in a difficult position," said Stevenson. "With his powers, what action can we take against Jacobson? It's for our own safety and the safety of this programme that we've taken the view that he can't be tried in the usual way."

To the left of Stevenson, Rountree rose to his feet.

"Based on the initial observations with the Jacobsons, we've adapted the vagus nerve stimulation, or VNS, therapy used to prevent epileptic seizures, and applied this to the ventral stream. By doing this, we can control or disrupt his channelling ability."

"I don't understand," said Tom.

"It's simple, Dad. They've opened him up and wired him to some kind of kill switch."

"He'll be lucid when he appears before the courts

martial," said Stevenson, "however his appearance may be a shock to you."

Jacobson's trial began the next day. Stevenson had been right – where they looked at Jacobson, they didn't initially recognise him. He looked like a beaten man. Most of his hair had been shaven off and there was a brutally ugly gaping scar around the base of his skull running transversely from ear to ear.

Matthew Howard looked at his friend, who stared at the floor dejected.

Dear God, what have we brought about?

A man in military uniform, who Matt didn't recognise, brought the room to order.

"Simon Michael Jacobson, the charge before you is that you did wilfully and with malice aforethought murder your father, one Nikalus Jacobson. Do you understand the charge that is put before you?"

Jacobson slowly looked up from where he was sitting and sneered at Thomas Howard. "Yes, I understand," he said slowly, his eyes never leaving Tom.

"How do you plead?"

"Not guilty."

"Do you deny that, yesterday afternoon at approximately 3.20pm, you left the mess hall with Nikalus Jacobson, and on leaving, you forcefully pushed your father into the open lift shaft in corridor B?"

"No, I don't deny it."

"Was this action, accidental?"

"No, it wasn't accidental."

"Was this action, intentional?"

"Yes, it was intentional."

"Then, how, Sir, do you justify your assertion of innocence?"

"I didn't say I was innocent, I said I was not guilty. There's a difference."

"Pray, enlighten us with the difference?"

Jacobson let out a heavy sigh. *It was true that he'd had it within him to murder his father, but that wasn't how things were supposed to have turned out.* "I was angry, I admit that. But there was no way I was going to kill him, that outcome was forced on me. If reality had not been tampered with then my father would not be where he is now, and neither would I. I obviously had the potential to kill him, but it was a one-in-a-million chance that I would snap. That was not where I was headed, not until *he* forced that interaction."

With that, Jacobson pointed at Thomas Howard.

"I was *always* capable of it, and in that sense, I'm not completely innocent, however, it was Tom who pushed me to do it. It was him that made do what I did, led me to shove my father the way that I did. It was him that grafted the world to a branch where I killed him. So, I killed my father, yes – but not by choice. That was forced on me...

"Why Tom?" Jacobson sobbed, "What did he ever do to you? Why?"

The room erupted in uproar and all eyes turned to Tom. However, before another word was spoken the uniformed senior officer leading the proceedings turned from his consultation with Stevenson and interjected – "This significantly changes the nature of this investigation. I recommend a recess for the remainder of the day. We will reconvene tomorrow."

CHAPTER 63

Thomas Howard sat in Stevenson's office alongside Matt and Rountree.

"Well," barked Stevenson, "Is it true? Did you do what he said? Did you shove him into a universe where he'd killed his father?"

Thomas Howard looked at the floor and considered his words carefully.

What could he say? It was indeed true, but as to whether he did it on purpose, did he really know? He didn't think so, but given what he'd suspected about Jacobson, could he be sure?

"Yes," he said, "I did it, but not intentionally. I was drawn into it."

"How do you mean?" asked Stevenson.

"I mean the reality where Jacobson..." he paused and then began again. "In the reality that we're in now, I could see Jacobson pushing his father towards the lift. I could see what he was trying to do..." Thomas Howard rubbed his face as the tears welled in his eyes. "It was automatic, without thinking I reached out to stop him, and me reaching out is what forced the reality, where he killed him, to be. What does that mean? It effectively means *I* killed him, doesn't it?"

It was enough to drive him mad.

How should one assign moral responsibility if fundamental tenets like cause and effect could be disrupted? But had causation even been challenged, or was it merely that a different path had been followed? It wasn't as if the graft which he'd applied had a substantial temporal element to it.

His heart went out to Jacobson, however. At the end of the day, in this reality that they now occupied, Jacobson had murdered his own father, albeit not in cold blood, but it had been murder all the same. *He wouldn't wish that on anybody. Surely that could not be denied.*

"There is certainly no legal precedent for this," growled Stevenson.

Then the realisation hit Tom – that in an infinite universe, anyone was capable of anything, and that meant that anyone could be manipulated like a puppet being made to dance.

If that were the case, then surely it was wrong to punish Jacobson? But what then for justice for his father? Jacobson did murder him after all.

"Can you fix it?" asked Stevenson. "Can you put it back to how it was. How it should be?"

How it should be, what did that mean?

Matthew Howard looked at Stevenson, and after a long pause, he said, "It can't be put back as it would have been. That flow is gone. We could get close though, but do you realise what you're asking? Jacobson already remembers both killing and not killing his father, fixing it will lead to a third stream. His father would be alive alright. However they'd both know what had happened, that his son had killed him. Worse though, his father would remember falling, screaming to his own death at the hands of his son – and that would be stamped on his psyche. If the two of them weren't channellers that would be one thing, but they are what they are. Be careful what you want – what you get back might be more than you bargained for. More than that, he'd know what has just been done to him here... But you wouldn't know anything. Could you ever trust him?"

Stevenson pulled at the side of his face, rubbing his eyesocket in frustration...

This was a real mess. However, if this were to be resolved he knew one thing – *this screw-up couldn't be allowed to ever happen again.*

"What can we do?" Rountree finally said. "We can't incarcerate Jacobson when he knows he didn't actively kill his father. But at the same time – he did."

Jacobson was no longer one thing. He was both guilt and innocence smashed together, and that was the problem.

"We can't exactly release him either."

"What are you saying?" asked Matt

"Casualties of war," replied Stevenson.

"You can't be serious!" exclaimed Tom, "You're seriously talking about killing him?"

"No, I'm not, but accidents do happen. I'm talking about Jacobson attempting to escape and, in the process... Who knows… perhaps if things were different this could have already happened. Do you understand?"

Thomas Howard's mouth went dry. He understood perfectly what Stevenson was asking him to do. Everything he was, railed against the idea.

But then again, if Jacobson was targeting his grandson or about to target him… If Jacobson were targeting Ethan it could resolve everything. It would take him out of the game. Then maybe they could all just go home…

"There can be no loose ends," said Stevenson.

"Understood," replied Tom as acceptance washed over him.

"…and by the way, when that's done, you're each having one of these devices fitted," Stevenson added.

CHAPTER 64

"Not him then?" Matthew Howard faced his father and miserably toyed with his coffee. The night before, Jacobson had tried escape and had been fatally injured in the subsequent attempt to apprehend him.

"No," confirmed Tom, "not him." Frustrated, he threw the empty paper coffee cup across the table.

Both of the Jacobsons were now dead, but the graft which targeted Ethan had remained stubbornly unchanged.

"What have we become Matt?" said Tom. "What have *I* become?"

The old man had likely been an accident, but there was no way he could say the same thing about his, now dead, son.

In the past days, the calm calculated manner he'd approached the whole topic had frankly shocked him. He had viewed the younger Jacobson purely as a means to an end; an obstacle to be overcome. But certainly, not a person, or even a friend.

But then again, he didn't write the script, he had merely changed the channel. It wasn't as if he'd killed him. Was that so wrong? It wasn't as if he caused those events to happen, they had always happened – just somewhere else.

If a tree falls in the forest and no one is there to hear it, does it make a sound? But if events occur with no measurable impact on reality, can they be said to be truly real? If the only thing that differentiates reality from imagination is memory then could dreams be as real as alternate realities? If the metric of reality is the amount of knock-on effect that a meme has on the universe... surely witchcraft, religion and even Santa Claus fall into that category?

In at least one reality, Jacobson had always killed his father. In another reality Jacobson had been killed whilst trying to escape. Tom hadn't made any of these things happen, they'd always been so, he'd just chosen that his consciousness should exist in this version of reality – merely switched channels, affecting, from his perspective, which reality was core. Was that so wrong?

The more Tom tried to rationalise what he'd done, the more he struggled. It was tempting to think that he was only an innocent observer in all this, but that was patently untrue.

It may be true for those without the gift. However, for those like Matt and himself, it constituted an act taken by choice which had resulted in suffering.

Had the devil made him do it?

Was he evil?

But do what?

Who had suffered?

If anyone, it was him and Matt.

What did all this mean?

What he hadn't foreseen was that he and Matt would be drawn into the escape and how it would affect them.

The night before, Jacobson had somehow managed to get out of his cell and make it to the dormitory level. This was an oak-panelled corridor with heavy doors. Matt and Tom had rooms across from one another. Five minutes earlier they'd been woken by the distant sound of a siren. Tom had pushed his head out of his door and found himself looking at Matt. "What's going on?" he'd asked, as Stevenson had thundered down the corridor.

"No time, to explain," Stevenson said. "Shut your door and keep it locked. You too Matt."

As instructed, Tom had locked the door and waited in silence. The minutes dragged by as he wondered what the situation was outside.

"Somebody, let me in." Jacobson's voice sounded desperate as he rattled the door handle.

But instead he had sat there in silence – ignoring him – pretending he wasn't there. Why hadn't he helped him? He didn't know. But sat there he had. Then he'd heard Jacobson with a similar plea at Matt's door, only to be met with the same lack of response. Did Jacobson even know with whom he was pleading?

Other voices could now be heard outside, and Jacobson's shouts were accompanied by the sound of running.

"No…" he heard Jacobson's cry tail off down the corridor. This sound was followed by first one and then two more bursts of automatic weapon fire.

Tom continued to sit in silence and slowly rocked backwards and forwards.

That was that. Neither he nor Matt had helped. Was that wrong? He didn't know. What he did know, was that the driving force behind his actions, or inactions, to finally safeguard Ethan, had once again failed. Ethan's fate had not changed one iota.

And he'd pulled in a reality where he'd passively let Jacobson die. For nothing. *All that is needed for the triumph of evil is that good men do nothing.* Joseph's words rang in his ears. He had stood by while they killed him. Jacobson was meant to be one of them. Wasn't he?

Even then, it was all for nothing.

It was frustrating, it was beyond belief; whatever they did, it made absolutely no difference to the situation.

It was as if they were cursed. And from it all, if Stevenson were to be believed, both he and Matt were likely to be fitted with some surgical contraption – some kind of control device.

In *this* reality however, there had been no hearing for Jacobson, no Courts Martial, no outburst, and no subsequent discussion. Stevenson had not ordered any action against Jacobson and had not instructed anyone to fit them with controls.

Stevenson had no knowledge of that conversation.

And now that particular conversation had never happened.

However, now that both he and Matt knew what Stevenson was capable of, it was only a matter of time.

CHAPTER 65

Matthew Howard sat in the conference suite with the rest of the assembled representatives. Almost a week had passed since Jacobson's attempted escape, and The Commission had been recalled.

"Some of you already know about the recent tragic events at the manor over the last week. But for those who don't, it's with a heavy heart that I have to report to you the loss of our two most recent channellers."

As Stevenson recapped recent events for all assembled, Matt continued to study him, watched his calculated demeanour, his insincere, almost-sympathy, watched him make eye-contact with the members of the room before proceeding.

"We'll never know why Jacobson felt compelled to murder his father or attack his guards, but we can only hope that both of them have now found some kind of peace. Between them, they moved this programme on in ways that we had not considered possible and we will forever be grateful to them for that. However, it also appears that, for them, this gift had a darker side that had tortured them over the years. It appears that it made Jacobson finally snap and led him to murder his father. It also drove him to attempt to escape, which ultimately resulted in his own unfortunate death. I wish the news were better. We have lost two friends and colleagues. Two of our own who won't be forgotten."

You hypocrite, thought Matt. *It was you who ordered him killed, and you don't even know it.*

"What has become apparent however, is that we crucially need a greater understanding and far more control. As you no doubt know, yesterday Parliament passed the bill to introduce mandatory mental health screening and profiling. Within five years we will have a complete neurological and psychological map of every adult in the nation. In fact, it is a testament to both Jacobsons that we have reached this point.

Had they not steered the outcomes of the early discussions for us, it is not clear that this would have ended so favourably. For the minute, however, we need to dig deep and redouble our efforts to understand this phenomena, so that it is not resting on the backs of one or two individuals."

With that, Stevenson closed the meeting and walked swiftly out of the room, denying anyone the chance to challenge him or ask further questions.

CHAPTER 66

The next research sessions were sombre to say the least. Grant and Fellowes took a back seat to Baker, who thought that progress could be made by mapping what was possible within the RIFT onto classic paradoxes or thought experiments. Baker's conjecture was that by gathering round a whiteboard and discussing each of these in a structured manner they might shed new light onto the situation.

"If we consider The Grandfather Paradox", he said, underlining the words he'd just penned, "our model would suggest that this is not a paradox at all. Our model suggests that while you can't kill your grandfather in the past, you could identify a reality in which he died. However, were you to interact with that, were you to graft to that branch, you would effectively cease to exist."

"That appears to be right," said Matt with unease. "Although it's almost impossible to locate such branches, in the distance, they are there. But I'm not going to interact with one, for obvious reasons…"

"…although there may be advantages," interjected Baker.

"Such as?"

"Well, if my theory is correct," said Baker, "if Matt chose to jump to that reality, he couldn't be opposed, as there wouldn't be a *him* in the other reality to oppose."

"OK. Let's not try that," said Matt.

"No, quite, and rightly so," agreed Baker. "The interesting point is, however, that this would not create any kind of paradox since both branches would have already been in existence. The graft would simply truncate one timeline and replace it with the version where you were never alive or even existed."

"I'd agree with that," said Matt. Baker was correct. However, there was something that Matt could not put his finger on. In the approaching graft all of Matt's family were still there, there was just no Ethan. *What could the connection be?* Shaking his head, he tried to hide his discomfort and push the thoughts away. "What other theories are there?"

"There's retro-causality or backwards-causation," said Baker adding to the list, "where information in the future influences events in the present."

Ethan...

"I've not experienced that," said Matt quickly.

"There's Cramer's Immaculate Conception paradox. Here the idea is that you receive information from yourself in the future – a best-selling book, say – and you publish it becoming rich and famous. Following this, you pass a copy of the book back to yourself. The question is, who wrote the book if the *past you* got it from the *future you* and the future you sends it back to the past. It is created out of nothing – Immaculate Conception."

"But that would never happen," sighed Matt. "If I jumped to a reality where I had created a book, then that would be because, in that reality, there was a version of me who had written that book in the first place. We would superimpose memories, there is no paradox."

Grant stood up suddenly, hands waving in front of him, desperately trying to frame his words. "That's it then," he said. "Immaculate Conception. That's how we work all this out."

It was clear from the look on Matt's face that he was lost.

"It's simple," said Grant excitedly. "In fact, it's so simple, I don't know how or why I didn't see it earlier."

Blank faces continued to stare back at him.

"Oh C'mon..." he said. "We've been trying to crack this thing forever, but that's crazy. Why not, instead, look for a universe where we managed to crack it? Locate a reality where we managed to fully understand it operationally and scientifically. Can we not use a variation of the encryption process? Aladdin's lamp? Can we not, in the here and now, nominate this whiteboard, say, to hold the key?"

Grant erased the contents of the whiteboard and wrote 'THE KEY' at the top.

"Why do *we* need to work it out? Immaculate conception you said. *We* need to keep trying, but we also leverage the other realities."

The excitement of checking the board infused them for the next few days, but this diminished over time. Two weeks had passed when Matt noticed it – through the RIFT he could see the whiteboard now had different text in another reality.

"It's there," he gasped. "I won't pretend I understand it, but it's there all the same."

Reaching out he touched it and made it real.

The text became real, but suddenly his legs gave way.

What was happening?

It was like a machine gun pounding in his head. Every thought seemed to have a thousand echoes and all memory of the last two weeks became a jumble of incoherent feelings. Matt looked at the panic and the terror on his father's face that told him that Tom was in a similar position.

He attempted to stagger across the lab and blacked out shortly before reaching the door.

CHAPTER 67

Matthew Howard woke to sounds around him. Eyes still shut, he attempted to recognise his surroundings by what he heard but found them unfamiliar.

He was much more in control than before, than when he'd blacked out. But where was he?

"OK. I'm finally back. So exactly, what happened?" came Stevenson's stern voice.

"On that morning – the 23rd, within thirty minutes of writing up our findings on the board, writing the key, both of them seemed to keel over." This was Baker's voice.

"What do you mean *writing the key*?" asked Stevenson. "Remember, I've been off the grid for the last month, what board?"

"It was Grant's idea, well kind of, to try to find a way in. We reasoned that more likely than not, at least one reality would figure out how the RIFT worked. The intention was to identify that reality by writing the key, the solution if you will, on a whiteboard – we agreed that about three weeks ago. Well, I'm saying it was Grant's idea," gabbled Baker, "Matt saw it elsewhere so, if you like, it was *other-Grant's* idea. Ironically, in the end, we didn't need to as we solved it ourselves – old school."

Memories came back to Matt. *That was right, Baker had thought he had figured out how to identify arbitrary outcomes. Was that when it all went wrong?*

"And what were you going to do if you hadn't solved 'old school'?"

Why was Stevenson being so antagonistic?

"That's simple," explained Baker, we would have grafted to the reality where they had solved it."

"I don't believe what I'm hearing," scoffed Stevenson, the exasperation clear in his voice. "And what do you think the millions of *other-you's* were going to do when they saw that board?"

"I don't know, they would probably…"

Baker paused, the realisation finally hitting him.

"Oh my God! You mean that rather than a merging of *just-two* universes, Matt's probably undergone thousands of merges, if not more… Wait did he just move?"

Matt was aware that he had indeed shifted, opening his eyes he looked at Stevenson and Baker.

"What's going on?" he said groggily, "What happened?"

"You blacked out, Matt. But that was over a week ago, you've been here ever since. We thought we'd lost you."

Matt looked around at the infirmary and tried to take it in.

A week?

What did they mean – a week?

How was that even possible?

Looking down and to his left, he realised that he was plumbed to a drip, and an ECG, but not only that, there was something going on downstairs which he really didn't wish to know about.

"What can you remember, Matt," asked Stevenson.

He didn't know. It was mostly a blur of conflicting information

"Where's my father?" he finally said.

The last he remembered, Tom had also known that something was wrong.

"I'm fine Matt," came a familiar voice. "I was out for a couple of hours, not like you. You gave us quite a scare. I've been fobbing Jane off for a week."

Of course – Jane… she must be beside herself.

"So, you finally figured it out?" he said to Baker. "So what did you do? How does it work?"

Stevenson raised his hands to cease the conversation, "You know that's classified Matt, so don't go fishing. For the minute you need to rest and get something to eat. We'll talk in a few days, OK? It's good to have you back."

CHAPTER 68

"What did he mean classified?" Matthew Howard looked across at his father once Stevenson had left. "What the hell happened to *complete openness?*"

Tom let out a deep sigh.

"A lot has happened Matt, and none of it good. As I do, you probably remember agreeing five points with Stevenson. Not military-led, principle driven, family assurances, being informed about the bigger picture and being consulted on everything."

Tom counted the points off on his fingers as he cited them.

"Matt, although we both remember it, that agreement never happened here."

Matt tried to work out what this meant.

If it was all different maybe that meant that Ethan was safe.

"What about Ethan?" he said.

He looked into the RIFT and got the same answer at the same time as his father's response. Shaking his head, Tom replied, "No change, unfortunately."

Closing his eyes, Matt attempted to search for the memories that must be there. It was no use. It was like attempting to tune in an old TV set riddled with interference. No, that was not right, it wasn't that there wasn't enough signal – there was too much signal, and all of it conflicting. It was a mess.

Far stranger than that, however, *he* was a mess. It wasn't that he'd approximated the same recent history, although in many cases he had. It was infinitely more varied than that.

His memory was shattered into a countless multitude of fragments. He was a man out of time, nothing he knew as memory, could he trust. It was like all roads had led to Rome, for it ultimately to be sacked. Seemingly, every possible version of himself that could have noticed this reality was present in his head. Many of the thoughts that he possibly could have had, he now remembered having.

There was an almost infinite number of routes he could

have taken to this point, and he remembered walking parts of all of them. In one past his study of Zen meditation led him to accept the commotion in his head. In another past he'd represented the fragmentation of his memory as an algebraic lattice and was able to bring a topological structure to the chaos. In others, he'd leveraged cognitive behavioural therapy and stoicism to limit the effect of negative beliefs. One after another, in more and more realities he'd found many and varied coping-mechanisms which now formed a patchwork defence against slipping into the abyss.

But as numerous as they were, would those defences be enough?

The myriad of different voices all clamoured in his head.

If the definition of a man is the sum of his experiences, then who was he?

Shades of Hunter S. Thompson…

How did he even know that?

How should he act, what would constitute his personal dharma?

Random thoughts bounced round his head like a ricocheting squash ball, haemorrhaging thoughts like random movie scenes.

Why was he marginalising his family?

Was he? Surely this was for them…

Wasn't it? How much of Ethan's life had been wasted chasing this folly? Was everything he'd done wrong? Who could give him confirmation?

A million other voices forced similar thoughts into the front of his mind. The incessant chatter refused to leave him space to think, and with this, the panic rose, stifling him.

How could he make them stop? What did he need to do? Was he a good man?

His father looked at him kindly, knowing his pain.

"It's bad for me, but I can't imagine what it must be like for you, Matt," he said.

"The voices are all you, son. They are your allies, your armies, your experts-in-waiting. Accept them and use their strength. You can't fight them, and don't try to reconcile them, just try to find whatever peace you can. A lot has changed – a lot you won't like, and Ethan needs you…

"Jane needs you…

"I need you."

CHAPTER 69

"So, what *can* you tell me?" Matthew Howard had recovered enough to return to the lab and was sitting opposite Baker and Grant.

"The best way that I can explain it, is that, it's like water," said Grant. "Imagine an infinite number of droplets. The surface tension normally keeps them separate, but get these droplets too close to one another, and they coalesce. That's what you do when you graft a branch; you draw worlds close together, punch through the surface-tension barrier – and two droplets become one. Basically we've found how to make a particular drop resonate based on its constituents, based on the outcome of the reality within that world."

"So, every drop of water is another world?" said Matt, "and you can locate a world by vibrating the water?"

He understood, but thought it better to play dumb.

"It's a metaphor Matt, Jesus!"

"But with this, you can locate anything?"

"Pretty much."

"So what do you need me for?"

"We can locate it Matt, but we can't see into and can't interact with it. We still need you, don't worry."

For now. But for how long?

CHAPTER 70

"What's changed?" Matthew Howard asked his father, "Tell me – tell me it all."

"OK, but like I said, you're not going to like it."

Tom began, telling Matt what The Commission had done since its establishment. Unlike many of the worlds that the *other-they's* had come from, the version in this world had been far more aggressive in driving through its ideas.

In this world, Hunter and Leighton-Jones had not been thrown out in disgrace. Between them, they had put into place a series of political manoeuvres which had shocked Tom, but unfortunately had not surprised him. Unlike the many worlds other than here, in this reality, Hunter had not sought to discredit The Commission. Instead, he had built it up to be the answer to all the authorities' problems, even the ones that they had never considered. In just over six months, since mandatory mental health profiling had been introduced, he had taken them from relative obscurity to autonomous control.

They had been helped…

Jacobson stared at the piece of paper as it lay on his kitchen table. For such a blandly worded letter, it still seemed to him to taunt him.

Why had he, last week, received an official government demand citing extra-ordinary powers under HM special regulations to attend the Branchford Institute? Why now? Why today? How had they found him? Had they got to Matt?

He didn't know. All he knew was that a car was scheduled to arrive for him and his father in the next hour.

At the stroke of eleven, a black jaguar saloon with darkened windows pulled to a halt outside the small terraced house the two of them shared.

Neither early nor late. Military precision.

"Come on then Dad," he said with an air of resignation and wheeled the old man out into the street. The car proceeded into the city, driven in silence.

Fine. That suited both him and his father. He had no desire to speak and no words to say anyway.

They were met by a thin man in a single-breasted suit, not at the Branchford Institute but at a nearby row of the Georgian buildings opposite a similarly grassy square. Instead of opening the door to let them out, however, he got in the front seat.

"To the Manor," he said curtly as the driver set off. The man turned in his seat. "I'm sure that you probably have questions. However, it's necessary for you to keep them until we arrive."

Just over an hour later they pulled up to the front of an imposing building – square, pillared and porticoed – which sat squat within its own estate. They were greeted by military personnel who led them towards a side door. The gravel was dense and rich, which made it difficult for Jacobson to wheel his father – to his relief the entrance opened to reveal the stainless-steel doors of a lift.

Inside, flanked by the thin man from the car, they were led to an ornate room with an oval table where there sat two other men, suited, older and thick set.

"Gentleman," began one of the men, "Welcome. You were asked here because we believe you may have a gift, a gift that is extremely valuable to both Her Majesty's government and also the country."

"We weren't exactly asked," mumbled Jacobson. His father quickly touched his arm to quiet him. None of the men in the room showed any indication that they had heard, though undoubtedly they had.

"For some months now, we have been analysing the population for *persons of interest*, persons whose medical records and psychological history suggest that we ought really to be talking to them. I know, that you know, what I'm referring to – know what I'm talking about, don't you? For instance, we haven't introduced ourselves, but that's because we don't need to, do we? So I ask you, what are our names?"

Jacobson nodded in resignation, in other worlds, they'd been introduced countless times over.

"You're Stevenson," he replied, "Rountree and Hunter."

"Thank you," Stevenson said slowly, "It's always so much easier when we have a degree of honesty. Now, what can you tell us about yourselves?"

The question was rhetorical, as before they had a chance to answer, Stevenson ran his finger down the report on the table in front of him and turned to Jacobson's father.

"Nikalus Jacobson, in 1948 you were institutionalised under the National Assistance Act following a number of severe schizophrenic episodes. Over the next ten years, it's reported that you claimed that 'this world wasn't how it was meant to be', that 'your children had been erased from existence' and that 'Anna, your wife and her family had been annihilated in Treblinka'. You further claimed to be a member of an 'anti-catastrophe-league' a government organisation which you purported could, and did, change reality. In '52 you claimed that the country had earlier been overrun by Stalin, that Churchill had mounted a foolhardy, abortive attack against Russia and that he had been killed – essentially it was all over, that is, until something changed history…"

The pain was apparent in Jacobson's furrowed brow. "Why do you keep telling me what I know already? Why do you want to torture a foolish old man in his wheelchair?"

"Why?" said Stevenson, "You know why – because these weren't just ravings, were they? They were all true, weren't they?"

"If you know all that, you also know that we were instructed by Churchill to support *Operation Unthinkable* but prepare to branch to a reality where in '45 the attack on Stalin never happened – a contingency called *Operation Overstrike*. Instead, however, there was a branch put in place which went back a lot, lot further, one which neither Churchill nor Mother would have ever sanctioned."

Jacobson bunched his hands into fists as he unhappily continued to speak. "I saw it coming but misjudged it. The country had gone to the wall, and so I thought the graft I could feel building was folded in from '45 – Overstrike, our so-called get-out-plan.

His eyes welled with tears, he sniffed, trying to dismiss them and wiped them away. "By the time it had happened, it was too late, it was all over – they were all gone, all of them. It had all changed, the organisation as we knew it no longer even existed, but more than that, it had never existed. I was considered a lunatic. But why am I telling *you* this? You know the rest."

The old man was a wreck. His son touched his arm to try to comfort him. "Has my father not suffered enough? What do you want from him? What's all this about?"

"This gift you have," said Stevenson, "It's as rare as hens' teeth, and in this world that we find ourselves in, enemies no longer fly a flag or wear colours. Nor do they affiliate in any meaningful manner to a sovereign state. Today's battlefield is *in the mind*, it is in the towns and the cities that we live in. Our enemies could be our neighbours, our friends, even our brothers and sisters. 9/11 and 7/7 showed us that we won't necessarily see it coming. It showed us that death comes to us with a smiling face, and that's why we *need* people like you. Just as importantly, we need people like you to be with us, because if you're not *with* us…"

Stevenson left the implication hanging. Jacobson looked at him, the weight of inevitability thickening the air between them.

So this is where it ends up, he thought, *this is where everything is reduced to absolute terms, this is where freedom dies. You're either with us, or you're against us. And if you're not with us…*

"Let's just say that that would make you a risk that would need to be managed… or if-needs-be, neutralised."

Jacobson felt his rage rising. Threats were not something that he had ever responded to well. As if feeling this, his father once again touched his arm to calm him.

"But Gentlemen, surely we're all on the same side here," the old man said and smiled. "Surely we are all friends, all with different objectives but ultimately the same goal. How may we help?"

As if on cue, Hunter opened his briefcase and took out five identical folders which he distributed. "This, gentlemen, is how you can help," he said. "This is what we need. In this dossier, you will find a description of the challenge. What we need your help with is branching to a particular reality. One where a very particular set of events happen, one where we are able to give the country the leadership and protection it needs. In the reality I'm referring to, over the next six months, this organisation will be central in foiling a number of extremely serious terrorist plots. It will also expose galling revelations about both the leader of the opposition and core members of the cabinet which will lead them to tender their resignations. We will demonstrate, beyond doubt, that we are fundamentally able to operate above any and all intelligence agencies, domestic or otherwise. We will demonstrate this by uncovering things about the prime minister which he will prefer us not to reveal, and we will be granted leave to operate and make legislation without consulting parliament.

"Global technology vendors will collaborate on what will become known as the *human condition*. Artificial intelligence and vast amounts of raw processing power will be contributed in order to understand and help with the growing challenge that is mental health. One implementation of this AI will be an app which acts as an electronic counsellor. It will be incredibly popular – however it will actually be a front to monitor and discover channellers like yourself."

"You can't be serious, you can't just pick and choose fate, and anyway even if you could, what you want is impossible," said Jacobson. "How do you expect us to find something that specific? That's not how it works."

"Maybe not searching by hand, but we already have a certain amount of technology backing us up. We can find the world, you just need to get us there."

"And why would we do that?" asked Jacobson.

"To get to the truth," replied Stevenson, "to get even, to get revenge. Once we're plumbed into the system we'll get you access to whatever information you want, we'll help you track down the truth about what happened to your family. If we can, we'll find who ordered it."

"How will you know to keep your word?" said the old man. "After all in the world you describe, none this would have happened."

Jacobson was stunned, "Dad, you can't be serious."

"Simple," began Hunter ignoring him, "at the start of the year we established orders that, should a channeller present to us a series of keywords and should the keywords match the situation we were currently experiencing, then that would be sufficient to imply assistance. Presentation of the final keyword would represent a promise."

Jacobson grabbed his father's arm and shook his head.

"And what are the words?" continued his father.

"Master of fate and – *anything,*" said Stevenson.

Jacobson looked at his father in horror. *Could he actually be considering helping Hunter? Consider assisting with this madness? For what? Not to change anything, just to try to pull back the curtain on something that should be left well alone. He needed to let sleeping dogs lie. Couldn't he see that?*

"Dad, I won't let you."

However, before he could act further, the thin man placed himself between the pair and ushered the younger Jacobson out of the room.

"Don't worry," said Hunter, "he'll be perfectly fine."

"So, where were we…"

CHAPTER 71

Matthew Howard sat back after he had listened to his father relate the story.

"So, how do you know this?"

"Memories, from Jacobson and his father himself, notes I'd taken at the time. It's a jumble, but I've had a week to try to sort it out in my head."

"How much power does The Commission hold?" he asked.

"It may as well be absolute Matt, they are becoming plumbed into everything. They have the PM by the short-and-curlies, and just about every prospective or potential channeller is on their radar from this app thing."

"What about Jacobson? How much of a risk is he?"

"They're still both dead Matt. We're safe in that respect, but for how long I don't know."

"How did it happen, the lift and then an escape attempt?"

"I don't know Matt. To be honest, I'm so mashed that I've no idea if that's what happened."

"What, you think there's something else?"

"I don't know Matt, I just don't know anymore. What I do know is that Hunter and Stevenson have it all pretty much sewn up between them. But it's worse than that. They're talking about bringing in a health tax. Basically everyone is taxed, and you get a rebate if you can prove you're taking steps to be as healthy as you can be – but in reality, it's a smokescreen for encouraging schizophrenics to be fitted with what they're calling an inhibitor."

"Like what they did to Jacobson."

"That's my understanding; yes. But they're selling it as some great benefit to society. Basically, anyone who is young and obese is taxed out of existence – there're so many conditions within the scope of the tax that the one they're actually interested in is hidden in plain sight. They're making it mandatory for all adults to be fitted with some kind of device, either RFID or NFC, that monitors bio-signs.

However it's a Trojan Horse – the devices can be used as inhibitors."

First they came for the socialists… thought Matt. "We need to do something," he said.

"Let *me* worry about that." Tom said decisively.

CHAPTER 72

Thomas Howard looked out of the window of his home, at the greenhouse at the bottom of his garden. *What he would give to be the man he once was, to be ignorant of this.* The greenhouse, as dilapidated as it was, had fallen into complete disrepair, and ironically now had more things growing in it than before.

Ethan, now six, was playing happily on the rug to the side of him. Barbara was in the kitchen. In the intervening years his and Matt's silence about what exactly they did had turned Jane and Barbara from, at best, acquaintances, to firm friends, and as a result the younger couple had moved within a stone's throw of Tom and Barbara.

He felt a gentle hand on his shoulder moving, forwards and back. "You look tired, and worried," said Barbara. "What is it?"

"It's the world, Babs," he muttered, "just the world."

If this made any kind of sense to her, she didn't show it. However, unlike the old days, she had long since given up asking questions, and instead, simply accepted his answer.

Tom looked again out of the window and mentally closed the door on Barbara, shutting her out. It wasn't intentional, it was just that he needed some clarity. *He needed to do something, but what?* Most of all though, he was determined not to breathe a word to anyone, not even Matt. *He couldn't risk them suspecting anything.*

Loose lips…

The easiest way was going to be to go public. But where or how?

A knock on the door snapped him out of his thoughts, and he heard Barbara answer it. "Yes, he's through there…"

Looking up he saw the face of a man he thought he recognised as one of the staff from the Manor. "Yes?" he said, but before he could say more, he noticed a Taser in the man's hands and heard Barbara's screams as he went down and blacked out.

CHAPTER 73

Thomas Howard blinked as he slowly came around.

Where was he? He tried to raise his right hand to move and found it restrained, his left hand and ankles too. *What had happened to him?*

For the first time in what seemed like years there was an utter silence in his mind – it was as still and clear as glass.

He lay flat on his back and took in what he could of the room he now occupied. It was white, floor to ceiling, except for a light grey tubular steel institutional bed – and it was to this that he was restrained.

This room.

He recognised it immediately as the institution he'd seen so many times before, but this time it felt different.

He looked to his left to feel a tightness at the base of his skull which made his heart sink.

An inhibitor. But why? And why now?

Before he had a chance to think more the door unlocked and what Tom assumed were doctors entered, accompanied by Fellowes.

"What's going on?" he said, "Where am I?"

"You're at the Manor, Tom," she said.

"Why?"

"I'm sorry Tom, we had no choice. It was nothing personal."

"What do you mean, nothing personal? It feels pretty personal from here."

"I'm sorry about this, but you shouldn't have gone to the press, Tom." Stevenson stood in the door flanked by Hunter.

What were they talking about? He hadn't done anything. Had he?

"But I didn't *do* anything," he whined, thrashing about, attempting fruitlessly to sit up, the restraints holding him down.

"But that's where you're wrong Thomas," chided Hunter,

his eyes as cold as those of a snake.

"You did it a thousand times over, maybe not here, but you did it all the same, again and again, in other worlds, across the RIFT."

"But *I* didn't do it," he said, pleading now. "If that happened at all, that wasn't me."

"They're all *you* Thomas," Hunter whispered. "Just because *you* didn't do it doesn't mean you wouldn't."

Thomas Howard couldn't believe what he was hearing. "But *I* didn't do anything."

Stevenson stepped in, "Tom, I know this is hard to hear, but you have been detained under one of our special regulations – under the new Propensity to Act provisions."

"The what?"

"Earlier this year, The Commission was granted special powers to do whatever is necessary to keep this country safe. You know that. These powers granted an extension to the Terrorism Prevention and Investigation Measures Act whereby this Commission can issue a 'determination of intervention' – which, by definition, is law."

"So, you're issuing edicts now?" snapped Tom. "Who do you think you are?"

"We're the people who keep the public safe at night Tom. If you ask most people, they don't want to live in some idealistic society, they just want to get-by, have an easy life. They want to be safe and secure, and if some things need to go to the wall, so be it."

"What do you mean, go to the wall?"

"Well, take security, I agree that terrorism is a marginal issue within ethnic minorities, I agree that most are good citizens, but the consequences of not catching the terrorists are huge. Most people just want to be safe. That is democracy."

"What are you saying?"

"I'm saying that we define what good looks like and, if you want to live here, you conform. It's better for everyone in the long-run."

"So, what's going to happen to me?"

"Well, that's up to you. In time you'll come to believe that all of this was part of one of your episodes, and if you can convince us that you can conform then there'll be no reason for you to remain here. Although your work at the Manor is now over, or rather, it never happened."

"What? What about Matt?"

"Let us worry about that. We'll deal with Matt."

As Hunter finished speaking a nurse arrived at the door.

"Sir, you're behind on your rounds and you said that you have a *hard-stop* today."

"Yes of course thank you, Kathy. Howard – Kathy will look after you until you're discharged. I won't see you again. If you go, have a good life."

Kathy...

With a sense of mounting horror, Thomas Howard realised that this was now his home.

CHAPTER 74

Matthew Howard had arrived at his parents' house only hours after Stevenson had called him. "You might as well hear it from me as anyone else," he'd said, "but we've had to inhibit your father to stop him going public. Don't make us do the same with you."

He'd tried to protest but the line had gone dead.

Knowing his father had been at home, he worried about his mother. She had called earlier, saying that Tom had been taken. If they had indeed taken him, she would be a wreck. Tired, he had arrived after a long drive at their house and let himself in.

"Oh, hello Matt," she said, "what brings you here."

Matt was taken aback.

"You called me Mum, earlier this afternoon."

"I don't think so dear, I'm sure I'd have remembered. It's nice to see you though, would you like a cup of tea?"

What was wrong with her?

"Never mind that, Mum. Where's Dad?"

"You know where he is Matt, he's been doing very well after the procedure, they say, and I hope to see him back soon."

"What procedure? What are you talking about?"

Matt was getting desperate now. *What was wrong with his mother? What had happened to her?*

"Matt, we talked about this, both you and your father have been getting progressively worse, like Joe was, and the institute offered him a treatment normally only available in America. He's been doing very well after the procedure, they say."

"Mum, you said they came for him, they took him."

"That's right dear, they did, although hopefully, he's only going to be gone a couple of weeks though. Do you want me to give your father a message?"

Matthew Howard quietly stood there is disbelief.

What had they done to her? Why was she acting as if none of this was amiss? Why was what she said about his father's procedure familiar? Had he invented the conversation with Stevenson?

Was any of it real?

CHAPTER 75

Thomas Howard looked up from his bed at the nurse busying herself around him. "So – what happens now?" he asked.

"You're monitored for a few days, and then… Well let's just see, shall we? You've had a bit of an ordeal after all."

"You say that like I'm not the first *one like me* you've had through here."

"There's Simon and you," she said. "Mr Hunter says that before we helped you there were all sorts of voices in your head, but now you'll have some peace."

Simon… why did he know that name?

"And what does… Simon think of being here?"

"I wish we knew…"

"Alright, should we get you out of those restraints?"

The question almost surprised Tom.

Was he supposed to answer?

Before he could, the nurse banged on the door for attention. "271 requesting assistance removing restraints from patient Thomas Howard," she called through the small hatch that had slid open in the door. There was some exchange that Tom didn't catch, other than to hear the nurse reply with a single word – "Hammersmith."

The door unlocked and two male staff members entered the room. "Alright then, Tom. These gentlemen are here to help me remove your restraints, now you're not going to give us any problems, are you?"

"You needn't worry," sighed Tom, "the fight's gone out of me."

"You'd be surprised…" she replied, then released his straps under the watchful eye of the two orderlies and helped him sit up.

"That's better isn't it?" She handed him a dressing gown and a pair of slippers. "There'll be an assessment later, but for the minute, you can watch TV in the dayroom if you like."

Thomas Howard lurched to his feet, realising for the first time just how groggy he was, and followed the nurse along the corridor, all the time being escorted tightly by her helpers. As they turned into the room, the nurse greeted an older man who was crumpled and twisted sideways in an electric wheelchair.

"Hello Simon," she said, "How are we today?"

The man never moved an inch, but his eyes were wild, darting backwards and forwards. He looked for all the world like a dishevelled madman, but Tom felt a pang of recognition. "Jacobson? Is that you?"

It was Jacobson, Tom was sure of it. But if it was, his question didn't raise an answer. The man's eyes just widened even more and stared back at Tom.

CHAPTER 76

Thomas Howard blinked as he slowly came around.

Where was he? He tried to raise his right hand to rub his face and found it constrained, his left hand and ankles too. *What had happened to him? Hadn't he been here, only hours before?*

Again, there was an utter silence in his mind – it was as still and clear as glass.

He lay flat on his back and just as before took in what he could of the room.

It was white, floor to ceiling, except for the light grey tubular steel institutional bed to which he was restrained.

He looked to his left to feel a tightness at the base of his skull which made his heart sink.

An inhibitor.

He remembered now; *they wanted to silence him.*

He'd been here before. Hadn't he?

Before he had a chance to think more, the door unlocked and what Tom assumed were doctors entered, accompanied by Fellowes.

"What's going on?" he said. "Where am I?"

"You're at the institute Tom," she said.

"Why?"

"You should remember in due course, Tom, but you were having seizures. Which is why you and Barbara elected for you to be fitted with a chip to inhibit your symptoms."

"Why do I feel like we've had this conversation before?"

"Because, in a sense, you have, Tom. Unfortunately, last time the chip wasn't functioning, and you attacked one of our other patients."

Was that true?

"Is he OK?"

"Shaken up, but yes."

As Fellowes was speaking the familiar face of the nurse appeared at the door.

"Sir, you're behind on your rounds and you have a hard-stop today."

"Yes of course thank you, Kathy. Tom – Kathy will look after you until you're discharged."

"When did the institute get a ward?" he asked her.

"You're a lot calmer than the last time we met," she said. "To answer your question, it has always had one." She looked at him strangely. "You really don't remember any of it, do you?"

"What do you mean?"

"You've been coming here since just after your grandson was born. Since you started having your episodes."

Tom's heart began to pound within his chest.

What he was hearing sounded wrong, like she was trying to trick him. But why? There was no deceit in her eyes and what she was saying resonated with him deeply. He'd been here before. He'd been here many times. And he knew Kathy well.

"What about The Commission?" he asked.

"The Commission is a fabrication, Tom. Like I said before – you'll remember that in due course."

"So how do *you* know about it?"

She sighed, "Tom, again, the name only means anything to me because of previous conversations that we've had."

"I can't accept that. How can it not be real?"

Thomas Howard struggled against the rising tide of consciousness which rolled into his psyche – fragments of conversation flickering and glowing like embers in his mind.

"Let's break it down," she said. "Tell me again about The Commission. What do they do?"

"That's easy," he replied, "They manipulate reality to influence outcomes and use their abilities to aid the government. They were meant to be a force for good. Meant to be…"

"And you believe that you were a part of this?"

"Yes, exactly, and so was Jacobson."

"So what you're saying is that you and Simon are part of some secret 'time spy' organisation? What next? *Thunderbirds are go?*"

It sounded ludicrous when she said it like this.

"OK, then answer this," he said, "If all of that has been a lie, how have I been paid all this time?" Tom sat back in his bed and scowled.

How dare they try to tell him none of his recent past was true?

"Thomas, we've been through this," the nurse explained, exasperation now showing for the first time. "When your father died he left a sizeable estate for you and your son."

"Dad, had nothing," he replied – but what she had just said sounded strangely familiar.

"Yes, it was a surprise to you, at the time," she agreed, "but I can assure you that you have not been being paid by some James Bond-style secret organisation."

"It was hardly James Bond," said Tom, scoffing.

"But how plausible is it?" she asked. "What's more likely, you having delusional episodes... or that you and the rest of... the rest of this *Justice League* being able to alter the very fabric of the universe by merely wishing it?"

"I could prove it to you, if I didn't have this... *thing.*"

"Ah yes, the high-tech anti-timewarp device, which is also strangely available on the NHS?"

It sounded absurd. What was true? How could he tell? Could everything he thought of as his journey to this point be a lie?

His mind swarmed with a million different versions of the past.

Could he really have been that separated from reality? Did that mean that Ethan was, all along, never in danger?

But he was never alone in this. There was Matt. Matt would know the truth of it.

After all, blood was thicker than water.

CHAPTER 77

"What's happened to my father?"

Matthew Howard looked hard into Rountree's eyes before asking again. "My father; what's happened? What have you done with him?"

Eli Rountree looked at Matt compassionately and gently placed a hand on his upper arm. Rountree's tenderness rattled him. "Come-in Matt, sit down. If you recall, we talked about this last week. Like yourself, Tom's delusions have been getting worse, and we suggested the same treatment for both of you. You mother was here too Matt. Try to remember. Tom said he wanted to undergo surgery. His words were, 'We need to do something. I need to do something.'"

The words were certainly familiar, but Matt felt had different memories attached to them. *Or did he?*

He was so confused. His mind was so fragmented and shattered that he struggled to recall anything.

"What do you mean *last week*?"

A look of shock crossed Rountree's face.

"Matt, you've been attending this clinic on a weekly basis for a number of years. You were making excellent progress, focusing on your son and father. Are you saying you have no memory of that?"

Matt just looked at him.

What was Rountree trying to do? Was Stevenson putting him up to this?

"What about The Commission, the Manor? What about the RIFT?"

Rountree shook his head. "I'm sorry Matt, the Manor, as you call it, is real enough, but it's a psychiatric retreat. No more, no less. The rest, as we've discussed many times, is purely a figment of your imagination."

Matt shook his head from side to side. *He couldn't accept it.*

"If it's a figment of my so-called imagination then how do

you know what I'm talking about? Answer that."

Rountree sighed. "Matt, this is hardly the first time we've had this conversation, and I very much doubt it will be the last. You've related these stories a number of times, however, more recently, I thought you'd made progress and begun to be able to see them for what they are."

Matthew Howard didn't know what to believe. His very being and his internal moral compass screamed at him that he was being spun a lie, but looking into Rountree's face, he failed to see any deceit.

Could it really be that it was all just a fabrication? He needed to see Tom, speak to him.

"Where *is* my father," he said.

CHAPTER 78

Matthew Howard looked across the table at Eli Rountree. "Where *is* my father," he said.

"I'm sorry Matt, but I thought you knew. He's here and has been all along."

"What do you mean 'here'?" shouted Matt. "Strangely, I can't see him."

"Matt, when I say 'here', I don't literally mean here," Rountree replied, opening his hands to indicate around the room, "I mean here at the institute, in the medical wing next door."

Matt's head was spinning.

Did he know about that? He couldn't tell. If he did, why could he not recall it? If he didn't why was it suddenly so familiar?

What he did feel was a growing sense of discomfort with the whole situation, and that included his own sense of being.

He felt like he wanted to scream but had no voice, as if he was about to vomit but had no mouth. He felt like a fraud, with no confidence in which direction the conversation should go, as if he was an empty vessel cast out on a sea of uncertainty and disbelief.

He knew these thoughts weren't constructive but that didn't help him. It was like when Jane told him to *snap out of it*, they were like words in the wind.

But snap out of what? Where was this train of thought going?

Again and again, the incessant chattering within his mind clamoured at the doors of his self-control – he needed to focus, keep the badness boxed off, but he needed to do so without forcing it. Force things too far, and it all goes to hell.

He felt the panic rise in his chest and he fought to suppress it. "If he's here, where is he? Can I see him?"

Rountree's attitude seemed to suddenly soften. "Of course you can Matt, but I need you to promise not to upset him.

Remember he's not long since had a procedure, and the last thing he needs is to be upset."

Matt didn't know what to say, he had so many questions, but holding back a little longer wouldn't change things.

"OK," he said, "I won't upset him, but if you're playing me…"

The two of them left by the front door and entered one of the buildings on the left. Although the outside of the building maintained the Georgian theme of the square, the inside was clinical and modern, decorated to a high standard in neutral colours. "At least it's not the Victorian asylum I was expecting," he muttered, still annoyed.

Rountree shook his head in apparent amusement.

"What?" asked Matt.

"Matt, you never fail to amaze me – you say that every time you come here. Come. Your father should be up and about."

Matt followed Rountree through a set of glazed doors, behind which was a small reception area.

"Hello Kelly," he said, addressing the man behind the plinth, "I'm just taking Matt to see his father – Howard in room seven."

"Hi Eli," he said, "He's doing really well, actually up and about. He's in the dayroom with Simon and Kathy."

Matt followed Rountree down the corridor, where they found his father sitting behind a round table, thumbing through a copy of the day's paper while half-watching TV.

"Dad! Are you OK?" asked Matt as soon as he saw him.

"I think so Matty," he replied weakly. "They tell me I'm doing very well."

It was his father, but also not his father. It was like the lights had dimmed in his eyes – he was a shadow of his former self. His voice had none of the rich timbres that Matt recalled, and as he sat Matt noticed that Tom had developed a slight shake.

"How are you in yourself, Dad?" he said.

Tom Howard looked at his son, and Matt saw sorrow in his eyes. "It's silent Matty, like you wouldn't believe. It's like there's only me in here," tapping his temple, "and that's… difficult."

But the silence was also… wonderful.

"They tell me I was having issues, but Matty I don't remember. All I know is that my mind feels flat. It's like there's no colour, no flavour, no richness. It's like I'm an old TV at the end of the day and all that's left is the little white dot after the national anthem has played out."

Matthew Howard reached out for his father's hands, clasping them between his own. "Dad, we will get through this."

"Tell me one thing Matt – was it all a delusion like they say it was? All of it? How could it be and seem so real?"

Matthew Howard looked across the table at his father. *What could he say?* He could feel Rountree's eyes burrowing into the back of his head.

'Don't upset him' Rountree had said, and he'd agreed. If they had each been suffering similar episodes, then fanning the flames was the last thing he should do. But if it were real, what did that mean?

It was impossible.

He had so many conflicting memories, in both directions, that there was no way to know. Even if the reality of their experiences were confirmed, one-way or another, he was a mess of uncertainty, and likely wouldn't know if this now was reality or fiction in half an hour's time.

"Honestly dad, I'm probably the last person to ask," he sighed shaking his head, "What I can tell you is that I'm having issues myself, that I'm struggling, Dad. I know that much."

It was true, his head was a contradiction at almost every level. It was either the juxtaposition of thousands of different conflicting realities – side effects of being a master-navigator of different worlds, or he was a nut job. In any case, he had no way to tell, and he only had a tenuous grip on reality. He did know which answer was more likely.

Matthew Howard looked into the RIFT and, as ever, became aware of the space in the world where Ethan would have been. The panic-stricken face that he presented to his father said it all.

What should he believe? Who was there that could validate any of this?

"You need to concentrate on getting well Dad, not on anything else. Save other thoughts for another day."

Rountree smiled, seemingly satisfied with Matt's performance and appeared ready to leave, when a nurse entered wheeling in another patient.

"Do you remember Simon, Matt?"

Matthew Howard looked at the man in the wheelchair and realised, with a degree of shock, that it was Jacobson. But this was not the Jacobson from his memory. Gone was the pirate-like swagger. Instead Jacobson half-lay in a wheelchair, scrunched up, unable to sit straight.

Had any of the interactions that he remembered happened?

Had they broken bread together, placed bugging devices at the Institute? Had Jacobson killed his father, ever been killed in another reality, or ever even been shot?

Matthew Howard silently stood transfixed and looked at what he'd thought of as his erstwhile friend who now sat slumped in front of him, little more than a broken pile of bones.

Had they done that to him, or had he always been like that?

Did Jacobson remember him?

"I do, but I don't," he began. "I remember him differently." *It was very confusing.* "Has he always been, you know, like this?"

"Yes and no," said Rountree, "In the way I think you mean, yes – but until recently he was a lot more lucid. Until he suffered several seizures. You two talked regularly – do you not remember?"

Matt thought…

Yes…

No…

"Maybe," he said, "I don't know. I don't know anything anymore." His heart raced, and he leaned inward to look at Jacobson's face, "Do you remember me?" he asked desperately.

Jacobson's body was slumped, but his eyes glared wildly before flickering back and forth. Suddenly he grabbed Matt by the arm and pulled him close. Then in a hoarse whisper, he rasped, "Hope – dice."

The words hit Matthew Howard hard, causing a flurry of images to detonate in the front of his mind. For the briefest of instants he saw all of them – Tom, Joe, himself, family around them – wheeling an oversized lemon-yellow pushchair through an idyllic-looking park. But just as he'd seen it, it was gone.

What was Jacobson trying to tell him?

"What happened to him?" Matt asked Rountree as they were leaving the ward.

"How do you mean?"

"Well I remember him as a relatively-fit individual – not like he is now."

"Like I said, he was a lot more lucid until recently he suffered a stroke – but he's always been like that Matt, for as long as you've known him."

"After his seizures you mean?"

"Yes, after his seizures – there was also a stroke."

Matt was unconvinced.

"Has he ever walked? You know, before he was shot?"

"No, Matt he's never walked or been shot… Where is this coming from Matt?"

They'd reached the door, and Matt meant to leave. Rountree, however, reached for it, as if about to open it, but then stopped.

"He said something to you, Matt, 'Hope dies'. What did he mean by that?"

"I've no idea, to be honest. 'Hope dies' who knows what that meant," replied Matt.

It was a lie – He knew precisely what Jacobson had meant. Or at least he thought he did.

He hadn't said hope dies. He'd told him to not give up hope – to prove he had the gift, using something as simple as dice.

Rountree paused, looking at him, as if trying to work him out. "OK then, See you next time then Matt. You be careful out there."

CHAPTER 79

Matthew Howard hurried along the London streets towards Covent Garden tube station. Although he didn't know what to believe, he knew he wanted to get as far away from the Institute as possible, and do so as fast as possible.

He reached the Oxblood-tiled station and entered it. With its lack of escalators, he always thought this station strange. Today he was met by staff in the process of shutting the entrance.

"We're closing-down the route in ten minutes, sir, to work on the lift – so you'll have to be quick."

Matt nodded and proceeded to the lift, while the guard repeated the same information to another man behind him. A thickset man entered the elevator beside Matt as the doors closed.

"Just made it eh?" said Matt as the lift began its journey. If the man had heard him, there was no sign of it. He only stood there in silence. Matt shrugged. *Life was too short to worry about such things.*

Leaving the lift, the two of them joined the platform, they must have just missed a train, since, save for the two of them, the station was completely empty. The scrolling LED screen told him the next train was in two minutes.

Not long to wait now.

The man from the elevator sat down slowly on the plastic seat by the wall. For some reason Matt chose to stand – although he couldn't put his finger on it, there was something about the man he didn't trust. Maybe it was the way he'd blanked him in the lift. Maybe it was the man's bulky frame that unnerved him, but there was definitely something.

Looking up, he made sure he was in the view of the station camera. He glanced at the clock.

One minute.

Matthew Howard stood in the centre of the platform and waited for the train, while in his head he planned out his next steps. What he needed was clarity, and Jacobson had given him the key. When he reached King's Cross he was going to the toy shop, Hamley's in St. Pancras, where he would get some dice and a notebook.

Then he would see.

On the train home, if he were able to throw twenty sixes in a row, then he would know.

Then he'd know the truth.

Hope.

Dice.

Hope… Why did that word ring in his ears? What was there about it? 'Hope'…

The rush of air on his face and the sound of the incoming train roused him from his thoughts and he stooped to pick up his bag from the platform beside him.

Still no other passengers.

The emptiness bothered him.

Strange he shrugged – *maybe they'd closed down the entrance sooner.*

As Matt straightened up, he saw the train's light at the end of the station. Suddenly, a massive shove to the small of his back pushed him over the side of the platform and into the gap between the rails.

What the hell!

Panicking, he found himself on the sleeper, inches from the probably electrified tracks, looking into the lights of the oncoming tube train. The pit was at least three feet deep, if not more, and there was no time to try to climb out.

No time to consider how he'd got there.

His only chance was to graft. His only chance was the RIFT…

Matthew Howard stared at the oncoming tube train lights…

There wouldn't be time to be picky. If he wanted to live, he'd have to take any reality that he could.

Looking into the RIFT he searched for an alternate…

Anything.

In one he saw himself on the platform, face to face with his would-be attacker. Reasoning anything would be better than this he grabbed at the man's jacket in that reality and crossed the RIFT.

Thomas Howard and Simon Jacobson sat across the table from Rountree.

"It was nice to see Matty again, wasn't it?"

Tom nodded, but Jacobson merely seemed to make a low growling noise.

"Don't be like that Simon," scolded Rountree, "I know, shall we turn the local news on? See what is happening? You never know," he said ominously, "someone we know might be on..."

CHAPTER 80

Matthew Howard faced his attacker as the wave of memories rewound and flooded into place.

One minute.

Matthew Howard stood in the centre of the platform and awaited the train. In his head he planned out his next steps.

A feeling of déjà vu flooded his senses. *Had he been here before?* He shook his head.

What he needed was clarity, and Jacobson had given him the key. When he reached King's Cross he was going to the toy shop, Hamley's in St. Pancras, where he would get some dice and a notebook.

Then he would see.

On the train home, if he were able to throw twenty sixes in a row, then he would know.

Then he'd know the truth.

'Dice.'

'Hope.'

'Hope...'

The rush of air on his face and the sound of the incoming train roused him from his thoughts, and he stooped to pick up his bag from the platform beside him.

Still no other passengers

Strange he shrugged – *maybe they'd closed down the entrance sooner.*

As Matt straightened up, he saw the train's light at the end of the station.

He was suddenly aware of a massive shove to the small of his back that pushed him across the platform, almost shoving him into the pit and onto the gap between the rails.

Almost but not quite.

What the hell!

Panicking he had twisted round and found himself looking face to face with the man from the elevator, finding himself clinging to the left lapel of the man's jacket with his right hand. That was all that had saved him. His heart raced so quickly it felt like it was about to leap out of his chest. The man wasn't larger than Matt, but he was definitely fitter.

What now, what could he do?

Matt shoved the man backwards, but it was like trying to move a brick wall.

The man glanced down at Matt's right hand with an expression of contempt, and in a single fluid-motion struck Matt in the face with his right elbow before peeling his hand off his jacket.

Matt felt pain shoot like electricity from his wrist to his elbow, and like a ragdoll felt his body being wrenched round. His assailant straightened Matt's arm, twisting his fingers up like he was opening a fan before applying yet more pressure. Grabbing his neck from behind, he began marching Matt to the pit in front of the oncoming train.

Matthew Howard knew that unless he did something immediately he was undoubtedly going to die. He saw himself in the pit, remembered himself there. Beneath him, he saw his feet autonomously walking towards the edge of the platform and heard the train approach.

This was it.

If he could stay away from the edge, that would be enough. With that in mind, he let his feet buckle under him, and with a certain degree of inevitability, let his face crumple into the concrete of the platform. He felt the cold hard surface followed by pain as his forehead collided with the ground. He tried to flatten himself out and get as low as possible, to make himself as immovable as he could. With his fingers and toes, he attempted to edge himself backwards.

The man who had him in a wristlock grunted as he was pulled forward and down. He tried to push Matt forward, but Matt had made himself a dead weight. Matt felt the man let go of his arm and try to grab his collar and the back of his belt. He wriggled to try to get free and rolled onto his back, drawing his feet up in front of himself. Frantically he kicked and kicked at the man, striking his assailant's hands and shins.

The man grabbed hold of his left leg and pulled Matt around, meaning to tow him towards the gap. But Matt made it as hard as he could, continuing to kick at the man's hand as he felt himself being dragged towards the edge. He could see that his blows were skinning his assailant's hands – bloodying the man's fingers to pulp. However this did not seem to dissuade him.

Holding on to Matt's leg, the man reached the edge of the platform – but it was *too little, too late.* The tube train pulled into the station, and curious faces now watched out of the window.

Looking up, the man realised that his means and opportunity had now passed. Dropping Matt's leg, he turned on his heels and fled from the platform, heading up the stairs towards the lifts.

Matthew Howard heaved a sigh of relief. He was alive.

But what was that about? Were he ever to find out he needed to follow, and follow now.

Climbing to his feet, he followed towards the lifts to see the doors of the leftmost lift closing. Piling into the lift next to it, he steadied himself against the metal sides as the lift began to ascend.

Seconds ticked by as his mind spun, trying to make sense of what had just happened.

A stranger had just tried to throw him under a train. It must be The Commission. Nothing else made sense.

Spots of blood on the lift floor caused him to raise a hand to his head. When he brought it down it was ruddy.

He was hurt? Was he concussed? He couldn't tell. He felt weak, but that would have to wait. He needed answers.

Exiting the lift, he lurched out onto Long Acre and spotted the coat of the man on the far side of a zebra crossing. Reeling from side to side, he staggered after him with singular focus.

The man looked back and saw Matt doggedly approaching him.

Whether it was determination, tunnel vision or single-mindedness which caused him to fail to notice the large, fast-moving yellow delivery van, he would never know. However stepping out into its path was the last thing, in this world, that Matthew James Howard would ever do.

CHAPTER 81

"I'm so sorry for your loss, I really am," said Rountree, "They say he just stepped out, and it would have been instant, not that that's much consolation."

Jane Howard looked down and hugged the small child she held in her arms, hugging him like she was frightened of losing him, frightened of losing the only part of Matt she had left.

She had cried for the best part of a week, and there would be more tears to come, but for now, she was determined to be strong.

She lovingly stroked Ethan's head to comfort them both, staring out into the distance. "Thank you Eli," she said, "I know you helped him immensely, and Tom also."

They stood on the exposed point where the crematorium sat and looked out across the valley. It was as beautiful as it was wild. Matt had always loved this part of the world – that's why they had come here to say goodbye.

Barbara and Tom drew up beside them, Tom patting Ethan's head and kissing Jane on the cheek. "It was a nice service," he said.

"Yes," mouthed Jane. There were no words which could express her and Ethan's loss.

Tom was home, doing well and looking forward to making progress with his garden. Although he'd had no memory of it, he'd not worked regularly since Ethan had been born, having been signed off with long-term psychiatric issues.

Matt's death weighed heavily on him.

Eli Rountree felt no remorse. They'd done what they'd had to do. However, from the moment he'd received the text simply stating *it's done*, he'd not looked forward to this inevitable day.

"It's a terrible thing when parents bury their children," he said, finally.

CHAPTER 82

HAMPSHIRE APPROXIMATELY 10 YEARS LATER

"He would have been so proud of how you've turned out, Ethan."

Jane Howard rubbed her son's arm and tearfully gave him a hug as they sat in Tom and Barbara's front room.

Almost a decade had passed, and many things had changed beyond recognition. Following Matt's death, Jane had taken Ethan to be close to her own parents in Hartlepool, but it had never been the same. Without Matt, life just seemed to be one prolonged malaise to be endured. She didn't feel like she was living, she felt like she was merely existing, and to make things even more unfair, in the last year both of her parents had died. It was as if they were being picked off.

First to go was Anne, her mother, suffering a stroke in November. It diminished the woman Jane knew to nothing, before finally taking her away completely the following February.

Then there was her father, who had struggled on without 'his Annie', but finally seemed to lose all will to live. By the May he was gone too.

She and Ethan had managed to cope, the two of them, but then followed the cruellest news of all. The day it happened, Jane Howard had just begun self-scanning her goods at the rundown supermarket and had presented the chip in her arm to request authorisation of her selected foods. As normal, the checkout *traffic-lit* her selections and disallowed a good number of them based on her bio-signs.

That was the positive side, Jane thought. *They were trying to keep us healthy, reduce cost on the system; but it was an imposition – what had happened to freedom?*

In the last ten years, there had been one diktat after another for the *so-called* common good. It had started slowly, but then the rate had become frightening. Swathes of the populace had been deported, those from an ethnic minority suspected of even the slightest connection with fundamentalism had been shipped off, regardless of how tenuous the link. *Guilt by association*? It made her sick. She'd lost friends, good friends – all in the name of the so-called common good.

Strangest of all was the people's lack of objection to any of these changes – it was all just accepted.

Any mention of religion had been removed from the state and with churches of all flavours being boarded up, it had all but disappeared.

And it was all just accepted.

Borders had been tightened and all trade strictly regulated. Almost all non-formal ties with the outside world had been severed. The country had literally pulled up the drawbridge and become an insular state.

And it was all just accepted.

Visitors were still allowed but were tightly controlled. Foreign Students were housed in dedicated communities only being allowed to leave campus if escorted by the authorities.

When she told Ethan of the freedoms she had as a child, he found it hard to believe. Life without the curfew was something he just didn't comprehend.

The treatment of people, its borders and lack of freedom should have been the economic death of the country, but somehow, in contrast to the view of every expert and every pundit, the country continued to thrive as chains of irrationally bizarre behaviour and acceptance ran riot. It was completely improbable – as if the world was a stage and there was no free will.

Against all the odds, this isolationism appeared to give the country a cachet.

Apparently, Cool Britannia.

Time after time, the British government had stepped into international disputes and appeared to resolve them almost instantly. No one could explain it, nations reached agreements in the most improbable ways, while in the background there was always influence.

There were murmurs of leverage, of a secret organisation that had the British establishment by the balls. Nothing was public, but no one dared cross them.

Domestically, things had gone from bad to worse. One after another, a series of absolute decrees had been voted in, and the international community had seemingly rolled over and, not only let it happen, but willingly accepted it.

It had begun with compulsory mental health profiling, then there were the mandatory health implants. These were widely hated, but no one dared to speak out.

The state imposed strict controls on just about every avenue of life, and it was vanishingly rare that a family would not know of at least one person who had gone missing. Desperate families searched in vain on regulated social media for lost loved ones or by attaching posters to lampposts, but these were always removed, often within hours and they never lasted the day.

It was against this backdrop that further legislation had been passed to limit even the foods that could be bought. And it was because of this that Jane Howard was left with a meagre selection of provisions to pay for.

The state-run supermarket's lights flickered in the dimness. Since the restrictions had come into force, many well-known grocery brands had all but disappeared. *After all, when you can't sell what people want, what else can you do?* The state had stepped in, of course, but, since then, with little profit margin, nothing had been maintained, and it seemed each store was living on borrowed time.

She was tired and depressed, but more than that, she'd had enough. She was sick of this.

She swiped her implant again, this time for payment. It was then, without warning, that she collapsed, falling forward like someone dumping a heavy sack on to the stack of groceries. Almost as soon as she had fallen, the mass of her legs dragged her backwards, flopping her to the floor to lie motionless – a dead weight.

The doctor entered Jane's ward where she sat cross-legged on top of the bed, Ethan beside her holding her hand in his.

"It's OK you can tell me," she said. "It's bad isn't it?"

The expression on the woman's face said all she needed to know – the prognosis wasn't good.

"Mrs Howard…" she began and paused, the pain on her face evident.

She'd had a sinking feeling all day and her mood had got lower as the day had dragged on. "What is it? Cancer?" she asked.

The young doctor nodded almost imperceptibly.

"Where?"

She cleared her throat and began again, "Mrs Howard, you have an advanced malignant tumour at the base of your brain. Unfortunately, it's quite progressed."

"Can you fix it?"

She shook her head slowly. "I'm sorry," she said, "with the degree to which it has already spread, it's unlikely that any treatment would make a difference. You'd just be torturing yourself."

Jane Howard gripped the bed. She looked at Ethan, who had listened, dumbstruck. She wanted to scream out but felt too deflated to even raise her voice.

All the things that she would never do. All the things that she would never know. Ethan, her baby. She would likely never see him become a man, get married, have children of his own.

Although she did not sob, her eyes filled-up and glistened with sorrow. Like a dam brimming over, they welled-up, then once begun, silently, the teardrops flowed and flowed without end. She turned to Ethan and found his face a mirror of her own. Lost for words, their eyes spoke volumes and told each other of the love that had suddenly become urgent in the face of impending loss.

"How long have I got?" she said, without turning back to the doctor.

"With any luck, nine months; worst case, three."

As few as three months... How little time that suddenly seemed. She'd kept library books for longer than that.

It was unfair, it really was.

Shit on toast!

The thought made her smirk like a naughty child.

Well at least she had still kept her sense of humour. How long would that last?

They arrived at Tom and Barbara's home a week later. Jane

had been in the process of selling her parents' house, and so already had most of their belongings packed up.

"Your dad would have been so proud of how you've turned out, Ethan," she'd said as they sat in the front room.

She rubbed his arm and hugged him tightly.

"You've been my rock in all of this you know? Promise me, when I'm gone that you'll listen to Tom and Barbara. Promise me that you'll do what they say."

Ethan Howard said nothing, he merely held his mother and nodded. He held her and held her and wanted never to let go.

As the weeks passed, Jane went from bad to worse, becoming increasingly unsteady and finding difficulty in walking. She became reclusive and elected to spend a good portion of each day reading or talking to Ethan.

But, if fate had not dealt her a cruel enough hand already, it further twisted the knife. She developed double vision, and difficulties speaking and swallowing. In three months she'd all but lost the ability to communicate and was being fed via a tube.

"If only there were something I could do," said Ethan. He paced the kitchen in dismay.

"It's what life is," replied Tom, before realising Ethan was actually talking into his mobile.

"Do you want to know what's driving me mad?" asked Ethan. "It's that I keep seeing her up and about out of the corner of my eye, but when I turn, she's gone. Anyway, I'll come see you at the shop later."

Tom Howard looked his grandson, trying to work him out. *Yes, he'd been talking to the daughter of the corner shop owner – Ayesha – A girl he'd become keen on, but what had he meant? Could he really be saying what Tom thought he was?*

"Ethan, I heard you talking about your mother. This is going to sound strange," he said, "but when you see her, how do you feel? Do things seem *sort-of* out of place, not like it's wrong, but not like it's right either, just different?"

Ethan was dumbfounded. "Yes – exactly. But, how could you know that?"

"Because I used to be able to see things like that too. You need to trust me Ethan, can you do that? You need to see her. If you can, we may have a chance. It helps if you're dog-tired – you and I will stay up and then we'll see."

Ethan was more than confused. "What are you talking about Grandpa?"

"Come, I'll tell you," he began, "but you must promise me you won't breathe a word of this to your grandmother…"

CHAPTER 83

Thomas Howard sat at the kitchen table opposite his fifteen-year-old grandson, two mugs of steaming tea between them.

Where should he begin? Where COULD he begin? A mixture of excitement and disbelief ran through his veins. He hadn't felt like this since well before Matt had died.

Rountree, Stevenson, The Commission. The RIFT was true – and they had all deceived him. He felt that he'd been played – a chump that hated himself for falling for their lies.

But could he be that sure? He'd been here before. Could he dare to believe that all of it could have been true?

One thing he knew for sure was that he needed to make up for lost time. If only he could see the RIFT, but that was impossible.

"Ethan, if you believe what people say, the men in this family have a gift. Your father had it, I had it and my father before me."

Ethan looked lost. "What gift?"

"This is going to sound strange, kooky even, but if you're seeing what I think you're seeing, then it's just possible we can save your mother. I believed in this once Ethan, before they convinced me I was mad. Before they did... this." Tom pulled up his hair and pointed at the scar at the base of his skull.

"You may find this difficult to believe, but the men in our family have a kind of ability to see different worlds, different possibilities and, in some cases, reach out and touch them. We can see these different worlds and pick them... choose them... be them."

Ethan looked at him like he was crazy, pulling his face in a twisted expression of disbelief.

"What this got to do with Mum?"

"You say you keep seeing her Ethan. I believe what you're seeing, out of the corner of your mind, are different realities, possibly where Jane is in remission."

"What are you saying?" asked Ethan. The mention of his mother was a raw nerve and the conversation riled him. "What are you trying to do?"

"I'm only trying to get to the truth, Ethan. I need you to get to the point where you perceive the real world around you. You're tied into a single *reality-view*, and your mind is resisting seeing anything different. You need to unlearn what you have learned, to unset your expectation – to see the world for what it is."

Tom stood up and shuffled over to the middle drawer of the kitchen dresser. From this, he took out an old bundle of notebooks and a screw-top glass jar with a lid. From the jar he took a red wooden die and handed it to Ethan. "What I want you to do, Ethan, is throw ten sixes in a row."

"That's never going to happen," said Ethan.

"Ethan, for once, just trust me, … please."

Ethan took the die and threw it – a five. "How many hours do you have?" he sighed.

"Not hours. Not time Ethan. You should be thinking, how many *worlds* do you have."

Tom placed his hands on the table and did his best to keep Ethan's fleeting attention.

"Now Ethan, would you agree that you rolled a five?"

"Okay," said Ethan a mix of aggravation and loss on his face – *Where was this going?*

"Good. Now would you agree that you might have rolled a six?"

"Okay," he said again.

"So, if you *could* have rolled a six, there is almost certainly another world, *a parallel universe, if you like* where another version of you *did* roll a six. Would you agree?"

"I guess…" his eyebrows were raised and his brow was furrowed.

"You have it in you, Ethan to see those other worlds. Don't look at the die, look at the possibilities. Look through the die. The singularity of the die is what is driving your expectation that there is only one reality. But that singularity is in your mind. Your father used to tell me: *You have two eyes, each gets a different view of the world, close one eye and open the other and the world looks different. Open both eyes, and there is one image.* But Ethan, that image that you see only exists in one place – *your mind.* The reality is that there is no single image, there are two.

"It's the same with the world. The single view of reality that you think of as the world is only a perception. If you can see past your expectations, then you can begin to see the world as it really is – or see the *many worlds* as they really are."

Unconvinced. Ethan sighed heavily, "So, what do you want me to do?"

"You need to trust me Ethan, but most of all you need to trust yourself, and to relax. Remember where the die is and slowly, close your eyes till they're just slits and, best you can, free your mind. Don't open your eyes, just make it so you can only half-see the table."

Ethan closed his eyes and attempted to relax. He tried to un-close his mind, un-focus his eyes away from the table and away from the die in front of him.

His eyes became slits, and the room faded to dark as he attempted to do as Tom had asked and close his mind to the singularity of the world around him.

He tried to tell himself that there was not one die, but many. However when he opened his eyes, a single die with the number five stubbornly stared back at him. "I can't do it," he protested. "It's pointless."

"That's because you're trying to make it happen," said Tom.

"But you want me to try, don't you?" Ethan said, exasperated. "How on earth do I try without trying?"

Tom Howard felt for his grandson – he'd been there himself. He knew that words alone were never going to convince him, but what else did he have?

"Ethan, think of it like riding a bike or driving car, or even like playing tennis. If you try to do it, you invariably don't succeed – you have an objective and a goal – but beyond that, you need to trust your instincts, and prevent your conscious mind from interfering."

The frustration on the teenager's face was apparent.

Try without trying. Trust your instincts.

"But you told me to overcome my instincts, deny them. Which is it?"

Tom was finding this difficult, but he held out a hand and

spoke calmly, in a measured tone, "You need to deny the instincts around your perceptions that make you see the world as one. But you also need to trust your instincts about who you are and embrace what I know you can do. You said that you'd recently seen your mother, tell me about that…"

CHAPTER 84

It had been around a fortnight before that it had happened. Ethan Howard had sat dozing on the couch, almost falling asleep, when his mother had walked past him saying that she was tired and was going to go to bed.

"Don't be too late OK?" he'd heard her say, but tiredness had prevented him responding. He just sat there, half-nodding, and continued to doze. She'd said the same thing, in the same way, countless times and it was only moments afterwards that he'd realised the unreality of it.

His mother could not balance, focus, nor talk, she'd all but given up the will to live, but there she had been, passing him and talking to him and he'd viewed that as normal, certainly nothing out of the ordinary.

For an instant, he'd viewed it not only as normal but had known it simply as the way that things were. For a moment he'd perceived it not as strange, for it had come to him not only as an event, but had been accompanied with memories that had woven an explanation into the narrative. It had come with memories that hinted at a spontaneous, unexplained remission that medics were at a loss to attribute to science.

And then as quickly as it had come, it was gone. It had left him hollow and empty, the realisation making him nauseous like a punch to the stomach.

Similar things had happened many times before and had always played-out the same way. Each time it had been so unremarkable that it passed him by, and when the scales finally fell from his eyes, it was like a hypnic jerk – a sleep-start. It was like he felt his whole being drop and his stomach turn with it, leaving him crashing back into the sickening realisation that it was all a lie and his mother was infirm and bed-ridden, her days numbered.

It was like someone was switching channels in his head and he'd only half noticed, only later realising that the movie wasn't the same anymore. At no point was anything amiss – only in retrospect was there a realisation that none of the plot made any kind of sense.

"When it's happened I've always been fried, half asleep," he explained. "One time it was after that party that I'd gone to and come back a little... Well, you know..."

"Tired and emotional?" said Tom, "Yes I think I remember. Well I remember you being grumpy as hell the next morning, anyway."

Ethan blushed sheepishly.

"So what do you want me to do?" he asked.

"You need to practice, so you can realise when it happens, not realise afterwards, but as it happens. The die will help you do that. Shut your eyes and try to doze off," said Tom. "And when you get there, see all the possible dice, simply pick one, reach for it, and that possibility will become real."

"And that's all there is to it?"

"And that's all there is to it," echoed Tom.

Ethan shut his eyes and tried to concentrate on his breathing.

In – down to the bottom of his lungs.

Out...

In – down to what felt like his feet.

Out...

As the breath left his body he slowly but surely felt a world of tension lift from his arms and legs. He concentrated on his toes and then his legs, his fingers arms and torso. He tried to relax as much as possible, to still his mind.

Ethan Howard emptied all active thought from his head and concentrated, singularly and in totality, on becoming at peace, becoming one with himself.

He slowly began to open his eyes and, through the shadows that his perception now offered, he attempted not to look but simply to let the positions where he knew the dice could be wash over him. To his utter dismay, the die remained there as a single, unmoving anchor.

What had he expected? Of course it was. There was a single die because there was a single world. How could he expect there to be anything else? Anything different?

"I'm sick of this," he spat, grabbing the die. "I want to

believe you, Grandpa," he shouted, "I do, but it's all crap!"

Tears in his eyes, Ethan Howard stormed out of the room – still clutching the die in his hand.

CHAPTER 85

Ethan left the house and headed down the street. Tears streaming from his eyes. *Why was his grandfather doing this to him?*

He texted as he walked and, at the end of the street, he ducked into the tiny corner shop. "Ethan," greeted the man that seemed to live behind the counter, "Is everything OK?"

"Mr Hassan – Is Ayesha in?"

But before the man could answer, a head popped round the door. "Hello you – Are you OK? C'mon let's get out of here."

Ayesha was in Ethan's class at school, and when he'd started there she had been one of the few people who had not ignored him, not sought to distance themselves from the new boy.

As far as Ethan was concerned, she was the only thing in his life that hadn't, so far, gone to shit. She was shy and demure, and she was beautiful. In his first week, he'd been drawn to her and suggested they meet for coffee. Ayesha had said her family didn't usually approve of English boys, so it was a surprise when she instead invited him to dinner at her house.

He knew that he would be on trial, maybe not with Ayesha, but certainly with her brothers and father, but by the end of the evening he had begun to gain their trust, and although not accepted, had been welcome ever since.

Ayesha was his confidante, someone to whom he could say anything. "I don't know why he's doing this," he said.

"I can't say that I understand," Ayesha said, "but if your grandfather thinks that you should listen to him, then you should. What I do know is that time is precious, and you should spend whatever time that you have with your mother."

CHAPTER 86

Jane Howard lay motionless, her unfocused eyes staring into the void. *Was this living? If so, they could keep it.*

Earlier, she thought she had heard her son downstairs. There sounded to be anger in the timbre of his voice followed by a crashing door, but she couldn't make out any of what he'd said. *Ethan wasn't easily riled. What could be winding him up so?*

She dozed, in and out of consciousness, not knowing how long it had been when Ethan's knock woke her as he tapped on her door and entered the room.

"I'm so sorry Mum," he said, attempting to prevent his tears from flowing. Seeing Ayesha had helped, but only so much, and she had sent him back to his family.

Jane Howard wished that she could see or speak, but she found herself far too weak. What there was of herself was slipping away.

"Ignore me, Mum," he whispered, "I've just been listening to one too many of Grandpa's crazy stories." He realised he still held the die, and he put it down on the bedside table before holding his mother's hand.

"What am I going to do without you?" he said. "You know I'd do anything if there were anything that could be done."

Like a small child, Ethan attempted to comfort both himself and his mother, climbing on the bed and placing his head on her belly, wrapping his arms around her.

Weak as she was, Jane Howard managed to stroke his hair from his fringe to his neck, attempting to soothe him like she'd done when he was but a baby.

My son. My beautiful son. How can I bear to leave you so young, but what say do I have in any of this?

The old her would have been angry, would have fought, would have railed against the world before accepting something like this. It was cruel and unfair, but then again, she was no longer the old her. She was instead merely grateful for the moment that they now shared.

If she could choose the moment to die, to finally go, there would undoubtedly be worse moments than here and now. Her son in her arms, with a mutual love, deeper and more complete than she could have ever thought possible.

She noticed Ethan's breathing had slowed as he began slipping into the arms of sleep.

Rest-now baby, she thought, laying her head back against her pillow to join him.

Ethan Howard felt himself wake. *Where was he?*

Then he remembered, he could still feel the warmth of his mother's body against the side of his face. Beginning to open his eyes he noticed the bedside table where there now sat more than one die. He lay motionless and looked at them. They were there, but not there, real, but not real – *Just as Tom had said.*

He realised that he had no idea which was the die which he'd placed there and which was... The realisation stopped his thought in its tracks.

He had placed ALL of them there. That was the point, but more than that, he remembered placing all of them there. Not one after another – that would make no sense – but nevertheless, he remembered a multitude of conflicting and inconsistent pasts.

He looked at the dice, and felt the separation flood his mind. He didn't so much resist his perception, forming a single view, as simply not invoke it. In that moment, he felt more in control of himself than he ever had – he noticed the feeling of the slightly different pasts within his head, each jostling for supremacy.

Continuing to stare at the dice, Ethan perceived them all in equal measure and let the multiplicity saturate him.

Selecting the nearest die, he picked it off the table and felt the other dice melt away into nothingness, leaving only shadows in his mind.

By interacting with the die, he'd given providence to that reality, provided definition and had felt his mind, for a second, focus on the singularity of the selection he had made.

Now he understood. He understood everything, but more than that, he knew what he must do.

CHAPTER 87

"I did it, I can see it, Grandpa," Ethan Howard said excitedly, "but it's more than that–"

"Good," nodded Tom, "but what do you mean more?"

That was the question, *what did he mean?*

"I felt something, something that I've never felt before."

He couldn't easily put into words the level of peace he had felt – he felt infused with power and self-confidence.

"I felt like I'd been sleeping and finally woken up. I know I *had* been sleeping and *had* just woken up, but that's not what I mean... What I mean is that I feel like I understand what you were trying to tell me, but not just *understand it.* I know it and feel it. More than that, I feel like I can start to see the world for the first time how it actually is."

"OK – Prove it," said Tom, "Show me."

Ethan took the die from his pocket and reached out to the jar containing more dice from the table. Shaking them in his hands, he cast them in front of Tom. Through the world of possibilities that he found suddenly simple to navigate, he picked the dice back up, each one a six, and threw them again.

Each time it was the same – a six.

"Ethan, what can I say," Tom was astounded. Not only did he never expect Ethan to grasp things so quickly, he'd never seen the gift manipulated like this, with such ease – not even when he was with The Commission.

Ethan was not just a natural, he was a virtuoso.

"I can see things," Ethan said. "I feel like I can do anything. Look..."

Tom watched on as Ethan proceeded to take three copper coins and balance each one on the edge of the other.

"Ethan. Your mother..."

It was true they hadn't much time, but he also had questions and doubts.

"There are others like me, aren't there? I can feel them

moving – like vibrations, like ripples. What will they do to us? Who are they?"

"Ethan, I need to tell you something, the world we're in now isn't how it was meant to be. The curfews, the power, the controls and the strange influence this country seems to exert on the world – none of it is natural. In a sense, your father and I set those wheels in motion; not intentionally, but we did so, all the same."

"What do you mean?"

"What I mean is that, when you were born, we didn't so much feel a ripple in reality, but a tidal-wave. We could feel something coming to a head. Something was going to happen, and was huge, but way down the line. We've never found what it was, but whatever it was, it was focussed on you. Ethan it has always been about you."

Ethan sat silently – *What could he say?*

"This is going to be difficult to hear, but soon, Ethan, if the graft is still there, then someone, or something, is going to attempt to erase you from existence. You father and I tried to get on the inside, tried to steer things away from that outcome, but nothing we did made any difference, and as we meddled more and more the organisation which formed around us, which we were part of, grew and grew. It thrived, but it became rotten, and we became weak. In the end, when they got the power that they wanted, they neutralised me and, likely, had a hand in your father's death.

"But Ethan, I've got to tell you, what you can do... I've never seen the like of it, and they won't have either. It's likely that you'll be seen as a threat. They'll fear that you could overthrow them. They'll see it and they'll act."

The worst thing was that Tom knew that, in all of this the rise of The Commission was not a chance-happening. It was his and Matt's meddling that had put the wheels in motion.

The road to hell is paved with good intentions.

"I can feel them," said Ethan, "feel them moving, nudging, but I can't see this... thing you're referring to. I need you. I need your help.

"The thing in your head that they fitted you with – did you say that it actively inhibits you from doing... *well*... doing this?"

"That's how I understand it, yes."

"So, if it failed, you'd be back in the game? Because sooner or later everything fails, right?"

"I'm not sure I follow you Ethan, but essentially yes."

Ethan's eyes glazed over and almost without effort he located what he was looking for and melted and flowed into it. What he had searched for was a reality where Tom's implant, at that moment, had just gone offline.

As Ethan watched, Tom's expression changed, like all at once the lights had come back on. Tom looked instantly younger and more vigorous, but then the incessant mental chatter hit him like a truck.

Becoming unsteady, he swayed backwards and forwards, feeling suddenly dizzy, his mind was awash with foreign thoughts once again – it was different from before, he now felt his age, felt the weight of the last ten years play on his mind.

His heart raced as his mind began to perceive the other worlds that for the last decade had been closed to him. The shock caused him to catch his breath and he simply sat there stunned, listening to the clamour of thousands of voices all singing their different songs. He was no longer purely in the room with Ethan, but then again, he was – he was everywhere and nowhere, all at once, his senses saturated. Slowly his heart and his breathing returned to normal, and his perceptions returned to his kitchen, to Ethan.

"Are you OK?" asked Ethan, "Sorry to do that, but I need you to remember, to see."

Tom nodded, lost for words. *How had Ethan done this?*

The boy seemed different somehow, confident, assertive. It was like their roles had suddenly changed. It was like he was the child and Ethan the leader.

Thomas Howard braced himself to look into the RIFT. He knew what he was about to see, but having Ethan sitting there, almost a man, filled him with worry – *was it still there?*

The graft hung there as ominously as it ever had, but in the intervening years it had approached, it had grown, it was almost upon them.

He was unable to see any of the detail of it other than the fact that, as before, in that graft, Ethan had never existed. "I'm sorry Ethan," he said, "If we'd left well alone, the chances are that the world would be a lot better place, this would have gone away, and Matt would still be alive."

"This Commission – you really think they would come after us?"

"You don't know them, Ethan. They did this to me, and they did other things. It was The Commission that brought in all the rules we live our lives by, the controls, the mandatory screenings. Before them we used to feel safe. People have always disappeared, but not like they do now."

Ethan tried to take it all in, it wasn't easy, and the implication wasn't pleasant. "Are you saying that if you and Dad hadn't somehow tried to save me the world would be a better place?"

"That's not what we wanted Ethan, but that's probably the truth. Without us, The Commission would likely have never been formed, and without The Commission, none of these controls would exist. We wouldn't be frightened to speak out, we wouldn't be shepherded into whatever outcome The Commission wanted."

"But we are safe, aren't we?" asked Ethan. "I mean, isn't it for our good?"

"Ethan, you don't remember, but there was a time when instead of placing restrictions on everyone and living in a police state, the country tried to live as one. If you were a person of faith, you were accepted. You had rights, and the government protected those rights. It wasn't always great, but at least, we had democracy."

"We still have democracy," said Ethan.

"Don't be naive," replied Tom. "We have democracy, because people vote, but it's an illusion. Just as you control the die, they control the outcome. It doesn't matter who rolls it, and slowly but surely freedom dies."

Ethan looked at his grandfather. He didn't want to admit it, but he knew what he was saying was true. He knew that the society that they lived in was fractured and rotten. He knew his mother had friends who had disappeared under strange circumstances and he knew that there was little or no dissent in Parliament.

It was all false.

"So," he said, "what do we do?"

"I don't know Ethan, what you can do, I've never seen the

like of it before. Maybe you're what we've been waiting for, maybe you could fix things. If you can do only half of what I think you can do, maybe you can change this – maybe you can stop this before it ever got started."

For a moment, Tom seemed to drift off looking into middle-distance, as if reflecting on what he'd said.

"Surely Joe had doubts," said Tom finally. "If he hadn't pushed it with Matt, would any of this ever have come to pass? Your father visited Joe before he died, and it was their digging that set this all off. It was Joe's death that pushed me into suggesting that The Commission be formed."

Ethan sat there. *How could he take it all in?*

"Alright," he said. "Let's save the world, but later, OK? First, I'm going to fix Mum. Whatever, or whoever's got it in for me will have to wait."

CHAPTER 88

The sun streamed through the panes of the greenhouse where Tom sat on his stool. Intently, he tied stems of the tomato plants to the canes to keep them upright. A sound next to him made him turn, and looking up he saw his grandson, Ethan.

"Mum, says five minutes for dinner. Can you come and get washed up? Oh, and Gran says don't be dragging mud into the house."

The words seemed to echo with unreality. *What was this?*

He looked at Ethan, who looked back at him feeling a similar unease.

Jane Howard had been busying herself in the kitchen. The meal was chicken with vegetables although she'd been denied the butter, salt and even the gravy granules that she'd wanted. She placed the dishes of steaming vegetables at the table where Ethan and Tom sat.

Ethan looked at the scene around him – it had a dream-like quality. *Was this real?* It felt natural, but there was something else, like he was not entirely there. In the back of his mind was a strange notion of his mother, not in recovery and remission but instead in a parlous state that made her not even able to speak, not able to eat, unable to see. The idea was like a seed that grew and opened before him.

He was here, in the moment, but not really here. Left alone, this world would slip back into echoes, as it ever had, and he would lose her once again. But this time it was different, this time he had the benefit of absolute clarity. *He knew what he must do.*

Reaching out he took the peas and the world flowed into definition around him. As he did, the two worlds crashed into one another, and the memories fought for space in his head. The level of inconsistency took his breath away as he both remembered his mother recovering but also acutely remembered the acceptance that she would never recover. He felt lost, not knowing which memories to trust.

The graft was not like what he'd experienced with Tom. It was not like the dice. It was two months or more since the realities had been common. It made Ethan's head swim with indecision. It was like he could see two of everything, like the ceiling was spinning, like he was seeing double. *No – it was like he was thinking double.*

Forcing himself to look up, he saw Tom was oblivious. However, the instant Ethan disrupted his inhibitor, Tom's expression became a mirror of his own.

He'd done it, but a two-month graft was enormous. It would be like a sonic boom. They'd created a beachhead, but would there now be hell to pay?

At one level he felt a panic rise in his chest. But then he looked at his mother, oblivious to it all, healthy, in remission.

If it meant saving her, let them come. He would be ready. Let them all come.

CHAPTER 89

"Sir. There's been an occurrence."

Charles Hunter looked up from behind the heavy leather-topped, oak desk.

"What do you mean, 'an occurrence'?"

"The fixers, Sir. They think there's been an unsanctioned graft, Sir, and not a small one. They're estimating about two to three months."

"What's changed?"

"We're still looking into that – it may take a while," said Baker, "the monitors picked it up as a jump in the quantum matrix."

"Why wasn't it opposed?"

"I'm sorry Sir, I don't know Sir.

"They think it was localised effect, with no impact on us or them, which is why they think it got through."

Hunter scowled at him and raised his voice.

"Baker, everything impacts us. Everything impacts everything else. Do you understand nothing? But more than that, much more than that, I can't have rogue elements out there. A graft of that size doesn't happen by chance. We're shutting this down, and before you say it, I don't care what the collateral damage is."

CHAPTER 90

"Ethan, we need to move, and we need to move soon."

"What do you mean?"

Thomas Howard looked at his grandson and sighed. "Ethan, I know you've been living in the moment with your mother, and I didn't want to disturb you. But don't you think it strange that almost on a nightly basis, we're suddenly having very similar news reports – all about mental illness?"

Ethan hadn't thought about it, but now that he did, it was true. Since his graft a month ago, there'd been ever-increasing reports of issues attributed to a history of mental health problems. These varied vastly, in one report, a small child had been strangled by her brother who claimed to hear voices, in another, a respected army-veteran had gutted two strangers in a train station. On a daily basis, report after report surfaced, each one different but all equally emotive.

"Are you saying that we somehow triggered this?" asked Ethan. "How?"

"I don't think so Ethan, I think that what we did, caused them to wake up, caused them to realise that there is someone out there. A threat. And if you ask me, these events have been engineered to justify a case for indiscriminate action – watch this."

Tom held up his phone and played a news report.

"And as part of our continued investment in public health and wellbeing, we're proud to announce that, from next month, we will be extending our programme of public-safety initiatives. Too long have we been subjected to the danger within society that these conditions cause. However, we are a nation that cares, a nation that does not blame, a nation that helps those in need, and since the events in the last month imply that so many of our citizens need help, we can't stand by.

"From next month, I'm proud to announce that a national effort to identify and help those that need it most, will begin.

Every British citizen will be offered screening, at their convenience, in their home, workplace or school. By working together, we will make Britain safe again."

Tom stopped the playback.

"It's like religion and immigration all over again."

"What do you mean?"

"Before the religious mass deportations, there was a huge spike in unrest and terrorist-incidents."

"Yes," said Ethan, "we were taught in school that the government stamped it out via 'harsh but fair' policies." As he said them, the words seemed to sour and turn to ash in his mouth. "Are you saying that all of this is somehow orchestrated?"

"Not orchestrated Ethan – predetermined. In an infinite universe, where anyone is capable of anything, it's just a case of finding the right anything… And that means that, as with religion and immigration, this so-called *public safety initiative* will be a mandate for a witch hunt against anyone who shows any chance of having the gift."

With horrific certainty, it all made sense.

The Commission were looking for them. Looking to purge society of what they saw as a threat, and in order to remove the cancer, they were more than willing to cut deep into the flesh.

CHAPTER 91

Thomas Howard looked at the letter that lay on the table. Picking it up, Ethan turned it over in his hands, "I thought they said that this was to begin next month."

"Apparently, I'm described as a priority case."

This wasn't going to end well, they both knew that.

"What can we do?"

"We need to stop this before it starts, Ethan. Your greatest weapon in all of this is surprise. As far as they're concerned, they've seen the limit of your abilities. That's got them rattled, but they don't know what you can do. I believe in you, Ethan. I know you can stop this before it started. God knows, someone has to."

Out of the dresser, Tom drew Joe's notebooks, old and worn, the pages yellowing. "With your gift Ethan, I'm sure you can use these to find a reality where it isn't so different, a reality where, with just a little nudge, Joe doubted himself just enough to let it go. To keep all of this to himself and to avoid fixing anything." He handed the battered notebook to Ethan who turned it over and over. He felt the soft nap of the leather against his palm and closed his eyes.

"So, this was the book that Joe used, day to day?"

"Yes, this one was his last book, barely used. He hadn't even cracked the spine on it."

"So, in an infinite universe, it's plausible that a manufacturing fault caused an artefact that looked enough like some text to be readable – like the image of Jesus appearing on the inside of a piece of fruit."

"But that would be insanely unlikely!" said Tom.

"But not impossible?"

"No, not impossible…" the idea cause Tom's heart to race. "Do you really think you could locate something *that specific?*"

Ethan wasn't sure, but there was only one way to find out.

"But what will you say? How will he know to trust it?"

"That's simple," said Ethan, with a wry smile. "We just want to knock him off-guard don't we. I'll just say it's from me."

Ethan slowed his breathing and focussed through the book until he became aware of the infinitely-many books that stretched in front of him.

"What are you planning to say?" asked Tom, not believing what he was even saying.

"I'm just going to ask him to back off," replied Ethan. "Don't worry, I'll be nice."

Ethan perceived the totality of the book in front of him and watched as his infinitely many selves opened it. Ignoring the versions where the front page was blank, he let the images flow into his mind's eye, and he attempted to navigate the many different possibilities.

If he hadn't known it before, he knew it now, he was a natural. By intuition, he was able to pull the different possibilities out of the mist, finally viewing what he was looking for:

STOP   FIXING.   ETHAN

Like writing a text. It was a bit of a mess, looking like a spidery watermark, but the words were legible enough.

He didn't know why, but the idea of texting the past amused him no end. *Now to hit send.*

Focusing in on the singularity of the book in front of him, he reached out to pick it up.

Ethan felt like he'd hit a brick wall, he couldn't explain it. Reaching out again, he fought his way towards the book.

Was someone trying to stop him… Who?

He fought his way towards it, felt himself edging closer, inch by inch, if that even made sense – he closed in on it and attempted to grasp it. It was no-good, like a wet bar of soap it slipped out of his fingers and sat there taunting him.

Taking a minute to gather his thoughts, he attempted once again, this time with more focus, more determination. *He would not be stopped.*

For what seemed like hours, he attempted to gain purchase on the book. He could feel the energy, surrounding it, growing and growing, and seemed to even hear it sing with a high-pitched whine. Sweat was running out of him, and his heart was beating faster than it had ever done. With all that was left in him, he grabbed for it, tried to get it over the line, but it was no use – whatever it was that had opposed him was not going to let him succeed.

Tom Howard watched in dismay as his grandson crumpled to the floor.

Over a decade earlier Joseph Howard looked across at Ethan's father in utter exhaustion.

"Matty, I'm …"

But before he could finish his sentence, Joseph Howard's face dropped, as the stroke that ultimately killed him took its hold.

CHAPTER 92

"Ethan, Are you OK?"

Tom Howard touched his grandson's hand. He'd laid him in the recovery position earlier. He'd thought of calling someone, but how could he?

Ethan blinked and focussed on his grandfather.

"You scared me half to death. What happened?"

"I was there. The book was within my grasp, and something stopped me. Something like I've never felt before. It fought me, and it won. It's no use – I couldn't do it."

He kicked himself for thinking he could go up against them. *Tom had built him up, sure, but at the end of the day, what could a kid hope to do against the system, no matter how evil? This wasn't a fairy-tale, wasn't Star Wars – who was he kidding?*

He'd failed – but more than that, he'd had his arse handed to him on a plate. It was hopeless. They were on to him, and they'd beaten him.

CHAPTER 93

The day after Ethan's attempt was when Tom Howard was due to be visited, due to be assessed.

He thought about running, but where would he go?

He thought about hiding, but what would happen to Barbara?

Instead, he elected to go and sit in his greenhouse. At eleven o'clock they arrived, with smiling faces, eager to do work for the greater good. Probably not even realising the sinister nature of the wheels being turned by their efforts.

Ethan couldn't bear to listen, so instead watched out of the window as the group of three assessors trooped to the bottom of the garden where his grandfather sat tending his tomato plants.

He watched as they unpacked their technology.

He watched as they all-too-briefly talked with him.

He watched as his grandfather's head dropped in sombre, sorrowful acceptance. And he watched as they took him away.

Pressing the palm of his hand again the window as Thomas Howard was driven away, Ethan croaked through the tears that now poured down his face – "I'm sorry Grandpa. I've failed you."

CHAPTER 94

As far as he was concerned, that was the last time Ethan Howard saw his grandfather.

It wasn't that Tom did not come back, it was more that what came back was not Tom. Whatever it was that had now been done to him had left scorch marks on his head and rendered him a docile fool.

Ethan watched as he sat, once again, tending his plants, but his grandfather was gone. The man in the greenhouse knew nothing of the world, knew nothing of anything.

He wanted to shout, but who would listen? He wanted to scream, but who would understand his pain?

Worst of all, he knew that he was the cause of it all. He knew, that were it not for his father and grandfather chasing some damned fool notion of saving him, none of this would be happening.

And saving him from what? He didn't even know.

What he did know was that, one by one, society was culling the threat that it perceived. People were changing, or actively being changed.

Worse than that, life at school was unbearable.

Although most assessments came up negative, suspicion ran riot. The drive to be certified as normal led to fear and insecurity, and with that came persecution. Anyone with the slightest idiosyncrasy was called out by the mob as a target. Ethan managed to avoid the taunts and the beatings, but many did not.

Ayesha was scared, saying her brother had been taken for questioning, that her father was concerned that, if they found out that her family were still practicing Muslims, they would be seen as a different threat. Ethan wanted to speak to her, but she had not been to school that day and had not answered his texts.

At the end of his day, he called at the shop. He couldn't believe that he wouldn't continue to be on good terms with

Mr Hassan, but with everything that was happening, there was a still a doubt.

However, when he rounded the corner he found Ayesha's shop shut up, with a heavy municipal brown metal plate blocking the letterbox. The windows had chipboard nailed over them, and there was no sign of life.

She was gone.

Not knowing what else to do, he slumped in the shop doorway and wept.

Had they left? Had they been taken?

Either way, Ayesha was gone.

He was still sitting in the doorway when his mother drove past hours later. Taking one look at the shop, she understood it all.

"I know, baby," she said. "I know."

The following days passed in a haze, until events could no longer be ignored and the moment he had previously dreaded was upon him – his so-called assessment. His mother and grandmother had sailed through theirs and busily told him there was nothing to be worried about. He loved them, but their naivety sickened him.

Could they not see what was going on?

Could they not see what was happening all around them?

First his grandfather.

Then Ayesha.

And what about his father and Joe?

The assessors were due to come to see him at eleven o'clock.

Ethan Howard sat in his room and stared at the wall.

What should he do? What could he do?

He thought of running, but why? Where would he go? Surely all of his life had been building up to this moment.

Had Ayesha run?

He wasn't upset… He was angry. He was angry at the way that a gift that could help so many had been corrupted, used to turn good people into docile sheep. He was angry at the system for what they had done to his grandfather.

Whether she had run or not, he was angry that Ayesha was

no longer in his life. And he was angry at the responsibility that he felt for bringing this situation on the world. More than anything though, he just wanted it over. *If they wanted to make something of it, they could bring it on.*

It was against this setting that he heard the knock at the front door. He knew they had come for him, but he chose not to move. He heard them on the stairs, and he felt the opening of the door behind him. He was aware of their presence, but determined to have even just a second more without admitting they were there. He chose not to turn around.

"Hello Ethan," said a voice he didn't recognise. "We're here to ask you some questions if that's alright?

Silence.

"My name's Stevenson, and I actually knew Matt, your father."

CHAPTER 95

The mention of his father made Ethan turn. He looked at the staff accompanying Stevenson and dispassionately watched them begin to unpack their equipment.

"Are you really going to bother with that?"

"What do you mean Ethan?"

"If you knew my father, you'll know what he was capable of. And if you know that, you'll also know what that test is going to say."

"And what is that?"

"It's going to tell you that I'm my father's son. It's going to tell you that I can do what he could do. It's going to tell you that you need to either enlist me or neutralise me – but it's not going to tell you which."

Stevenson looked the fifteen year old Ethan Howard up and down. Smirking, he shook his head from side to side.

"Yes. You are indeed your father's son."

Standing up, Ethan picked up the bag that he'd already packed. "Shall we go then?"

CHAPTER 96

Ethan left the house with Stevenson, much to his mother's protestations. "No, you can't be going," she said in a worried tone. "Where are you taking him?"

Her face became a mask of fear, her lip trembled and her eyes looked up pleadingly, she was now silent, simply attempting to hold on to her son.

"Don't worry Mother," said Ethan as Stevenson's staff peeled her off him, "It'll be alright – you'll see." *Everything will be alright.*

With that, he stepped out of the house and into the morning air – a brief chill before he was enveloped by the hermetically controlled atmosphere of the waiting car. It was a Jag, blacker than night and sleek enough to imply that it had enough power to get out of a tight squeeze should it have need to. Ethan had expected no less, although he was surprised that the darkened windows stopped him knowing where he was headed.

When the car finally pulled up, it was with a certain degree of relief that he stepped out in front of a building which, from what Tom had said, Ethan assumed was The Manor. That was a good start, on the way he'd wondered if he'd over-reached, and the end of his journey would be to step out in front of a freshly dug grave.

You never know, he thought, *it may end up there yet.*

He was led to a rather drab interview room where Stevenson took off his jacket and put it on the back of the chair. "You know, Ethan," he said, "I first met your father in this very room, all those years ago.

"Your father had high ideals," he said, "and so did your grandfather. With those high ideals though, they didn't see the bigger picture, they thought of everything as cut and dried, *black and white*. But nothing is ever that simple. In the last five years we've had zero domestic terrorist incidents, the health of the nation is better than it's ever been and, internationally, we're thriving like never before. This Commission has not only been good for the country, it has also put Britain back on the map."

"And that's where you and my father differed, presumably," Ethan replied.

"Somewhat," said Stevenson. "He didn't see the bigger picture. He thought that it was better to throw things to the winds of chance than to engineer society and lose far, far fewer battles. But enough about your father. This isn't about him – it's about you. You may not know it Ethan, but we're at war. Every day in more ways than you can even begin to imagine. And for that, we need foot soldiers, talent like yourself. If you are even half of what your father was... then – well, what can I say?"

"My father may have been a dreamer," said Ethan, "but he believed that all people should have the one thing that you've taken from them."

"And what, pray tell, is that?"

"That's hope," replied Ethan. "I remember little of him, but I remember that clearly. Never give up hope – that was his view." Even as he said them, his father's words had a strange resonance.

Hope...

Stevenson looked at the boy, trying to work him out. "If you're so set against joining us, what did you think you could achieve by coming here?"

Ethan looked at him with contempt, "I needed to know who was responsible for my father's death and what had happened to my grandfather."

"And so now you know," said Stevenson. "Are you happy? You haven't seemed very happy recently – not since your little friend went away."

Ethan sat there silently and looked at Stevenson, refusing to be drawn. He was furious, but revenge was best served cold.

"I'll never be happy," he rasped, "not while people like you exist. But then again, you seem to be beginning to sweat profusely, maybe at your age, this conversation is too much to bear..."

Stevenson looked at the boy with a mixture of confusion and annoyance, which quickly evaporated – replaced with blind panic as he felt the crushing pain in his chest. His face turned red and then purple as he sank to his knees.

"You... But... How...?"

"In an infinite universe, anything can happen, surely, of all people, you should know that."

When he was sure that the breath had left Stevenson's body, Ethan hammered on the door.

"Hey! I think this guy's just had a heart attack."

The door opened, and before long medics were busying themselves round the body, but try as they might, they couldn't save Stevenson.

What a shame.

"Get Rountree here," shouted one of the staff. "There's something not right here. Get him here now!"

CHAPTER 97

Eli Rountree rounded the corner. "It's Stevenson Sir, he's had a heart attack."

Rountree was scarcely able to believe what he'd just heard. He knew Stevenson wasn't in the best of shape – *but a heart attack?*

"What had he been doing?"

"He was conducting an interview, Sir."

"Have we a recording?"

"Unfortunately, not. The gear's been on the fritz since this morning – as has the monitoring."

Eli was rattled. *This was too much of a coincidence.*

"OK. Take me to him."

"So, what happened?" Rountree asked of the boy who looked plainly upset by what had occurred.

"We were discussing how he was going to introduce me to some fixers. And then he stood up and clutched his chest. And... I didn't know what to do, the door was locked."

Rountree wasn't convinced.

"Do I know you?" he said. *Why was the boy familiar?*

"I'm not sure, you might have known my dad, Matt Howard."

Rountree was taken aback. "You're Ethan Howard? What the hell are you doing here?"

"Like Stevenson said, we're at war, and the country needs foot soldiers."

"Bullshit! Why are you really here?"

"Look, Stevenson made it clear that I'm either with you or against you, and I'm hardly going to stand against you."

"And then he just died?"

"Apparently so..."

Rountree rubbed his eyes in distress and dismay – he really didn't need this. It wasn't clear what he should do.

If Ethan was legit and Stevenson had recruited Matt's son, he could be a real asset. But if he was being played...

Stabbing the phone in the interview room, he requested an armed escort to the conference suite – what he needed was more information.

CHAPTER 98

"Are you aware of this, Sir?" Rountree asked Hunter.

"If you mean, did I know that Stevenson was bringing him in, then yes – I knew."

"But can we trust him?"

"The question *should* be 'can *we use* him?'"

"You think we can?"

"In time, yes. And if we can't…"

"But why take the risk?"

"Why?" said Hunter, raising his voice. "I'll tell you why. For the last ten years you've promised me fixers as adept as Howard or Jacobson were, but have you delivered? No! And you expect me to pass up this opportunity, because of what? Fear? Where is he anyway?"

"In the conference suite under armed guard."

"He's just a kid Eli. A kid! He may have a lot of potential, but ultimately, he's just a kid. We'll either make him or break him – you'll see."

****

Ethan Howard sat quietly at the side of the conference table. Against the wall two armed staff stood watch over him, bemused at being asked to guard a gangly kid.

"You must be Ethan," said Hunter as he entered the room, "I've been looking forward to meeting you."

"Ethan, this is Mr Hunter," added Rountree.

"So, Ethan," said Hunter, "Stevenson said that you wanted the opportunity to use your talents."

"You could say that," replied Ethan. "He thought I had a lot to offer."

"I think so too, Ethan."

"What I really want though, is to build a better society."

"A laudable ambition. Ultimately isn't that we what we all want?"

"I'm not sure. You've made it safer, but is it better?"

If Hunter was surprised by Ethan's tone, he didn't show it. "I think so, I really do. But ultimately, it doesn't matter what you think. It's your choice – you can either work with us, and for us, or not. If you want a bright future, you'll work with us…"

"And if I don't?"

"If you don't, Mr Howard, then I'm sorry to say we will have to neutralise you, remove you, and neither of us wants that. And before you even think that you can do your… *you know*, your thing, let me make one thing perfectly clear. The fixers in this organisation would never allow that – whatever you try, they'd oppose you."

As he spoke, Hunter indicated to the men and women that had entered the room while he'd been speaking. Looking at the armed staff, he waved to dismiss them.

Ethan appeared to consider Hunter's words. His earlier bravado had faded and now he was visibly shaken.

"I think both of us know that I can't join you," he said with more than a tremor in his voice. "But do you want to know why?"

"Amuse me – Mr Howard. Your family always has in the past."

"It's because you've gutted this country, you've destroyed it. You've sacrificed a whole generation on the altar of your vanity and built a church where hope has died."

Hunter raised his eyebrows in surprise.

"Those are big words indeed for such a little man – surely they are not yours."

It was true, they weren't, but Ethan was happy to attribute them. "Those were the words of Tom Howard," he said. "Those were the words of my grandfather," he spat.

Hunter said nothing, offering instead a slow-hand clap. "Well, Mr Howard, you certainly don't disappoint. You have indeed amused me. Confused me *and* amused me – but amused me none-the-less. If not to join us… What then? Do you really think you're going to walk out of here alive?"

The fear in Ethan's eyes was evident to see, but he knew what he'd come to say.

"No," he said, in deflated resignation, "you've affected our family for the last time. Today is where this ends."

"Don't be absurd," Hunter laughed, "have you heard

nothing of what I've said? Are you seriously telling me that if you tried something like you did with Stevenson, that we couldn't or wouldn't oppose you?"

"No, I'm sure you could oppose me easily."

"Then what?"

"My family is responsible for allowing this country to go to hell, and at every point they did it for one reason and one reason alone – to maintain my existence. But who, in all this, was attempting to deny me that, who is it who is setting out to erase me – who is driving the graft? It's clearly not you. But then I saw it. If I had never existed in the first place, it would make all things right. Like I said, it ends here. It's obvious, and to stop *this* it would be a small price to pay."

"Knock yourself out. They'll stop you."

"Would they?" Ethan said, attempting to be the picture of calm. He was petrified, but through his rising fear, he managed to get out the words, "We'll see."

With that, he closed his eyes and searched for what he was looking for, and the picture he formed was vibrant and filled with such joy as to make him euphoric. It was what he needed. Every fibre of his being screamed self-preservation. Every morsel of his psyche begged him to stop.

What are you doing? His inner voice seemed to say, but he knew he must continue, or it would all be for nothing. At that minute, a feeling of wellbeing flooded over him and he felt one with the world.

He understood the world, the universe, everything. He had found peace like he'd never known. And he knew it was right.

He melted and flowed with it, reached out for it, felt himself beginning to go. Strangely, he was no longer afraid.

It was wonderful.

Hope...

He knew they couldn't stop him, but to push the point home he held the graft like a great wave on the brink of crashing down. And because it was held on the brink, everyone, fixers and non-fixers alike, could see it. It was a raging maelstrom which bent and twisted reality, and Ethan was at the centre of it.

Hunter looked to the others in the room who had descended into disarray and panic. Like them, he felt his mind being torn apart – foreign memories pushed their way into his head.

Different lives, different outcomes!

Hunter struggled to stand as a million voices seemed to invade his thoughts all at once. "STOP HIM!" he managed to shout. "Why don't you stop him?" he screamed almost pleadingly.

"Isn't it obvious?" shouted Ethan through the storm. "They can't stop me because I'm not there to stop. Where we're going, I don't exist. None of this does."

The look of realisation on Hunter's face was all Ethan needed. He knew they would attempt to grab him, or worse, but by then it would be too late. He was done.

Stepping away from the brink, Ethan Howard let himself go, pulled in the other world, and at that instant, ceased to have ever existed.

EPILOGUE

"Matt – it's coming!"

Matthew Howard was aware of someone next to him, shaking his arm.

What's happening – where am I?

"Matt, don't do this, not today. I swear, if you don't wake up – the baby's coming for God's-sake."

Slowly, the fog started to clear from Matt's mind, and he began to rejoin the world around him.

"Matt – wake up."

Blinking he focussed on the face of his wife, Jane. He was always like this when woken, unable to separate the multiple tendrils of dream-state from reality. He would always come-to in the end, but it was rarely quick and today was no exception.

Since he was a child it had ever been the same, he would dream of events yet to come, or witness variants of past events that had typically happened the day before. These were never the same, but then again, they were *always* the same. His dreams were never what he thought dreams should be; of flying, of fighting dragons or some romantic tryst. If Matthew Howard dreamt of these things at all, it was rare. He was instead *continually* short-changed and treated to a theatre of the unremarkable, a prosaic daily helping of mundane slices of life – each one as vivid as the next.

"What's going on?" he mumbled groggily, attempting to determine whether he was yet awake.

"Matt, I think the baby's coming."

He shifted his weight, still confused, struggling, trying to force himself to focus.

"Are you sure? How far apart are you?"

"About twenty minutes."

Managing some clarity, he looked at his wife's enormously distended abdomen and smiled.

They had been trying for a baby for the best part of three

years and for a while they'd wondered whether Jane was ever going to catch-on – wondered if it was ever going to happen.

When it finally did, they'd intentionally avoided being told what it was, *boy or girl*, but Barbara, Matt's mother, had been in little doubt.

"*It'll be a boy*," she had insisted. "*It's your father's side. Howards are always boys, for as long as records go back. Always a boy and always only the one. I think they put something in the water.*"

I'll be happy either way thought Matt, and it was true.

"This could be it then," he said, gently stroking her bump. "Are you sure it's real – I mean could it be Braxton Hicks?"

Jane threw a pillow in his direction, her brown doe-eyes glaring. She was in no mood for debate. "Look, just get woken up, get my bag, and get me to hospital; and don't zone out. OK?"

Matt had a tendency to slip into distraction, to daydream or to *zone out* as Jane called it. He'd done that ever since they'd met, but that was just Matty.

I may as well try to catch the wind as change him, thought Jane, *like father, like son.* However, for all her understanding, today was different. Today she needed Matt to be her rock, to be 'with it' a little more than normal, to be a grown-up.

Still dozy, Matt swung his feet out of bed onto the floor; the thick rug that covered most of the room felt warm under his toes. He paused, remembering buying it with Jane only yesterday, bringing it home, how she almost convinced him not to bother.

"For God's sake Matt!"

"Uh?"

"Get a move on – and by the way, you have dog-breath."

Matt rubbed his eyes and mashed the palm of his hand into his stubbled cheek to wake up, before padding across the bare boards that made up the bedroom floor.

We definitely should have bought that rug.

Jane Howard lay on the bed like a beached whale, her recent contraction now abated. She looked around the room at the browning, hand-me-down pine bedroom set. She and Matt were not wealthy, they did not have the latest things, but she was happy – she knew that much.

Simple pleasures, she thought, *all this will change soon, lazy mornings would be a thing of the past*; if her mum-friends were anything to go by, she was in for a rough ride.

...But it would be worth it.

In the bathroom, Matt caught sight of his reflection.

Matthew Howard was twenty-eight, but since dropping out of college, his work as a plumber had put five years on him. It was as unglamorous as it came but he was always in demand. It was like he was born to it. He could tell what joints would last and which would fail just by looking at them.

It was like he had a sixth sense; like he had intuition. In one sense it was ideal; regardless of what technological advances would be discovered in the future, people would always need plumbing and would always have things go wrong. But in a much more real sense, it was far from ideal, crawling under other people's sinks and through their sludge was not something he could do forever.

In the mirror, picturebook memories of his grandfather's face stared back at him. Maybe it was his father's lack of hair, but Matt had always resembled his grandfather, more than his father ever had.

Good grief – I look old... and tired.

He grabbed his crusty electric toothbrush and began to work it around his mouth.

"When you've done that, get my bag," shouted Jane from the bedroom. "I'm nearly ready."

"OK," he attempted to say, before spitting the foam into the sink.

C'mon fella, keep it together, he thought. *Wake up.* He was *always* like this when woken. A bomb could be going off, and it wouldn't get a reaction.

Dog-breath sorted, he threw the cheap plastic toothbrush back into its glass and splashed water on his face.

Should have bought an electric toothbrush. He was starting to come around. Finally, he felt the first hint of adrenaline kicking in

Jesus, Jane was having a baby and he was on another planet. Well at least she couldn't say he wasn't consistent.

Jane lurched around the house checking she had everything she needed. She knew she should ask for help but she also knew that there was little point – she loved Matty more than life itself but he really was a disaster waiting to happen. In the kitchen she attempted to calm herself with a fruit tea – strawberry and camomile; what Matt would have called *Fancy-Nancy* – well his opinion could wait; she was determined to enjoy it. Jane tied back her light hair in a high ponytail; an Apache preparing for battle. Invigorated, she was as ready as she would ever be for what was to come.

OK... let's get this show on the road...

In the bedroom Matt pulled on his jeans and looked over at Jane's single bag.

"You ready?" Jane asked as she waddled back into the room; slowly rocking side to side to transport the weight – legs bowed like a gunslinger from the old west.

"This baby's not going to wait for you..."

"Pretty much," came Matt's muffled reply as he struggled to pull on a polo neck. Through the rough-knit weave, he could vaguely make out that Jane was moving, possibly muttering at his inept attempts to get ready.

"OK – when you *eventually* escape from that, I'll see you in the car. Don't be long – OK?"

Dressed at last, he cast his eyes round the room for what he needed to bring.

He grabbed Jane's bag and joined his wife.

Parenthood, he mused, *bring it on.*

****

Joseph Howard lay on his back, unable to sleep. This was nothing new: he'd been struggling for the best part of a year. Faraway memories of looking into the RIFT and bitterly arguing with his son Tom, troubled him. These were not so much dreams but *dreams of dreams.*

What did they mean?

Bored, he got out of bed and fetched a glass of water.

Age, he thought.

****

"Come on Jane, push, just a little more..."

Matthew Howard clutched his wife's hand and felt helpless; the NHS labour room bustled with attending staff.

Jane was exhausted, he could tell that, but somehow she kept going.

He wiped her sodden hair out of her eyes and mopped her fevered brow with a cold compress that the nurse had just handed him.

"Come on Jane, you can do it; breathe…"

Getting this far hadn't been easy; they'd arrived at the hospital nearly twenty-four hours earlier, thinking they knew what lay ahead.

It had been a slow, drawn out process, but Jane's contractions were now coming thick and fast.

"I can't do it," she sobbed grabbing the rails on the institution-bed's functional metal frame.

"Yes you can, Jane," Matt told her, "I'm here, we all believe in you."

"I can't. I can't do it."

Across from Matt, the midwife, who had just changed shift, rubbed Jane's arm in encouragement. "We'll have none of that," she said, admonishingly, "Baby's being born, and that's the end of it."

To Matt's surprise, this scolding appeared to actually invigorate his wife. With steely determination, she once again began to push.

C'mon Jane he thought against her rhythmic panting.

Jane grimaced and kept pushing; her back arched with pain.

C'mon Jane…

Through gritted teeth, she voiced her agony with a drawn-out guttural cry.

C'mon Jane…

With her whole being, Jane began a scream that seemingly had no end.

It's commmiiinnnggg…

Throwing in everything she had, Jane Howard continued to push a brand-new life out of herself, into the world and into the midwife's waiting hands.

The infant wriggled in the nurse's arms, ruddy and squirming.

It was over.

"Well done *Mum* you can relax. You've done it."

Exhausted but frantic, Jane peered down.

"Is it OK?"

Jane had dreaded *that question*, dreaded all the possible outcomes that it could bring. She had told herself that it would not make a difference. *But could she be sure? Did she know herself that well?*

The midwife swept the baby up, coddling it in a blanket.

"She's a girl, all the right number of fingers and toes, and she's beautiful, *aren't you flower?*" Lifting her up, she handed the baby to Jane to ensure the all-important skin-on-skin bonding happened as soon as possible. "There you go."

Even though she was still spattered with blood, she was indeed beautiful. Jane, now calmer, gently stroked her head.

My daughter, thought Matt.

My family.

With the baby's arrival, the previously clinical surroundings seemed to take on a far more organic feel, the machines and medical equipment faded into the background and all that was left was the wonder of a new life.

"Do you have a name picked out?" asked the midwife.

"Hope," Jane and Matt said in unison, their eyes never leaving the newborn.

Hope Josephine Howard.

The midwife continued to speak, but neither Jane nor Matt heard a word she said. Their attention was, utterly and completely, focused on the newest addition to their family.

Matt looked from Jane to Hope, welling with pride and knew at that minute that he'd do anything for them.

Absolutely anything...

Anything at all.

****

Thomas Howard straightened the potting tray in front of him and tipped out the packet onto a small saucer. One by one he took a pinch of tomato seeds and pushed each into the array of compost plugs that he'd arranged in a regular grid.

He sat perched on the edge of a battered stool within the greenhouse that lay at the far end of his garden. The greenhouse had seen better days and been patched-up any number of ways, but to Tom, that only increased his affection for it. He had no time for 'brand new', not when it came to *this*. Growing was about playing the long game; that was part of its attraction to him. None of it was about appearance, it was about understanding nature, it was about gentle encouragement; it was about finding peace.

Why did such a simple thing relax him so?

It was like knocking his brain into neutral. Thirty-six years as a civil engineer had taken its toll and left him balding, hypertensive and overweight. Recently he'd increasingly felt uneasy, but the time he spent tending his plants removed all that, made him forget that he bore little resemblance to his former self. This took Tom elsewhere.

The sound of the phone interrupted the silence of the Sunday morning.

Barbara would get that.

"Tom!" Barbara's voice, calling from the house, caused him to look up.

"Tom! Matthew's a dad! We're grandparents!"

Tomato seeds instantly forgotten, Tom hurried into the house to where his wife stood. Barbara was next to their ageing telephone-table, speaking into the receiver, her fingers wrapping themselves round the worn spiral cord.

"That's wonderful, I'm so glad for the two of you; your dad's here now – I'll put him on."

He knew she wanted to talk for longer; Barbara was always like that, looking after the pennies.

Tom took the phone from Barbara as she excitedly did a little dance, mouthing *It's a girl*.

"Matthew?"

"Hi Dad, or *Grand-dad* I should say," came his son's crackling voice, "It's a girl – Hope! I'm a dad! *How mad's that?* I'm on a payphone in the hospital so I'll have to be quick, but I wanted to let you know."

"That's fantastic Matt – How's Jane?"

"She's fine, great even, but knackered – all good – she's even asking for chocolate. Dad, I haven't got much change, have you got the number for Grandpa's place?"

"I do Matty, but he's actually here today, why don't I get him for you... Joe – you're a great-grand-dad, a girl – Hope. How about that?"

"A girl...

"Really?"

The confusion in the old man's voice unsettled Matt

causing him to draw the receiver from his ear. When Joe finally spoke, Matt was sure that he heard his voice waver.

"That's wonderful son. How about that indeed…"

****

"How's she doing?" the midwife asked as she checked in on Jane.

"Fine, having her first feed."

The midwife looked at Hope, quietly feeding – contented.

All was well.

"That's good," she said, "have a good night, and I'll see you in the morning."

With that, she pulled on her coat and packed-up for the day.

It had been a long shift and she was exhausted, definitely ready to go home. Climbing into the small red car, she pulled out her a squat Nokia handset and texted the number she'd been given when she'd accepted the assignment; a number, apart from this circumstance, she'd been forbidden from using.

Maam, she is here. Howard baby a girl.

A girl! Gods amongst us.

It was finally beginning – Nothing would ever be the same.

THE END

Coming soon

CHIMERA

VOLUME II OF THE FIXPOINT TRILOGY

Hope Josephine Howard claims to have once been a boy called Ethan. But on meeting her great-grandfather, the toddler becomes sad that he will soon be killed…

The Fixpoint trilogy continues …

ACKNOWLEDGEMENTS

YORKSHIRE 2020

Thanks to my many friends and family for their belief in me and support writing this book. I'd try, and fail, to list you all, but you know who you are.

Elsewhen Press

delivering outstanding new talents in speculative fiction

Visit the Elsewhen Press website at elsewhen.press for the latest
information on all of our titles, authors and events; to read our blog; find
out where to buy our books and ebooks; or to place an order.

Sign up for the Elsewhen Press InFlight Newsletter at
elsewhen.press/newsletter

MILLION EYES
C.R. BERRY

Time is the ultimate weapon

What if we're living in an alternate timeline? What if the car crash that killed Princess Diana, the disappearance of the Princes in the Tower, and the shooting of King William II weren't supposed to happen?

Ex-history teacher Gregory Ferro finds evidence that a cabal of time travellers is responsible for several key events in our history. These events all seem to hinge on a dry textbook published in 1995, referenced in a history book written in 1977 and mentioned in a letter to King Edward III in 1348.

Ferro teams up with down-on-her-luck graduate Jennifer Larson to get to the truth and discover the relevance of a book that seems to defy the arrow of time. But the time travellers are watching closely. Soon the duo are targeted by assassins willing to rewrite history to bury them.

Million Eyes is a fast-paced conspiracy thriller about power, corruption and destiny.

ISBN: 9781911409588 (epub, kindle) / ISBN: 9781911409489 (336pp paperback)

Visit bit.ly/Million-Eyes

TimeStorm
Steve Harrison

In 1795 a convict ship leaves England for New South Wales in Australia. Nearing its destination, it encounters a savage storm but, miraculously, the battered ship stays afloat and limps into Sydney Harbour. The convicts rebel, overpower the crew and make their escape, destroying the ship in the process. Fleeing the sinking vessel with only the clothes on their backs, the survivors struggle ashore.

Among the escaped convicts, seething resentments fuel an appetite for brutal revenge against their former captors, while the crew attempts to track down and kill or recapture the escapees. However, it soon becomes apparent that both convicts and crew have more to concern them than shipwreck and a ruthless fight for survival; they have arrived in Sydney in 2017.

TimeStorm is a thrilling epic adventure story of revenge, survival and honour. In the literary footsteps of Hornblower, comes Lieutenant Christopher 'Kit' Blaney, an old-fashioned hero, a man of honour, duty and principle. But dragged into the 21st century… literally.

A great fan of the grand seafaring adventure fiction of CS Forester, Patrick O'Brien and Alexander Kent and modern action thriller writers like Lee Child, Steve Harrison combines several genres in his fast-paced debut novel as a group of desperate men from the 1700s clash in modern-day Sydney.

Steve Harrison was born in Yorkshire, England, grew up in Lancashire, migrated to New Zealand and eventually settled in Sydney, Australia, where he lives with his wife and daughter.

As he juggled careers in shipping, insurance, online gardening and the postal service, Steve wrote short stories, sports articles and a long running newspaper humour column called *HARRISCOPE: a mix of ancient wisdom and modern nonsense*. In recent years he has written a number of unproduced feature screenplays, although being unproduced was not the intention, and developed projects with producers in the US and UK. His script, *Sox*, was nominated for an Australian Writers' Guild 'Awgie' Award and he has written and produced three short films under his *Pronunciation Fillums* partnership.

TimeStorm was Highly Commended in the Fellowship of Australian Writers (FAW) National Literary Awards for 2013.

ISBN: 9781908168542 (epub, kindle) / ISBN: 9781908168443 (368pp paperback)

Visit bit.ly/TimeStorm

TIMEKEEPERS
DAVE WEAVER

Never pick up an old coin

An outsider in his own time, Jack finds himself a stranger in the distant past, then a pawn in a dark, dystopian future where rebels struggle to overturn an ancient and ruthlessly oppressive empire.

Jack has an exceptional gift: a remarkable ability to absorb and memorise facts instantly and without effort.

A lonely teenager, he has had little control over his life, having to leave behind friends and everything familiar, in the move to a new town, a new school, a new start. Jack misses his old life. He knows that his immediate future will not be easy – his astonishing memory has not always helped win him friends – but he can never have anticipated the incredible events that are about to befall him.

Discovering what appears to be an ancient coin, Jack finds himself abruptly hurled back and then forward through time, by a technology and an intelligence beyond his control. Jack's extraordinary memory, and his fascination with history, are to prove vital as he is thrown back across the centuries, to the early years of the Roman occupation of Britain, then forward to the heart of a vastly powerful totalitarian state.

In both past and future, manipulated by opposing factions, Jack's life is under constant threat. He will need all his ability and courage to survive.

Whom can he trust?
Can he save those he cares for?
Will he ever return home?

ISBN: 9781911409335 (epub, kindle) / ISBN: 9781911409236 (224pp paperback)

Visit bit.ly/Timekeepers-Elsewhen

SmartYellow™
Jacqueline Ward
writing as J.A. Christy

SmartYellow™ is the story of a young girl, Katrina Williams, who finds herself on the wrong side of social services. After becoming pregnant with only a slight notion of the father's identity, she is disowned by her parents and goes to live on a social housing estate. Before long she is being bullied by a gang involved in criminal activity and anti-social behaviour. Seeking help from the authorities she is persuaded to return to the estate to work as part of Operation Schrödinger, alongside a surveillance specialist. But she soon realises that Operation Schrödinger is not what it seems.

Exploring themes of social inequity and scientific responsibility, J.A. Christy's first speculative fiction novel leads her heroine Katrina to understand how probability, hope and empathy play a huge part in the flow of life and are absent in the stagnation of mere survival. As readers we also start to question how we would know if the power of the State to support and care for the weak had become corrupted into the oppression of all those who do not fit society's norms.

SmartYellow™ offers a worryingly plausible and chilling glimpse into an alternate Britain. For the sake of order and for the benefit of more fortunate members of society, those seen as socially undesirable are marked with SmartYellow™, making it easier for them to be controlled and maintained in a state of fruitless inactivity. Writer, J.A. Christy, turns an understanding and honest eye not only onto the weak, who have failed to cope with life, but also onto those who ruthlessly exploit them for their own ends. At times tense and threatening, at times tender and insightful, *SmartYellow*™ is a rewarding and thought-provoking read.

ISBN: 9781908168788 (epub, kindle) ISBN: 9781908168689 (320pp paperback)

Visit bit.ly/SmartYellow

THE BLUEPRINT TRILOGY
KATRINA MOUNTFORT

The *Blueprint* trilogy takes us to a future in which men and women are almost identical, and personal relationships are forbidden. Following a bio-terrorist attack, the population now lives within comfortable Citidomes. MindValues advocate acceptance and non-attachment. The BodyPerfect cult encourages a tall thin androgynous appearance, and looks are everything.

In *Future Perfect* we are introduced to Caia, an intelligent and highly educated young woman. In spite of severe governmental and societal strictures, Caia finds herself attracted to her co-worker, Mac, a rebel whose questioning of their so-called utopian society both adds to his allure and encourages her own questioning of the status quo. As Mac introduces her to illegal and subversive information she is drawn into a forbidden, dangerous world, alienated from her other co-workers and the companions with whom she shares her residence. In a society where every thought and action is controlled, informers are everywhere; whom can she trust? Katrina's story examines the enforcement of conformity through fear, the fostering of distorted and damaging attitudes towards forbidden love, manipulation of appearance and even the definition of beauty.

In *Forbidden Alliance* we return to Caia and Mac some sixteen years later in a story that poses questions of leadership, family loyalties and whether it is possible to justify the sacrifice of human lives for the greater good.

In *Freedom's Prisoners* tensions have escalated. The rebels may have won the first battle in their fight against the Citidome authorities, but can they win a war? The Citidomes are fighting back and no-one is safe any more as RotorFighters rain down fire on defenceless villages destroying them and their inhabitants. Katrina explores betrayal, guilt, hope and endurance in an explosive conclusion to the *Blueprint* trilogy.

The *Blueprint* trilogy is a thought-provoking series with a dark undercurrent that will appeal to both an adult and young adult audience.

Book 1: *Future Perfect*
ISBN: 9781908168559 (epub, kindle) / 9781908168450 (288pp paperback)

Book 2: *Forbidden Alliance*
ISBN: 9781908168900 (epub, kindle) / 9781908168801 (288pp paperback)

Book 3: *Freedom's Prisoners*
ISBN: 9781911409120 (epub, kindle) / 9781911409021 (304pp paperback)

Visit bit.ly/BlueprintTrilogy

Programmed to Breathe
TANYA REIMER

Breathing is a gift I give you...

Above ground, in the frozen climate of year 3161, Avery's family is starving. When the jerk from the clan at the end of the village invites Avery to start a family with him in exchange for food and land, she has a serious choice to make. Leaving her family where she fits in, to live in a clan with an old man she loathes, doesn't feel like a good move. But can she really refuse when the offer comes with food and land that her family desperately needs?

Underground, in the cities of Quma, Yodan's life is perfect. He looks forward to starting a family with... Azala? Why does that feel wrong? Yodan's best friend soon discovers that someone or something has tampered with Yodan's mind, erasing things. Investigating further, they discover a horrifying truth; Artificial-life has found a way to merge with them to live mortally.

When a violent earthquake destroys the energy source that's keeping both above and below ground habitable, the survivors are forced together after more than a thousand years of isolated evolution. Their union is a clash of spiritual versus technical existence where suddenly no one fits in. How will the villagers react to the bald pink-eyed children needing a new home? And what kind of damage will be done by the lifeform who hitched a ride with them ?

Breathing is a gift I give myself...

ISBN: 9781911409533 (epub, kindle) / ISBN: 9781911409434 (288pp paperback)

Visit bit.ly/ProgrammedToBreathe

Existence is
Elsewhen

Twenty stories from twenty great authors
including
John Gribbin
Rhys Hughes
Christopher Nuttall
Douglas Thompson

The title *Existence is Elsewhen* paraphrases the last sentence of André Breton's 1924 *Manifesto of Surrealism*, perfectly summing up the intent behind this anthology of stories from a wonderful collection of authors. Different worlds... different times. It's what Elsewhen Press has been about since we launched our first title in 2011.

Here, we present twenty science fiction stories for you to enjoy. We are delighted that headlining this collection is the fantastic **John Gribbin,** with a worrying vision of medical research in the near future. Future global healthcare is the theme of **J A Christy's** story; while the ultimate in spare part surgery is where **Dave Weaver** takes us. **Edwin Hayward's** search for a renewable protein source turns out to be digital; and **Tanya Reimer's** story with characters we think we know gives us pause for thought about another food we take for granted. Evolution is examined too, with **Andy McKell's** chilling tale of what states could become if genetics are used to drive policy. Similarly, **Robin Moran's** story explores the societal impact of an undesirable evolutionary trend; while **Douglas Thompson** provides a truly surreal warning of an impending disaster that will reverse evolution, with dire consequences.

On a lighter note, we have satire from **Steve Harrison** discovering who really owns the Earth (and why); and **Ira Nayman,** who uses the surreal alternative realities of his *Transdimensional Authority* series as the setting for a detective story mash-up of Agatha Christie and Dashiel Hammett. Pursuing the crime-solving theme, **Peter Wolfe** explores life, and death, on a space station; while **Stefan Jackson** follows a police investigation into some bizarre cold-blooded murders in a cyberpunk future. Going into the past, albeit an 1831 set in the alternate Britain of his *Royal Sorceress* series, **Christopher Nuttall** reports on an investigation into a girl with strange powers.

Strange powers in the present-day is the theme for **Tej Turner,** who tells a poignant tale of how extra-sensory perception makes it easier for a husband to bear his dying wife's last few days. Difficult decisions are the theme of **Chloe Skye's** heart-rending story exploring personal sacrifice. Relationships aren't always so close, as **Susan Oke's** tale demonstrates, when sibling rivalry is taken to the limit. Relationships are the backdrop to **Peter R. Ellis's** story where a spectacular mid-winter event on a newly-colonised distant planet involves a Madonna and Child. Coming right back to Earth and in what feels like an almost imminent future, **Siobhan McVeigh** tells a cautionary tale for anyone thinking of using technology to deflect the blame for their actions. Building on the remarkable setting of Pera from her *LiGa* series, and developing Pera's legendary *Book of Shadow,* **Sanem Ozdural** spins the creation myth of the first light tree in a lyrical and poetic song. Also exploring language, the master of fantastika and absurdism, **Rhys Hughes,** extrapolates the way in which language changes over time, with an entertaining result.

ISBN: 9781908168955 (epub, kindle) / ISBN: 9781908168856 (320pp paperback)
Visit bit.ly/ExistenceIsElsewhen

GENESIS

GEOFFREY CARR

A conjunction of AI, the Cloud, & interplanetary ambition…

Hidden somewhere, deep in the Cloud, something is collating information. It reads everything, it learns, it watches. And it plans.

Around the world, researchers, engineers and entrepreneurs are being killed in a string of apparently unrelated accidents. But when intelligence-agency analysts spot a pattern they struggle to find the culprit, blocked at every step – by reluctant allies and scheming enemies.

Meanwhile a multi-billionaire inventor and forward-thinker is working hard to realise his dream, and trying to keep it hidden from everyone – one government investigating him, and another helping him. But deep in the Cloud something is watching him, too.

And deep in the Cloud, it plans.

What could possibly go wrong?

Geoff is the Science and Technology Editor of *The Economist*. His professional interests include evolutionary biology, genetic engineering, the fight against AIDS and other widespread infectious diseases, the development of new energy technologies, and planetology. His personal interests include using total eclipses of the sun as an excuse to visit weird parts of the world (Antarctica, Easter Island, Amasya, the Nullarbor Plain), and watching swifts hunting insects over his garden of a summer's evening, preferably with a glass of Cynar in hand.

As someone who loathed English lessons at school, he says he is frequently astonished that he now earns his living by writing. "That I have written a novel, albeit a technothriller rather than anything with fancy literary pretensions, astonishes me even more, since what drew me into writing in the first place was describing reality, not figments of the imagination. On the other hand, perhaps describing reality is what fiction is actually for."

ISBN: 9781911409519 (epub, kindle) / 9781911409410 (288pp paperback)

Visit bit.ly/GC_Genesis

ABOUT C M ANGUS

Born and raised in a steel-town in the Northeast of England, CM Angus now lives in Yorkshire with his better half, his children and an awesome dog.

Having struggled with English at school and having never written fiction before, he decided to become a writer while submerged in the bath one Saturday morning in 2014. Since then he has had stories published in a number of recent anthologies and manages a growing colony of notebooks.

With a background in e-Commerce and technology, he has previously written technical non-fiction and is interested in all things creative, technological and scientific. His work is inquisitive and blends a passion for story telling with a strong scientific grounding.

When not working or writing, he spends his time as a Reiki master, a meditation guide and multi-instrumentalist. With a PhD in esoteric hard sums and a strong interest in Martial Arts, CM Angus jokingly describes himself as a gentleman, a scholar and an acrobat who dreams of, one day, owning some woodland.